Hallie raised a brow in question.

"Come." Cooper gestured and led her outside the door with one hand on her upper arm. "There are the other men, Hallie. Once they know you're alone at night..."

She saw the picture. Remembering the way they'd ogled her at the trading post with lecherous eyes, she didn't need any more convincing. "I'll take a few things and stay with Chumani." The warmth of his hand burned through her sleeve. "Thank you," she said. "You always think of my safety."

His eyes dropped to her mouth, and she caught her breath at the heat she read in their depths. His other hand raised her face to his.

Hallie's heart set up a flutter. "What—?"

"You could talk a man blind, Hallie."

Her eyes widened and his face lowered.

"I don't think—"

"I don't care if you think or not. Just don't talk...."

SAFE HAVEN

CHERYL ST.JOHN

Badlands Bride

HARLEQUIN®

TORONTO • NEW YORK • LONDON
AMSTERDAM • PARIS • SYDNEY • HAMBURG
STOCKHOLM • ATHENS • TOKYO • MILAN • MADRID
PRAGUE • WARSAW • BUDAPEST • AUCKLAND

ISBN-13: 978-0-373-36189-2
ISBN-10:   0-373-36189-0

BADLANDS BRIDE

www.eHarlequin.com

Printed in U.S.A.

CHERYL ST.JOHN

is a peacemaker, a romantic, an idealist and a discouraged perfectionist. The author of both historical and contemporary novels says she's also been told that she is painfully honest.

Cheryl admits to being an avid collector of everything from dolls to depression glass, brass candlesticks, old photographs and—most especially—books. She and her husband love to browse antiques and collectibles shops.

She says that knowing her stories bring hope and pleasure to readers is one of the best parts of being a writer. The other wonderful part is being able to set her own schedule and have time to work around her growing family.

Cheryl loves to hear from readers. You can write her at P.O. Box 24732, Omaha, NE 68124.

This book is dedicated with appreciation and recognition to the distributors and booksellers who promote romance and romance authors, especially:

Nelson News, Omaha/read all about it! bookstores;
Kim Huebner, Terri Foster, Rosie Christensen,
everyone in the book room and all the drivers;
read all about it! bookstores, Nebraska and Iowa;
Karen Lafler, Jennie Mathison, Clay Nottleman,
Robbi Pozzi,
Matt Rohde, Laura Tadlock, Linda Theile,
Sue Turner, Kirk Utley,
Pam Williamson and the staff at each store;
Debi Jo Miner, 3R's, Omaha;
Linda Muller, Waldenbooks, Sioux City;
Terry Showalter, Lee Books, Lincoln;
Sherry Siwinski, Waldenbooks, Grand Island;
Penny Spoerry, Waldenbooks, Des Moines;
Kathy Uttecht, The Book Center, Norfolk;
Jo Lent, Waldenbooks, Mall of the Bluffs;
my friends at Baker Place, Omaha; and
Donita Lawrence, Bell, Book, & Candle, Del City, OK.

To all of you who order my books and recommend them to the readers, keep my backlist in stock and host signings, this doesn't begin to cover it, but here it is:

Thank you

Chapter One

Ignoring the reflection of the businesses across the street behind her and the words *The Daily* meticulously painted in gold and black lettering on the glass, Hallie Claire Wainwright observed herself in the window of her father's newspaper office. She adjusted the jacket of her carefully chosen two-piece fitted dress and smoothed a hand over her dark hair, fashioned into an uncharacteristically neat bun.

"I think I've earned the responsibility of reporting on the boxing matches," she said to her reflection. The sporting event would make the front page every day for weeks, and Hallie could think of nothing more exciting than seeing her name beneath the headline.

"I'm sure I could get interviews with the participants," she said convincingly. "Perhaps they'll share insights with me they wouldn't give the men." Forest green curtains obscured the interior of the newspaper office, but she didn't need to see in to picture her oldest brother, Turner, setting type and her father in the office beyond.

"I've been doing the menial jobs without complaint. It's time you gave me a chance. I'll do my best." Hallie gave her likeness a last confident nod and opened the door.

The reassuring smells of ink, paper and grease, which she'd grown up with, boosted her confidence. Turner didn't glance up as she strode pass the Franklin press to her father's office. She rapped twice and opened the door.

Samuel Wainwright glanced up and immediately returned his attention to the papers on his desk top.

"Father, I—"

"No."

Her mouth dropped open. "How do you even know what I was going to say?"

"You have that stubborn look on your face."

"I want to cover the boxing matches." She placed her fists on her hips. "Evan—" her lip curled around the name of the new apprentice "—gets all the good stories."

Samuel shifted his smoking cigar stub from one side of his mouth to the other and leaned back in his creaky leather chair. "Now, Hallie," he cajoled. "Don't get in a huff. You know it wouldn't be acceptable—or safe—for you to take up with that rowdy crowd in the Piedmont district. Any female in Boston with half a brain in her head wouldn't set foot within a mile of the place."

She rolled her eyes. "That's all the brain you give any woman credit for having."

He harrumphed, then shuffled through a stack of papers, finding one he wanted and ignoring her while he checked the list in his other hand against the sheet.

"Hello, Precious," Turner said, entering.

Hallie winced inwardly.

He'd rolled his white shirtsleeves back, and his dark hair stood up on his head in finger-combed waves. He handled the office work, overseeing the typeset and presses. "I want to check this against your copy," he said to their father.

Samuel extended a paper, and the two men concurred. Used to being ignored, Hallie sat on the corner of the ink-stained oak desk and crossed her arms over her chest, unwilling to acknowledge her father's wisdom in this particular case. So what if he was right for once? Her father and brothers, Charles and Turner, always came up with some inane reason that she couldn't handle a story, and ninety-nine out of a hundred times the real reason—the infuriating reason—was that she was a female.

Turner reached for a strand of Hallie's hair that had fallen loose. "You're a sight."

She batted his hand away.

"What are you pouting about now?"

"I'm not pouting."

He laughed. "You're mad as a March hare. Still in a fix over Evan? He says he can't sleep nights for the ringing in his ears. For the last week at supper, you've managed to discredit everything about the man, including his parentage."

Hallie uncrossed her arms and shot a glance at her father. He wore a smile of bored amusement. "I keep hoping *someone* around here will notice that he's not any more capable than I am."

"And as we've told you a thousand times," Turner said, raising a superior brow, "Father needed Evan."

She tried her best to swallow her resentment. Her father did need help, and she'd worked so hard to prove herself. Samuel had hired the young man to assist Charles with the reporting, so he could devote himself to the book work and editing. It hurt immeasurably that none of them had considered her for the position. And it frustrated her beyond words that they refused to listen to her reasoning.

It was one thing to constantly defer to her brothers, but now an *outsider* had displaced her! "Perhaps if I put on a pair of trousers, the lot of you will notice I have a whole brain in this head."

Turner scowled. "If you put on a pair of trousers, the men around here will notice more than that. And I'll have to turn you over my knee and discipline the object of their attention."

Hallie resisted the urge to stick her tongue out. Just because they treated her like a child didn't mean she'd give in and behave like one.

"Did you turn in the piece on the quilting society?" Turner asked.

"Now *that* was an unequaled challenge," she replied, tracing a worn scar on the desk top with an index finger. "Think it'll make the headlines tomorrow?"

"Look," her father said, interrupting. "Remember those classifieds we ran a while back? Here's more of the same."

Turner bent over the desk and read aloud. "'Bride wanted.' Another one—'Wife wanted to cook, do laundry and care for children.'"

"What kind of self-respecting woman would answer an ad like that?" Hallie asked, frowning her distaste.

"A woman who wants a husband," Turner replied, directing a pointed glance at his sister. "Unlike you."

She ignored the familiar taunt. "It's barbaric."

"But newsworthy," her father added. He caught his cigar between two fingers and squinted at her through curls of blue-gray smoke. "Some of the young ladies at Miss Abernathy's Conservatory answered the last ads. Why don't you do a story on them, Hallie?"

"Really?" she asked, jumping up.

"I haven't seen anything in the other papers," he continued. "Maybe, for a change, we can print a story before they get the idea."

The assignment filled Hallie with a new sense of importance. *The Daily* was always trying to get the jump on the bigger papers, and even though the other newspapers always managed to edge them out, the Wainwrights had increased circulation over the past year. Any newsworthy story that first appeared in *The Daily* was a feather in their journalistic cap.

"I'll work on it right away." She kissed her father on the cheek and smugly tilted her chin on her way past Turner.

Samuel and Turner exchanged conspiratory grins. "How

long do you think that will keep her out of our hair?"
Turner asked.

Samuel ran a hand over his balding pate. "Let's hope
until Evan has a foot in the door. It's hard enough being a
cub, without having to deal with Hallie when she's got her
hackles up."

"Well, then, we'll just have to keep her busy."

"Isn't it just the most romantic thing you've ever heard?"
The young woman with golden hair and ivory skin ignored
the cake and tea on the tiny table and stared vacantly across
the front of the lace-decorated establishment where the
ladies of Boston came to socialize over afternoon tea.

Hallie thought traveling to God-only-knew-where to
marry a man she'd never laid eyes on was the most asinine
thing she'd ever heard, but she politely refrained from saying so.

"Where *are* the northern Dakotas, anyway?" Tess Cordell asked, coming out of her dreamy-eyed trance. "One of
the girls said up by the North Pole."

"I don't think it's quite that far." Hallie tried to recall
her geography lessons. "It's far to the west and up north.
Quite remote, I'm sure."

Tess took an envelope from her reticule and carefully
removed and unfolded a letter. "His name is Cooper
DeWitt. He has a stage line and a freight company, so he
must be *very* wealthy." Her pale blue eyes took on that
dreamy quality again. "The only thing he requested in a
wife was that she be able to read and write. I think that's
good, don't you? He doesn't sound like a demanding sort
of fellow."

"Or discriminating," Hallie added.

"Right," Tess agreed, the comment apparently sailing
over her head. "He's not superficial like most young men
who care only that a woman be from a good family."

Hallie heard the resentment in her voice. Obviously Tess

was not from a well-to-do family, or she wouldn't have responded to an ad from a desperate frontier man. "Does he say how old he is?"

Tess frowned at the paper momentarily. "No." Her expression brightened. "But he does mention that he's never had a wife, so he must be young."

Or uglier than a buck-toothed mule, Hallie thought more realistically. What was this poor girl getting herself into? She almost wanted to offer her assistance if the girl needed someone to provide for her so badly she was willing to do this. But she held her tongue. Her family had told her often enough that her thinking was not that of a typical twenty-year-old woman. Tess was obviously delighted with her plan. "What else does he say?"

"Only that the country is beautiful and that I would have everything that I need."

"How romantic." Hallie made a few notes on her tablet. "Are you worried about being so far from anyone you know?"

"Well…" Tess chewed her lower lip. "I don't have family, but a couple of the other girls have accepted positions in the same community, so we'll be traveling together. I'm sure Mr. DeWitt will see that I can visit from time to time."

Hallie noted the term *accepted positions* for later reference. "Are the other girls as excited as you?"

"Oh, yes!" Her pale eyes sparkled. "This is an adventure of a lifetime!"

"I want to speak with the others, too. Can you give me their names?" Hallie scribbled a list and thanked Tess for the interview.

Hallie met the other young women, then hurried home to write her article. The enormous, masculinely furnished house was quiet, as usual. She slipped into her father's study and seated herself in his oversize chair, arranging paper, pen and ink on the desk top. She loved the room, did her best thinking among the familiar heavy pieces with the Seth Thomas mantel clock chiming on the half hour.

Nearly three hours passed before Hallie noticed the time. Double-checking the information, wording and neat printing, she blotted the pages. Her father would undoubtedly cut it in half, but, pleased with her work, she delivered it to his office.

He read the pages while she waited. "This is just what we wanted, Precious," he commended her.

Gladdened at the acknowledgment, she ignored the patronizing nickname.

"Keep on this," he said.

"You mean…?"

"I mean follow up. Go with them when they shop for the trip, watch them pack, all that. We'll run a series on the brides, right up until you wave them off at the stage station."

Surprised and more than a little pleased, Hallie nodded. "All right." She patted the edge of the desk in satisfaction. "All right."

Hallie read her articles in print each day, delighting in the fact that her father hadn't cut more than a sentence or two. She was so delighted, she didn't allow the fact that her father's new apprentice was covering the boxing championships and making headlines nearly every other day upset her—too much.

The day before her subjects were due to leave, she stepped into the office early. On the other side of the partially open mahogany door her brothers' voices rose.

"I'll take this sentencing piece," Charles said. "I'll be at the courthouse this morning, anyway."

"Right," Samuel said. "Evan?"

"I still have the lawyer to interview and, of course, the matches tonight. I'll try not to take a punch myself this time."

Male laughter echoed.

''That's some shiner!'' Charles said.

''Great coverage, son.'' Samuel added. ''You'll do any-thing to get an unusual angle. That's the stuff good reporters are made of.'' The aromatic scent of his morning cigar reached Hallie's nostrils, and she paused, a hollow, jealous ache opening in her chest at her father's casual praise of Evan Hunter. ''How many more matches?''

''Another week,'' Evan replied.

Hallie reached for the door.

''What're we gonna do with Hallie?'' Turner's voice car-ried through the gap beside the door. ''Her brides leave tomorrow.''

Hallie stopped and listened.

''That turned out to be an excellent piece,'' Charles com-mented. ''We've had good response.''

''Plus we got the jump on the *Journal*,'' Samuel agreed.

''Who'd have thought that when you came up with some-thing to keep her off Evan's back during the matches, we'd actually get a good piece of journalism?'' She recognized Turner's voice.

They laughed again.

A heavy weight pressed upon Hallie's chest. Hurt and self-doubt squeezed a bitter lump of disappointment into her throat. Of all the patronizing, condescending, imperious—

They'd handed her the story like presenting a cookie to a toddler they didn't want underfoot! And now they gloated over their own superiority. Hallie had never felt so wretched...so cheated...so unimportant.

''Do we have any sources in the Dakotas?'' Charles asked.

''Why?''

''The real story is on the other end of that stage line.''

A moment of silence followed Charles's comment, wherein Hallie imagined them nodding piously at one an-other.

''Yes, when the men who sent for those gals set eyes on

them,'' Samuel agreed. ''No. We don't have anyone that far west.''

''Too bad,'' Turner said.

''Too bad, indeed,'' Charles said. ''We could have had a real follow-up story there.''

''Let's just hope the *Journal* doesn't think of it.'' Samuel added.

Heartbroken, Hallie gathered her skirts and trod stealthily back out the front door. She walked the brick street without direction. It never entered her mind to go home. Her mother would only tell her as she always did that her father and brothers did such things for her own good. Clarisse Wainwright had been born and bred to be a genteel wife and a mother to Samuel's sons. The fact that Hallie had come along had been an inconvenience to all of them, or so Hallie saw it.

Hallie hadn't been born the proper gender to take a prominent place at the newspaper, as much as she wished to, as much as she knew the same amount of ink flowed through her veins as her brothers'. They'd patted her on the head and sent her on her way since she'd been old enough to toddle after them.

The truth lay on her crushed heart like lead. They would never see her as good enough, as equal, as valuable or necessary. Even Clarisse had been necessary only to the point of bringing Charles and Turner into the world. Now her mother lived the life of a pampered society wife, spending her days with her gardening club, at the tearoom and playing the latest vogue card game, bridge.

Hallie would never accept an invalid life like that. Surely there was some way to prove herself to her father. If only he would give her a chance, he'd see she was as capable as Charles and Turner—and more so than Evan Hunter—because she'd been born to the life.

If only she'd been born a man.

Her mother had forced her into dresses and threatened her

with Miss Abernathy's if she didn't take an interest in her hair and clothing. Hallie had conformed to their expectations—to the world's expectations—and resigned herself to her unchangeable, unappreciated gender. But she could not accept the role they wanted her to play. Hallie wanted more.

Should she give up or go on printing the same outdated page of her life over and over? Neither of the choices appealed to her.

Finding herself across from the tearoom, Hallie stared dismally at the brownstone facade beside the hotel and recalled her interview with Tess Cordell. Charles had said the real story was where Tess was going. There must be some way Hallie could keep in touch with her. Perhaps, even though the mail took weeks, she could convince Tess to correspond with her for future articles. Maybe Tess would send information about the other young women, too. It wouldn't be anywhere close to as in-depth reporting as she needed, but it was the only answer she had.

She set out for Miss Abernathy's, realizing she'd answered her own question. She couldn't give up. Not when the result meant settling for a superficial existence.

She found Tess Cordell hurriedly packing, arranging and rearranging, discarding items she couldn't fit into the two small bags open on the bed. Hallie surveyed the disarray in the small room. "Whatever are you doing? Yesterday you were all packed except for your overnight valise."

"I've changed plans, Miss Wainwright." Cheeks flushed, her fair hair atumble, she tucked a cotton night rail into the battered valise and clasped her hands together. Her blue eyes sparkled with excitement. "I'm going to Philadelphia."

"Philadelphia!" Disappointment sank in Hallie's stomach. "What about the Dakotas?"

Tess managed to look a little sheepish. She busied herself stuffing items back into the trunk against the wall. "I was engaged until a few months ago. Eric—he's my fiancé—

well, his family put pressure on him to call the engagement off. He did, and I was devastated.''

The strength left Hallie's legs and she wilted onto a wooden chair.

''Mr. DeWitt's ad seemed the only thing for me to do at the time,'' she explained. ''But last night Eric came to see me. He's taken a position in a Philadelphia law office, and he realized he couldn't go without me. You know that expression 'smart as a Philadelphia lawyer'? Well, that's Eric. Rich, too. And he loves me. So you see there's nothing else I could do but go with him.''

''But this DeWitt fellow...''

Tess reached toward the bureau and turned back, tossing two envelopes on the bed. ''Eric gave me money to replace what I spent. Of course, it must be returned to Mr. De-Witt.... Will you be a dear and see to it for me?''

Hallie stared at the envelopes, her plans dashed.

Tess buckled two leather straps around the last case. ''I've asked Miss Abernathy to store my trunk until Eric can send someone for it.'' She tidied her hair and settled her bonnet on her head. ''I hope I didn't ruin your story, Miss Wainwright, but this is the best opportunity I'm ever going to have. Please understand.''

In disbelief, Hallie watched her pick up her bags and hurry through the doorway. ''Good luck,'' she said to the empty room.

She sat in the silence, absorbing yet another wash of disillusionment. As far as she knew there were still three other women planning to leave on the stage the following day. Perhaps one of them would agree to help Hallie with her articles. None had been as young or as personable as Tess, but she would have to make do.

She moved from the chair to the rumpled bed and picked up the envelopes. One contained the letter she'd seen Tess with. Hallie unfolded it and read the scrawled handwriting.

Dear Miss Cordell,
My wife must be able to read and write. Enclosed is a
cashier's check to purchase whatever you will need.
There are no women's shops here. The Territory is far
from the life you are used to, but the land is beautiful
and you will have everything you need. I've never been
married. I trapped for many winters and now operate
a freight company and stage line. A justice will meet
us at the Stone Creek Station next month.

Sincerely,
Cooper DeWitt

Hallie tucked the letter back into the envelope and picked
up the other, pulling out a stage ticket and two hundred
dollars. No wonder Tess had been impressed.

She fingered the ticket, took it out and turned it over a
couple of times. *The real story's on the other end of that
stage line.*

With a little thrill of excitement, she realized what she
was thinking. No. It was too dangerous! She slid the ticket
back into the envelope. She would cash it in, buy a cashier's
check for the amount plus the cash and return it to DeWitt.

We could have had a real follow-up story there.
The voices from the other side of her father's door haunted
her. *Get Hallie off our backs…let's hope the* Journal *doesn't
think of it…* Turner's condescending tone came to her. *What
are you pouting about now, Precious?*

What if she did it? What if she used this ticket to get her
to the Dakotas? She could interview the men who sent for
wives. She could get the follow-up story on the other
women—the real brides.

But what about this DeWitt person? He was expecting a
wife. Hallie turned that question over a few times before a
solution came to mind. She could simply explain the situation to him, give him his money back and call it square.

She could get her story, and he could send for another wife. He'd have to anyway, since Tess had backed out.

Enthusiastic now, she planned her departure. She couldn't tell her family. They'd never allow it. Her mother would have a conniption fit. It would most likely take them a day to notice she was missing, and by then she'd be long gone. She'd write from the first station.

Satisfied with her plan, Hallie tucked the envelopes into her reticule and stood. She had packing to do if she was going to catch that stage tomorrow.

Cooper paced the dusty expanse of hard-packed earth surrounding the stage station and surveyed the broad horizon, temporarily forgetting its stark beauty. He saw only the barrenness of the land…the lack of people and buildings. He'd told her in the letter, but seeing was believing. And by now, wherever the coach was, she'd had time to see plenty.

Cooper frowned at the vista before him. The stage should have arrived sometime that morning. It was now early afternoon and there was still no sign of it. In his mind the delay signaled only one thing: trouble.

''Sky's clear here,'' Stuart Waring, another of the impatient grooms, said from behind him. ''But that don't mean they didn't run into rain or mud.''

Cooper turned to the two farmers sitting on crates against the log wall. Stuart wore a faded shirt with a string tie cinched around his scrawny neck. His scarred boots had been polished and shined. The ever-present wind snatched at his hat, and he secured it quickly.

''Coulda had a horse go lame,'' Vernon Forbes said. His jacket bore threadbare spots at the wrists and elbows, and he held a small, battered package. A gift for his bride? Cooper hadn't thought of that.

Angus Hallstrom, the station operator who worked for Cooper, leaned against the doorframe and picked his teeth with a piece of straw. "Fact that the stage's been robbed three times in as many months ain't sittin' well with me."

Cooper had been thinking the same thing. He didn't like the uncomfortable feeling that tiptoed up his spine and settled on his shoulders. Having money stolen or losing a month's mail was one thing…harm coming to the woman he intended to marry was another.

George Gaston, the portly justice, sat in the only chair and sipped black coffee from a dented metal cup. Cooper observed the motley group of men and imagined what the city women would think of them.

A strange uncertainty rippled in his chest, and he glanced down at his clean buckskin pants and fringed shirt. What would Tess Cordell think of him?

Fifteen years ago, even ten years ago, content living, hunting and trapping with the Oglala, he'd never have imagined he would pair himself with a white woman. Time had changed that, as it had the existence of his people—rather, the people of his heart—and most of them were surviving on reservation land.

Buffalo no longer roamed the grasslands in great herds, like rippling black seas. The Oglala, Santee, Yankton and other Sioux had been forced to make treaties in order to receive food.

Cooper paced to his team of horses, waiting in the shade of a wind-bent tree. He ran a hand down the black's hide and noticed his own skin, callused and rough, sun-darkened nearly to a shade like that of his Sioux family.

His white skin had given him an advantage over the men he called his brothers. He'd taken a land grant offered only to whites. He'd traded and sold years' worth of furs for wagons and tools, caught his own horses and purchased everything else he'd needed to start his business.

For now, he could only take food and winter supplies to the reservation, but someday, and he hoped it would be soon, he would be in a position to really help his people. And Tess Cordell would help him do just that.

Hallie covered her mouth and nose with her damp handkerchief and tried not to choke on the thick dust gusting in around the drawn shade. The wheels hit another gully and her groan was drowned out by the other women's cries.

Zinnia Blake held her wilted, green-feathered hat in place on her head with a dirty-gloved hand and Hallie tried not to laugh at the way the flesh beneath her chin jiggled. They hit another indentation and Zinnia flattened the hand over her enormous bouncing bosom. Even in the dim interior, her face glistened as red as a freshly washed tomato. "Isn't it awfully hot for this late in the fall?"

"It can't be much farther," Olivia Mason predicted. She pounded on the roof with the heel of her hand and peeled back the shade. "Mr. Tubbs, is it much farther?"

The monotonous sounds of the creaking coach and the horses' hooves were the only reply.

The wind stuck a coil of red hair to Olivia's pale cheek and she dropped the shade back into place. "He promised we'd be there this morning."

"Mr. Tubbs is doing the best he can," Evelyn Reed said, coming to the driver's defense. Hallie hadn't heard her speak more than a dozen words the entire ten-day trip and figured she must be as tired of the other women's complaints as she. Zinnia had been sick from the steamer's constant chugging up the river. Olivia had insisted on changing clothes twice a day, and then complained about having no clean ones.

Once they'd crossed the Missouri and boarded Mr. Tubbs's stage, things had grown progressively worse. Zinnia had a case of heat rash that drove her to tears. Olivia thought there should be a laundry at each rustic relay station. The meals were horrible, facilities for tending to nature's call primitive to nonexistent, and Hallie had a crick in her neck from sleeping sitting up.

But she was having a glorious adventure. She took copious notes, describing the weather conditions, the vegetation, the stark but beautiful outcroppings of stratum eroded by time and nature. She would have a story to beat all stories when she got home. Maybe she would even write an article for a magazine...or perhaps a book!

The jarring motion of the coach slowed, and the women glanced expectantly at one another.

"Thank God!" Zinnia panted. "We must be there. And, good heavens, I no doubt look a fright."

Olivia tucked stray red coils into her neat chignon.

The stage picked up speed again. Overhead, Mr. Tubbs shouted unintelligible orders to the horses. Inside the coach, the farers bounced and jostled. Hallie flipped up the shade and peered through the dust, gritting her teeth at the jarring of her backside against the poorly padded seat.

Appearing from a cloud of churning dust, horses and riders drew up with the stage. Shots were fired, and piercing screams erupted beside her. Heart pounding, she watched the riders gain on the stage. "Stage robbers!" she cried.

She'd stayed up many a night, thrilling to the excitement and action depicted in dime novels. Now, here was she, Hallie Claire Wainwright, participant in an adventure as exciting as those! Her heart pounded and terror shivered up her spine. She strained to see through the thick haze of dust, trying to impress each detail into memory for later.

Finally, after what seemed like hours, the stage slowed to a halt. The door was flung open and the barrel of a gun poked inside. Zinnia shrieked.

"Come out!"

Hallie glanced at the women's panic-stricken faces. As long as they were being delayed, she might as well make the best of it. Her father would love the firsthand story of a stage holdup! Let Evan Hunter try to top this one.

"Let's do as they say." She gestured to the others, gathered her skirts and stepped out into the sunshine.

Chapter Two

Three bandanna-masked men in sweat-stained shirts and ill-fitting trousers pointed guns at the women exiting the coach. With their hats pulled low, the invisibility of faces and expressions was as threatening as the weapons. Two others in the same disguising attire sat atop horses. Another, this one barrel chested and short legged, held Mr. Tubbs at gunpoint on the ground.

The grizzled old driver squinted from the bandits to the women, one side of his unshaven cheek jerking in a nervous twitch.

"White women," one of the three standing men said in awe. He wore a battered and wide-brimmed black hat.

The tallest, standing near Hallie, jerked his gun barrel toward the back of the stage. "The bags."

The riders dismounted and lithely leapt onto the coach, unfastening the leather straps and tossing trunks and cases to the ground. Jumping back down, they opened the bags and trunks, pausing only seconds to shoot off resisting or locked latches.

The bullets frightened Zinnia to hysteria. She threw her hands toward the sun and wailed.

"Quiet!" The black-haired man moved forward and

struck her with the back of his hand. Olivia couldn't support her, and she wilted into an unconscious heap in the dirt.

"Take what you want and go," Olivia objected. "There's no call to hurt women."

He yanked Olivia's hair. She yelped, and her red mane tumbled across one shoulder. Grasping a strand in his leather-gloved fingers, he tugged her closer.

She slapped his hand away and stepped back.

"Open that pouch." The man in front of Hallie, who appeared to be the leader, indicated her reticule.

He stood too close; his eyes were black and unyielding. The men's aggressiveness frightened her. She'd never seen women treated disrespectfully. This was what the papers called the untamed West. There was no law. No one would even hear the shots. They could die out here and not be found for days or weeks.

Wisely, Hallie chose to open her bag and withdraw the contents. Three men darted forward, taking the other women's possessions. At the same time, one climbed inside the coach.

The leader stuffed Hallie's money into his pocket. She swallowed her objections. It was only money, after all, and her life was more important.

"*You* don't cry."

Hallie stared into his black eyes, her heart jumping into her throat.

"Do you talk?"

She raised her chin without reply. He circled her slowly, keeping the gun pointed at her. Halfway around, she had to turn her head and wait for him to approach from the other side. The way he looked at her body sickened her and made her feel naked.

"Lift your dress."

She took a step back. "I beg your pardon."

"You do talk." He lowered the gun barrel to the front of

her open jacket and nudged the material where her blouse buttoned. "Lift your dress, or I will."

Nervously, Hallie glanced at the others. The bandits searched Olivia and Evelyn's bodies roughly through their clothing, and the women screamed. Stoically, rather than have this man touch her the same way, Hallie raised her skirt and petticoats to her waist.

He squatted and patted her cotton-clad hips and legs with gloved hands. She clenched her teeth, nausea suffusing her insides.

Beside her, Olivia cried out and sprawled on the ground. The man wearing the black hat straddled her. Her red hair spilled across the dirt, and her skirts bunched beneath her.

"Wait just a gol-durned minute!" Mr. Tubbs cursed from his prone position.

The leader, still in front of Hallie, paused with a hand on her calf. She could see plainly that the bandit on top of Olivia had no intention of stopping. The others stood watching.

Hallie had a good idea of what that ruffian intended to do to Olivia, and it probably wouldn't take long until the rest of them figured it was a fine idea and stopped being spectators. The leader, crouching before Hallie, bracketed one of her thighs with his gloved hands. With a strength born of terror, she kneed him in the face, knocking his hat off and releasing her skirts.

He yelped and dropped the gun, reaching for his nose and scrambling for balance.

Before he could stand, Hallie grabbed the gun and aimed it at him, securing both trembling index fingers on the trigger.

Since the bandanna was still tied across his face, only the top of his head, his black brows and obsidian eyes were visible. Hastily he grabbed his hat, jammed it over his black hair and stood, bright red blood soaking through the bandanna. He backed away.

"She won't shoot," said one of the others, now standing quietly.

If she didn't, one of them would take the gun away from her and she'd be in an even bigger fix. Before she could think about it, Hallie turned the gun toward the man on Olivia and squeezed. The weapon jumped in her hands, jerked her shoulders and set her off balance. Acrid smoke curled from the barrel and Hallie steadied herself. The black hatted man clutched his arm and backed away. "Kill her!" he shouted to the others.

Hallie's insides quaked and she waited for a bullet to impact with her skull. That shot had been a miracle. She could never shoot the rest before they killed her. A brief regret for the grief and shame she would cause her father and mother streaked through her head.

"No." The man with the bleeding nose raised an arm, his gloved palm halting the action. Across the distance separating them, their eyes met, and his penetrating black stare sharpened her already soul-piercing fear.

He grunted a command. Hallie couldn't tear her gaze away. If he'd told one of them to shoot her, she'd never see the bullet coming. Surprisingly however, the men gathered their stolen goods and mounted the horses.

With a final lingering perusal of Hallie, the leader leapt atop his horse and signaled. The gun trembled and her arms ached, but determinedly she kept it pointed at him. The bandits turned their horses and rode off, leaving a trail of dust on the horizon.

They were all still alive. Hallie shook so badly she finally dropped her arms, and the heavy gun barrel hit her knee.

A cackle rose on the air. "Whoo—ee!" Mr. Tubbs chortled, and spat a brown stream on the ground. "The fella what sent for you's got a job cut out for him!"

She swung her attention back to Olivia. "You all right?"

The slender woman stood and brushed her clothing off

without taking her eyes from Hallie. "Th-thanks t-to you," she stammered, and promptly burst into tears.

Hallie groped behind her for the coach and sat on the step. "I figured we'd all be next."

"I would rather have had them kill me," Evelyn said softly.

A moan rose from the ground. Zinnia unfurled from her faint and sat. She blinked about like an owl, rolled to her hands and knees and stood, wobbling. "What happened? Where are they?"

"Miss Wainwright scared them away," Olivia said, a look of amazement adding to her already bizarre appearance. Tears streaked her dust-caked cheeks and her bright hair stood out around her head like frazzled yarn.

"That she did!" Mr. Tubbs cackled and dusted himself off. "Whoo—ee! That she did!"

Zinnia's ragged hiccuping breath jostled her ample breasts.

What had she done? Hallie regarded the baggage strewn across the ground and their clothing flapping in the wind. What could possibly happen to top this?

Her mouth curved into a relieved but jubilant grin. Boston Girl Foils Attack On Women. What a story!

Cooper glanced up at the sun. He'd just decided to un-hitch the black and ride out to meet the stage when he spotted a cloud of dust on the horizon.

Anticipation rolled head over heels in his chest. He didn't have to like her. It didn't matter what she looked like. He didn't care how old she was or if she was a widow ten times over. All that mattered was that she could read and write, and she'd promised him that in her letter.

It would probably be easier if he didn't like her, since she was, after all, a white woman, and she would not like him. She didn't have to like him. City women were vain and shallow. Her reasons for coming out here probably bore as much desperation as his for needing her.

The small dot appeared on the horizon, and his gaze followed it. What would prompt a city woman to come to the Dakotas? Love for a man? Not in this case. Lack of funds? Probably. No other prospects for marriage? Miserable thought.

"They're comin'!" Stu shouted.

Slowly, Cooper strode to where the others stood watching the approaching Concord. He could make out the driver, Ferlie Tubbs, now, and sighed with relief.

Hooves pounded the earth, the jingle of harnesses and rings loud in the expanse of clear air. The stage drew near, distressed wood and leather creaking to a stop.

Ferlie squinted down at Cooper.

"Trouble?" Cooper asked.

The toothless ribbon sawer spit a thick stream of tobacco on the dusty ground and nodded. "Sonsabitches ran us down back at Big Stone Lake."

"Everyone all right?"

"Alive," Ferlie said.

"Hurt?" Cooper asked in alarm.

"Nah. Skeered the bejesus out o' the fat one, and the orange-haired crybaby bawled the whole damned way."

Cooper wondered whether he was marrying the fat one or the orange-haired crybaby.

"The hellcat's just madder'n a bear with a sore ass," Ferlie continued.

The door was flung open and, without waiting for assistance, a young woman in a dusty green dress with a matching hat askew on her head raised her skirts nearly to her knees and jumped to the ground. She wasn't fat and her hair, beneath the ridiculous hat and dust, was nearly as black as a Sioux's. *The hellcat.*

Her eyes, dark from this distance, surveyed the windswept vista and weathered log building and finally regarded the four men. Cooper met her stare. She was young, strikingly beautiful, with winged brows and a full mouth—definitely not a woman without better prospects in the city.

A sniffling sound came from inside the coach. She cast a significant glance over her shoulder and quickly stepped away saying, "One more mile in there and I'd have forgotten I was a lady."

The whining came from a short young woman whose drab dress resembled a sausage casing. She appeared in the doorway, another girl with wild hair the color of a stewed carrot holding her elbow. Tearstains streaked the dust on both their faces.

Ferlie jumped down.

"What happened?" Vernon asked, Stu and Angus at his side.

"Six of 'em," Ferlie said. "Rode us down at Big Stone. Robbed the womenfolk. Skeered 'em good. Woulda done worse."

Vernon clenched his fists.

"This brave young woman took a gun away from one of those border ruffians and saved us," the redhead explained, pointing to the hellcat. Beside her the fat lady sputtered into a fresh bout of tears.

The men cast one another skeptical looks.

Finally Vernon took the initiative and spoke. "Which of you is Miss Blake?"

The fat one sniffed. "I am."

Vernon reached for her gloved hand. "Pleased to meet you. Would it be all right if I called you Zinnia?"

A smile bloomed on her round face. She ogled Vernon as though he were rain for her parched soul. "Mr. Forbes?"

The hellcat stepped closer to Cooper—or maybe just farther away from the woman with the red and swollen eyes.

Vernon tucked his package beneath his arm and awkwardly assisted Zinnia from the coach. "You're safe now," he said. "You need a good hot meal and a night's rest."

"Miss Mason?" Stu asked, approaching the redhead.

She nodded. "Olivia."

The hellcat stepped back to the doorway of the coach and peered in. "Coming, Evelyn?"

Cooper stepped beside her and took the blushing young woman's gloved hand while she held her skirts and managed the step to the ground. She was painfully plain-faced and shy.

"Evelyn? Evelyn Reed?" Angus took her hand from Cooper's. He wore a nervous grin on his awestruck face. "I'm Angus Hallstrom. You musta been scared sh—" He stopped a second. "Real scared." The two stepped aside and the woman kept her head down as he spoke.

Amused at the station manager's enamored reaction to the plain-faced Evelyn, Cooper remembered the woman beside him—the only bride left. He turned and contemplated her.

"Someone must be notified," she said, looking up. "We were robbed."

Up close her sparkling eyes were three distinct colors. Gray ringed the outside, blending into green with rich golden brown at the centers. Her lashes were thick and black, and her brows arched delicately, heightening her refined beauty. "You're safe," he said, not knowing how to reply.

"She bloodied the big 'un's nose, grabbed his gun and shot the one jumpin' Miss Mason," Ferlie said. "You shoulda seen it, Coop. Hot damn!" He laughed again.

Cooper stared at her. This dainty creature had done all that?

"I may be safe," she went on, as if Ferlie hadn't interrupted, "but I'm poorer than Job's turkey! Those rowdies stole every bit of my money. They even took my jewelry. Someone will have to get it back!"

"I'm sorry." Again his words were woefully inadequate.

She positioned her full lips in an exasperated line.

Tess Cordell. And she was already unhappy.

"Mr. DeWitt?"

He nodded. "Miss Cordell?"

Her ivory complexion pinkened more deeply than the original flush of irritation. "Mr. DeWitt." She straightened her posture and lifted her chin. "I'm afraid Tess didn't come."

"What do you mean, Tess didn't come?"

"Apparently her fiancé had broken off with her sometime before she answered your ad. He returned just as she was preparing to come." She glanced over his shoulder and back. "She went to Philadelphia with him."

He regarded her. Four women had been expected, and four women had arrived. Confusion gave way to a sensation of rejection he didn't care for. "If you're not Tess Cordell, who are you?"

"I'm Hallie Wainwright."

He couldn't control the brow that rose in doubt. "And?"

"And…" Her glance skitted from his face to the driver who now made his way into the station. Angus left Evelyn Reed standing in the shade near the others, unhitched two of the six lathered horses and led them to the corral. "I'm a reporter."

He waited, taking stock of what he might read in her expression and movements.

"I'd been working on a story about the brides for *The Daily*. I wanted to follow up after the women got out here, and I'd hoped that Tess would be my contact. When she changed her mind, I didn't know what I was going to do. So, I took the ticket and the money and came in her place."

The Oglala didn't have a word for lie. Whites were the only ones Cooper had known to practice deception, and his lack of experience evoked an unfamiliar vulnerability. What purpose would a lie serve here?

Cooper didn't know which would be more disappointing: if she really wasn't his intended wife, or if she was and had come up with this plausible story to get out of an impulsive agreement she now regretted. In either case, he had no bride.

"You came in her place?" he asked.

"Well, I—" Her face grew a deeper shade of rose and she stammered. "I, uh, did use the ticket, yes. And I intended to pay you back for that as well as return the money that you sent Tess." Her gold-flecked eyes widened. "No! I did not come in her stead!"

Her horror at the thought of being his substitute bride didn't lend him any confidence. He took note that the other couples were already speaking with the justice. Stu glanced toward them expectantly. Cooper turned back to her. "All right. Where is it?"

"What?"

"My money."

Her mouth fell open. "They stole it! Those men who robbed us took everything of value they could carry on their horses."

"So you can't pay me back?"

She blinked. "No."

"Fair try, Miss Cordell."

Speechless for once, Hallie stared at the man. Beneath a fawn-colored hat, his blue eyes matched the endless sky overhead. He had a straight, stern nose and a shapely mouth with a tiny line at each corner. The deep dimple in his chin and the matching indentation beneath his nose lent authority to his serious expression.

"What are you saying, DeWitt?"

He scrutinized her face, and finally his expression changed. Drawing a breath, he said, "I understand why you don't want to stay."

"All right, why don't I want to stay?"

"You're a city woman. You've had a good hard look at this country…at the men…at me. And you're ready to go back to your comfortable home."

"It's not that at all. You can't presume to read my mind.

I never intended to stay here. I never intended to marry you.''

His gaze didn't flicker.

''Nothing personal, mind you. I am not Tess Cordell. I have a position at the paper back in Boston, and I'm not inclined to marry someone I don't know—or anyone, for that matter.''

He shrugged a broad shoulder indifferently, the soft fringe around his shoulders and his sleeve swaying with his movement, then turned and walked away.

His action surprised her, as did the thick, dark blond tail that hung down his back to his waist. She'd never seen a man with hair longer than her own.

The closer he got to the crude building, the more realization sank in. If she didn't intend to marry him, he didn't plan to waste time listening to her explanations. He hadn't exactly seemed the chatty, sympathetic sort.

Hallie sized up the situation. Here she stood in the middle of nowhere. The station and this handful of people were the only sign of civilization for who knew how far. She had a trunk full of dirty wrinkled clothes, a heavy satchel full of books and writing supplies, and exactly no money. He had every reason to think what he did.

''Wait!''

He paused and turned. ''Yes?''

Hallie caught up with him. ''I—uh, I have nowhere to stay and no way to get back.''

''Looks that way.''

''Perhaps you could loan me money for a room and a ticket home.'' His unyielding expression didn't give her much hope.

''There aren't any rooms, Miss...''

''Wainwright.''

''Wainwright. And I have better things to do with my money than give it to strangers without being sure of getting paid back.''

"My word is good," she replied indignantly.

"That's not the case with most whites."

Hallie gave him a curious frown.

Once again he scrutinized her face and hair, ran his blue eyes over her clothing. "How do I know you're not really Tess Cordell?"

Impetuously, she placed a hand on his arm. She thought he'd pull away, but her gentle touch held him even though the hard muscle beneath her fingers assured her no physical attempt on her part could stop this man if his mind was made up. He stared down at her fingers, and Hallie snatched her hand back.

She'd never met such a callous man. Her brothers may have been unsympathetic to her career plans, but they'd always been concerned with her safety and well-being. "So you're just going to leave me out here in God-knows-where, without a penny, to fend for myself?"

"I'm sure a capable reporter like you will come up with something. You got this far, didn't you?"

Yes, she had. Mustering her pride, Hallie stared at the dismal little station building and caught at her hat as another gale threatened to send it back to Boston without her. "Is there a storm coming?"

He glanced at the clear sky overhead and frowned. "There's not a cloud in sight."

"I just thought..." she mumbled. "The wind."

His attention wavered to her clothing flattened against her body, outlining her breasts and legs. She turned aside.

"The wind is always like this," he said.

"Oh." Hallie had never seen so much horizon. Land stretched in every direction. She'd never seen so much sky or dust or known so many insects existed. She'd never met an unyielding man like this one. Who knew? Maybe Tess Cordell would have made it this far only to change her mind.

She glanced at the others, still waiting near the building. "I'm sorry Tess didn't come."

He made no reply.

"Why don't you just take me to town? I'm sure I can make arrangements there." Perhaps she could sell something she had left, or make a trade for a ticket.

"There is no town."

"What?"

"Stone Creek isn't a town—yet. Besides my freight company, there's a livery, a trading post and a saloon."

She brought her attention back to his sun-burnished face. "And a post office?"

"Mail leaves from here." He nodded toward the station.

Hallie avoided his piercing eyes for several seconds. She ran through her dilemma in her head. No telegraph. No rooms. A fine fix. "How long until the stage goes out?"

"This one goes north tomorrow. It'll be two weeks before another heads back east."

"Is that mail, too?"

He nodded.

She stared at the tips of her dirty shoes. She could get a story in two weeks. But where would she stay? How would she eat? She was already starving. "Could you hire me? I'll help you with your business until I earn enough to get home, or until I hear from my father."

"You won't work off two hundred dollars plus the ticket in two weeks."

"I know that." She shook her head in frustration. "I'm not holding you responsible, even though my things were in the care of DeWitt Stage Company, am I? Why don't you give me the same courtesy?"

Hallie didn't know what other choice she had left. Unless she begged one of the newlyweds to take her home, and besides the embarrassing imposition, she wouldn't feel safe being too far from the stage station. It was her only link to home.

He studied her. "I don't claim to know much about city ways or what's proper and what's not, but you can't stay with me, even sleeping separately, without getting married."

He was right. No one would probably ever know, but even with the remote possibility that they would, Hallie couldn't risk the shame that would be placed upon her family, on her society-entrenched mother. "That is a problem. I don't suppose you have two residences?" she asked.

He shook his head and glanced away.

She couldn't help noticing his broad-shouldered frame in the soft leather clothing. Over six feet tall, the man was solid muscle. She couldn't allow his size or his gender to intimidate her. She was used to dealing with stubborn men.

He returned his attention and caught her observation.

"Marriage is out of the question. I don't want a husband."

Something flickered behind his blue eyes.

"You're insulted that I won't marry you," she guessed. She'd had enough experience with the male ego to know what she was dealing with.

"I need help. I don't expect a woman to fall at my feet." He took in her appearance again, from her hat flapping like a lid in the wind, to her clothing, and down to her feet.

Why should she feel inadequate beneath his stare? Hallie had never given in to the detriment of being a woman before, and she wasn't about to start. "I'm sure you'll find someone to help you, Mr. DeWitt. Just like I will find a way to get my story and go home."

She hurried back to the coach for her satchel, pulled out a tablet and pencil, and marched toward the small gathering in front of the building.

DeWitt followed.

"George Gaston, miss." The justice introduced himself nodded politely. "The ladies said Coop's bride changed her mind."

"I'm afraid that's so," she said.

"Well, let's go in, and the couples gettin' hitched should line up," he ordered.

Hallie joined the gathering inside the station. The rough log walls looked like the inside of every other stopover she'd been in since crossing the Missouri, but at least she was out of the wind and sun for a few blissful moments. The three couples took their places and the justice quickly performed the ceremony. Hallie's pencil scratched across the paper as she tried to take note of every last detail.

"You're the witnesses," the justice said, indicating Hallie and DeWitt. She signed three papers and handed the quill to DeWitt. He accepted it, carefully avoiding contact with her fingers, and turned his broad back to her.

Hallie stared at it only briefly before turning to George Gaston. "Would you be so kind as to give me a ride into town?"

He gave her a puzzled glance. "There ain't no town."

"To the trading post, then," she clarified.

"I only have the one horse, miss. Don't seem it would be proper." He glanced behind her. "Coop's the one with the rig."

Her body ached from the ride, and she was so tired she could have curled up right here and gone to sleep. She sighed in frustration.

"I'll give you a ride," DeWitt offered from beside her.

She slanted a glance up in surprise.

"Come."

"I need to post a letter to my father first." She scribbled on a piece of paper. "Do you have an envelope?" she asked the station manager.

"Nope."

Hallie looked at her letter in consternation.

"Just fold it and write the name and address on the back," he told her.

She followed his direction and handed the letter over.

"That's three bits, miss," Mr. Hallstrom informed her.

Distressed, she glanced over her shoulder.

DeWitt drew the change from a leather pouch and laid it on the wooden counter.

"I'll pay you back," she promised.

Hallie congratulated the women, promising to see them soon, and followed DeWitt outdoors.

"I'll pull the team over," he suggested. "You show me which bag is yours."

Though newly married, Angus jumped to the boot and performed his job, unbuckling the trunks and cases. DeWitt raised a brow at the sight of her trunk, but lifted it to the back of the wagon effortlessly, situating her valise beside it. She accepted his assistance and climbed up onto the seat.

Back aching, eyelids drooping, she rode beside him, desperately wanting to be able to eat and fall asleep. The man next to her made her feel even more helpless than her brothers did. If he believed her to be Tess, then he thought her a liar. If he took her word for who she was, he thought her a fool. Both assumptions got under her skin. "I'm a good reporter," she said at last.

From beneath the brim of his hat he cast her a sideways glance. She read neither skepticism nor belief.

"There have been plenty of women writers, you know," she said. "Mary Wollstonecraft wrote before the turn of the century. And there was Fanny Wright."

His expression didn't change.

"Anne Royall, too, but then she's not a very good example, with all that Washington gossip. And of course there's Lydia Maria Child's antislavery book. So you see it's not all that unheard of."

Hallie reached into her satchel and pulled out her clippings about the brides. "Here's one of my articles."

She unfolded a column and held it up for him to look at.

His attention flicked over the scrap of newspaper dismissively.

The wind caught it and tugged it from her fingers. Her

only copy disappeared into the vast countryside. Quickly, Hallie tucked the others safely back into her bag. "Those articles prove who I am, don't they?"

"Anyone could have cut them from a paper."

"You should have asked one of the other women who came. They could have backed up my story." She frowned thoughtfully. "I could have shown you my silver bracelet with my initials engraved on it, but by now some thief has probably given it to his... Do thieves have wives?"

He only glanced at her in silence.

"Well, he's melted it down for bullets, then," she said.

He turned his face away and watched the horses' rumps and the rutted dirt road.

Finally a few buildings came into sight, and the animals picked up their pace, heading for a long log structure with grass blowing atop the slanted roof. Hallie had never seen anything so strange.

"Is that your house?" she asked.

"The freight building. You can't see the house yet."

"You've planted grass on top!"

He cast her a curious look. "It's a sod roof."

An enormous barn sat beside it. Sectioned corrals holding horses and mules bordered the east side and the back.

He led the team through an opening wide enough to accommodate the horses and wagon, and stopped. Inside were rows of wagons, a wall of tools and the permeating smell of dung and hay. DeWitt unhitched his horses and whacked each on the rump. Placidly, they made their way through a doorway, where a short man wearing suspenders over his shirt met them.

"Hey, Coop! That the bride?"

Cooper hung tack on the wall. "No, Jack. She didn't come. This is Miss Wainwright. A *reporter* from Boston."

"Oh? Looks like this 'un would do." He tottered off behind the horses.

Hallie lowered her eyes and stretched her legs. Cooper

had called her by her name and identified her as a reporter. Did he believe her now? Her stomach growled, loud in the open room. "Why didn't you introduce me properly?"

His brows lowered. "Don't expect parlor manners out here, lady." He beckoned with an arm that sent fringe swaying.

Hallie followed. He led her across an open space near the big log building to a smaller one a short distance away. The logs were freshly stripped of bark. Behind it, two window-less sod houses stood, smoke curling from the chimney of one.

He opened a new door and ushered her inside, hanging his hat on a mounted set of antlers. The scents of wood and wax met her nostrils. The room they stood in had a glass window at each end. One side was for cooking, with a stove and table and chairs, the other a sitting area, which included a wide fireplace and a stone hearth. Overhead, a loft could be reached by a sturdy ladder made of saplings.

The stripped logs couldn't be seen from the inside. The walls had been plastered and whitewashed. Everywhere was evidence of recent construction and meticulous care. With new eyes Hallie took stock of the simple room and regarded the man who poked sticks into the stove and started a fire.

He'd built a home for Tess Cordell.

Did he feel cheated that she hadn't come? Resentful? An ache like that he must know sapped even more of her energy. Sight unseen, he'd provided the best his stark country had to offer. His preparations revealed there was more to the man than met the eye. He wanted a wife to share this home with. Hallie couldn't identify the lonely and disturbing feeling the thought wove into her empty stomach.

He'd only needed help, he'd said. He hadn't expected a woman to fall at his feet.

But he'd done all this in anticipation.

Somehow, perhaps unfairly, Hallie thought it was only right that Tess hadn't come. She hadn't cared if Cooper

DeWitt was old or young, hadn't thought of anything but herself and the fact that he obviously had a little money. She wouldn't have been happy here.

Would she?

He clanged a heavy black skillet on the stove and cut chunks of ham into it, his movements deft and sure. He looked different without the hat, less intimidating, more... approachable. His blond hair hung down the center of his back in a thick tail. He had a narrow waist and muscular buttocks and thighs.

Perhaps Tess had made a big mistake.

He glanced up and caught her looking.

Hallie met his eyes and willed herself not to think him handsome.

He dropped a heavy lid on the skillet. "I'll get you some water and you can wash before we eat. There's a privy out back."

"A what?"

He stood motionless, staring at the table. "A place to relieve yourself."

Embarrassment buzzed up Hallie's neck to her ears. "Oh—uh, a necessary," she said.

He brought water from outdoors and heated it on the stove. Carrying the metal pan through the doorway, he showed her into one of the two separate rooms. After placing the pan on a low stand, he left her alone.

Hallie surveyed the room. It held a wide rope bed covered with a rough blanket, a chest of drawers and an armoire, all new. There was no covering at the window, but wood pegs had been placed in an even row along the wall. All were empty. Waiting for a woman's clothing.

She loosened her hair, ran her fingers through it and re-pinned it as best she could, leaving her hat on the end of the mattress.

The water was a blessing. Even though it was warm, she scooped a palmful and drank it before she removed her jacket and unbuttoned her blouse, washing her face, neck, arms and hands. The rough toweling he'd provided exhilarated her skin, and, once finished, she felt refreshed, although she would've given anything for a bath.

Hallie replaced her clothing and carried the pan out, tossing the water on the ground.

"Next time water the vegetables with it," he said. Her nose nearly bumped his chest.

Next time? He took the pan and pointed to the table. Hallie sat obediently. Beside the plate lay a smooth white spoon and two-pronged fork. "These are lovely. What are they made of?"

"Bone."

She stared at the object in her fingers. "What kind of bone?"

"Buffalo."

"Oh."

He sat across from her and ate. She followed his example. The ham was a trifle salty, but the bread and eggs were filling. Hallie cleaned her plate, and didn't object when he gave her more from the skillet on the stove.

"I didn't see a chicken coop," she commented.

"Turkeys."

"Turkeys?"

"Wild turkeys. They lay eggs in the brush. I have some chickens coming this afternoon."

She swallowed her last bite. "Well, thank you for your hospitality. I'd best be on my way."

She stood.

He picked up the plates.

A thought occurred to her. "About my trunk…"

He looked up.

"May I leave it with you until I know where I'll be staying?"

He nodded and moved away from the table.

"Very well, then. Thank you again."

He turned back. "You know where to find me."

She nodded, picked up her valise and let herself out his door. Immediately the wind snatched at her skirts and blew dust in her face. Hallie drew her gloves from her reticule and pulled them on. The bag's weight brought an ache to her shoulder, but she made her way through the foot-deep dried ruts that formed a street of sorts, praying for success in finding somewhere to stay. Even an adventuress needed a rest now and then.

Chapter Three

The nearest building was a healthy walk, and exhaustion set in to Hallie's body and mind. She crossed the distance, thinking of her letter to her father sitting at the station for another two weeks until a stage came through to take it east.

She could probably walk faster.

Well, not unless she got a night's rest. And if she found her way. And if she could carry food and water to last weeks. And if she didn't run into those godawful robbers or others like them.

A shudder ran through her frame. She really was vulnerable. She'd never experienced the reality of it before. All of her father's and brothers' monotonous warnings came to mind. They'd known. But she'd led such a pampered, protected life, she hadn't thought any harm could actually befall her.

What an eye-opening day this had been.

The trading post was like nothing Hallie had ever seen. The building itself had been constructed of blocks of sod, and the cracks were chinked with mud. The thatched ceiling was suspended by a rough frame, weeds and cobwebs dangling over furs and tools and foodstuffs, everything covered with thick layers of dust. Besides dirt, the overpowering stench of tobacco and gunpowder and unwashed bodies hung in the cramped space.

Three men glanced up from their seats around a black stove in the center of the room. "Look, Reavis, it's one o' them brides. A purdy one, too!"

An unshaven man got up with stiff-jointed unease and took his post behind a laden counter. Obviously baffled with her presence, he scratched his head with bony fingers. Hallie stepped closer, so her words wouldn't be heard by the others. "Are you the proprietor?" she asked.

He chewed something that made a lump in his cheek and his whiskered upper lip puckered. His gray beard held a brown stain at the corner of his lip. He scratched his angled shoulder. "I'm Reavis. This here's my place."

Hallie glanced at the two men by the stove. They appeared eager to listen to the conversation without a qualm about rudeness. She leaned a little closer to Reavis and spoke softly. "Mr. Reavis, I seem to have run into unfortunate circumstances. Until funds are delivered to me or I'm able to secure wages on my own, I'm in need of lodging."

He worked over whatever was inside his cheek. "Huh?"

Hallie glanced from Reavis to the listening men and back again. "I need work and a place to stay."

"Why didn't ya say so? Somebody oughta told ya they ain't no place to stay and they ain't no work for womenfolk."

"No one has a room?"

"Everbody got a room," he said, and scratched between the buttons of his faded shirt. "Jest not one without a body in it already."

Hallie glanced around, thinking quickly. "Where does the justice stay when he's here?"

He jerked a thumb over his shoulder. "Throws down a roll in my back room."

"Could I do that?" she asked, hoping the justice wasn't staying long.

"Sure can." He exchanged a knowing look with the others and one of them snickered. "If'n ya don't mind my snorin'."

Warmth crept up Hallie's collar and heated her cheeks. "Oh." She mustered her dignity and peered around hopefully. "Why don't I clean the shop for you?"

He sized up the room defensively. "What fer? It'd jest get dirty agin."

Hallie's back ached and she'd never been so tired. She confronted the men eavesdropping. "And you, gentlemen? Would either of you have a job for me? I need to earn money to get home to Boston."

"Ain't no whores at the saloon," one of the others replied. His unpleasant smile revealed a missing front tooth. "You be fixin' to take that spot?"

She didn't care for the leering way he ran his eyes over her body. Refusing to show her mortification, Hallie turned away without giving his crude suggestion a reply.

They snickered again.

"Coffee there," Reavis said. "Or somethin' stronger if you hanker. You could sit a spell."

"Thank you," she replied, anxious to get away. "But I've just eaten." She ignored the men in the chairs and made a beeline out the door.

Just as well, she thought. From the appearance of the sales area and the vigor with which the man had scratched, she could only imagine what the back room and beds must be like. Hallie shuddered again.

Between the trading post and the next building, the wind covered her with as much dirt as she'd washed away at DeWitt's. Curiously she studied a large square tent with a sagging canvas roof as she passed. It appeared to have been there for some time, because weeds grew up around the bottom and a dirt path had been worn beneath the flap-covered opening.

In the open doorway of the next wooden structure the

bare-chested liveryman stood, watching her approach. Embarrassed, Hallie kept her eyes carefully focused on his soot-besmeared face. He stared at her as if she was an apparition the wind had blown in.

"How do you do?" she said.

A heavy-looking hammer fit like a child's toy in his massive hand. He bobbed his head in a nervous acknowledgment.

"I need a job and a place to stay," she said simply.

"Ain't no jobs, ma'am," he said. "Unless you build your own place, there ain't no work. Same for a house."

"I hadn't thought of building my own house," she said. "I'll keep that in mind." With little hope left, she asked, "Are you married?"

His eyes widened and the whites stood out in stark contrast to his dirty face. His attention dropped to the contours of her green traveling suit and the bag in her hand. "You askin'?"

Uneasily, she realized her mistake. "No. I—I'd hoped perhaps there'd be a woman.... Sorry to have bothered you."

She kept her shoulders straight and her head up, and hurried away. With his eyes boring into her back, Hallie was torn between turning around to look and running full steam.

Farther along the road and to the right, the land sloped downward and several trees grew along the bank of a river. Hesitantly she glanced back. The liveryman was still watching her from in front of his building. Hallie turned away quickly. The shade appealed to her, so she walked down the slope, dropped her valise and sat beneath one of the trees.

"Hellfire!" she said aloud. What had she gotten herself into? She could just hear Charles and Turner now, berating her for being ten kinds of a fool. Providing she made it back home so that they could yell at her. If wild animals or hostile Indians killed her out here, they'd lament forever about what a foolish, headstrong girl she'd been.

She'd sent a telegram from Buffalo, telling them her plan, and another from a place on the shores of Lake Michigan. It was purely conceivable that the letter she'd written today would never reach them. She could die out here and they'd never know if she'd arrived or what had happened to her.

Hallie snorted in self-derision. It would be the first time she'd made headlines. Foolhardy Daughter Of Newspaper Owner Perishes In Wilderness! Evan would probably write the damned piece.

The wind tore through the branches overhead, but down here near the bank, the air was calmer. Hallie laid her head on her leather valise and watched the leaves whip against the bright blue sky. When ticking off the pathetically few businesses, DeWitt had listed the freight company, the trading post, the livery and the saloon.

She hadn't seen the saloon, thank goodness. After that crude man's comment, she knew there were no respectable jobs or places to sleep alone.

She turned on her side and closed her eyes. This dilemma was too much to deal with right now. Perhaps she'd have a clearer head after a few minutes' rest.

Hallie opened her eyes to pitch-blackness. Her back hurt intolerably. Behind her, the gentle sound of lapping water blended with the exultant chirr of crickets and other, more unfamiliar night sounds. Occasionally, a loud croaking sound echoed across the river's surface. Something stung her chin and she slapped it.

Disoriented, she sat up. Her predicament came back to her, and fear trembled in her aching limbs. She was alone and unprotected in the untamed badlands of the Dakotas. Her very existence was at the mercy of Indians, wild animals and uncouth frontier men. What in the blazing Sam Hill had she been thinking of?

Hallie reached up for her hat and realized she'd left it at DeWitt's. She opened her valise. Once her eyes adjusted to the night, the moon provided enough light to see the contents and the nearby area. No wild animals lurked within eyesight. She withdrew her brush, unpinned her hair and brushed it out, securing the new braid with one of the ties from her reticule.

Gingerly, she picked her way down the bank and knelt near the water, scooping several handfuls and drinking deeply. A cool breeze blew across the water and she shivered. Her warmer jacket was in her trunk—in DeWitt's barn.

Nearer the water, mosquitoes feasted on her tender skin. Tall weeds nearby provided a place to relieve herself, though she worried more about having her backside chewed alive than someone seeing her. Quickly she finished and hurried up the bank to her spot beneath the trees, where she sat scratching her neck and wrist.

What should she do? Wait the night out here? Walk up near the buildings where it might be safer from animals? Perhaps she could find a spot in DeWitt's barn to hide for the rest of the night. Or did that Jack fellow sleep there?

Wings flapped overhead, and Hallie stifled a startled cry. She glanced around, searching the unfamiliar darkness. Just an owl. *Or a bat.*

An eerie hoot came from somewhere nearby.

Or Indians? Gooseflesh broke out on her arms. She'd devoured too many dime novels not to know that Indians signaled one another with animal sounds, and that an unsuspecting white wouldn't know the difference. They moved with stealth and silence and often took white women as slaves.

Maybe she would be safer nearer DeWitt's place. She stood again, picked up her case and hurried up the slope to the road. Men's voices came from the tent structure she'd seen earlier. Light glowed from inside. A revival tent?

Hallie hurried closer and listened to the voices through the canvas wall.

"Stood there pretty as you please with her skirts hiked

up and her prissy white drawers bared to all nature—whoo-ee!'' A gleeful cackle followed. ''And when that fella reached for her, she all-fired brung that skinny knee up and busted his nose! He couldn't absquatulate fast enough!''

Men's chuckles followed.

Hallie burned with embarrassment and aggravation. Why, that dirty, low-down coot! Mr. Tubbs had treated her with the utmost respect and dignity, only to turn around and make jest of her nearly disastrous episode with the bandits! She ought to go in there and give him a piece of her mind.

Glass sounded against glass and a belch erupted.

''Don't get too corned, Ferlie. You gotta head that stage out in the mornin'.''

''Never was a mornin' I couldn't sit atop a horse or a stage, no matter how many jugs or women I polished off the night afore.''

Laughter erupted once again.

The saloon. She backed away. She'd been around enough men in her life to know not to draw attention to herself when they were drinking.

Hallie stole away from the tent and found her way in the moonlight. The livery was dark. Imagining the huge black-haired man watching her from a crack in the wall, she switched her valise from one hand to the other and continued on. A beckoning yellow glow burned from the window of DeWitt's home, and she followed it easily.

She had no idea what time it was, her timepiece having been stolen, and wondered if he was asleep—she paused several feet away—or back at the saloon.

The barn wasn't lighted, but she found it easily enough. A sliding barrier now covered the wide opening he'd pulled the wagon through. A regular door stood to the side. She rested her fingers on the latch.

Did they tie their horses up in here or would she be trampled? Was Jack in here somewhere? This no longer seemed like such a good idea.

"We hang horse thieves out here."

Hallie gasped and dropped her valise, whirling to face the man who'd spoken at her ear. Beneath the palm she flattened against her breast, her heart beat wildly. A broad-shouldered, unmistakably masculine form was silhouetted against the moon. "Mr. DeWitt!" She dropped her hand and caught her breath. "You nearly frightened me to death!"

"Better than hanging."

"I wasn't going to steal a horse!"

"No? What are you doing sneaking into my barn, then?"

Hallie's confidence had taken a beating. She struggled for poise. "I—" she didn't want to admit this "—I was just going to spend the night."

"And abandon your cozy spot by the river?"

She gaped at him in the darkness. "You were spying on me?"

"Spying?" he asked, and his head tilted uncertainly.

"Snooping? Watching without permission?"

"I was spying," he agreed.

"Well!" She adjusted her jacket and stood straighter. Good heavens, had he even known when she'd hung her backside in the weeds? Hallie's posture went slack. She scratched absently at the place she'd just thought of.

"Come." He picked up the valise and reached for her arm.

Hallie pulled away. "What are you doing?"

He wrapped his fingers around her arm and hauled her forward. "You can't stay outside all night, and you can't stay in the barn."

Through her jacket his touch was just firm and unyielding enough to not hurt. "Is Jack in there?"

"Yes."

"Where are you taking me?"

"To my house. You'll stay there, and then I'll get some sleep."

"I can't stay with you! You've already said it's highly improper."

He stopped before his door and released his hold. "Proper doesn't hold much water out here."

She realized that. But she wasn't from here. She was from the East, where propriety meant everything. She glanced back out at the unending expanse of darkness. But then, Bostonians didn't have to deal with wild animals and Indians, did they? "Are there any bears near?"

He reached for the latch and opened the door. Welcoming light spilled across the threshold and revealed his muscled body in the buckskin clothing. "Grizzly."

More afraid of bears than of him, Hallie hastily stepped past him into the room. "You're right. Proper doesn't even seem wise at this point."

He carried her valise to the room where she'd washed earlier and returned with an enormous roll of furs.

"Go ahead," he said, gesturing to the room. "I'll sleep here." He pointed to the floor by the fireplace.

Hallie glanced from the room to the furs. She hadn't meant to put the man out of his bed.

"I'll sleep in the barn if you want," he said, as though he misunderstood her hesitation.

"No." She scratched at her jaw. "I don't want to impose on you. I could sleep here."

"You'll have the room to yourself. I've slept on the ground most of my life."

She looked at him curiously. What kind of family and upbringing had he come from? "You have?"

He frowned and stepped closer.

Hallie felt herself shrink from his immense form.

Gently, he took her hand and inspected the bites, dropping it to tip her chin up and study her neck and jaw with a warm blue gaze. He released her, and her skin tingled where he'd touched her. He brought water from the stove. For such a large man, he moved gracefully, without a sound. She glanced down at his knee-high moccasins. "This is still warm," he said. "Go wash. I have something for the itch."

Hallie accepted the pan and closed the door behind her. She stared in surprise. Her trunk stood against the wall. Why had he brought it in? Grateful he had, she removed the broken lock and opened the lid, sorting through the jumbled contents. Her clothing was dusty and wrinkled, but cleaner than what she was wearing. She slipped out of her traveling suit, washed and dressed in a nightgown and modest robe.

She opened the door and peered out.

DeWitt waited near the table. "Sit."

Approaching him made her feel small and at his mercy, a feeling she didn't like. Hallie studied his well-carved, sun-burnished face. Tonight she *was* at his mercy. She sat. Her heart fluttered nervously in her chest.

He dipped a broad finger into a small earthenware pot and retracted it smeared with a shiny yellow substance. Dotting it on her wrists first, he then rubbed it into her skin with his second finger. His touch was surprisingly gentle. Instantly the sting disappeared. The backs of her hands received his attention next. The intimacy of the situation struck Hallie, and she grew uncomfortably warm. She was alone with a man—a strange man.

She couldn't help studying his down-tilted face with its angled jaw and strong chin. Her attention wavered across his uncommonly long hair, still drawn back.

There was a perfectly good reason for the nearness they shared and the way she was dressed—or undressed. He couldn't have reached her wrists in the long-sleeved jacket. And the caressing touch he administered to the backs of her hands was merely an act of human kindness.

He tipped her chin up, and Hallie became aware of his hard, callused finger. Although the position brought their faces close, he focused his attention on her neck. His finger seemed to caress beneath her ear, along her jaw, the corner of her eye. His warm breath stirred the hair at her temple and an unexpected tingle ran through Hallie's body.

He dotted the end of her chin and their eyes met. He rubbed the spot absently, holding her gaze. "Anywhere else?"

Her gaze dropped to his lips.

"Miss?"

Hallie looked away. She shifted uncomfortably on the chair, the bites on her bottom driving her to distraction. In polite society one didn't even refer to a leg. She couldn't tell him where her worst bites were. "Uh…"

He handed her the pot, his callused palm grazing her skin. The corner of his mouth jerked, but immediately he flattened his lips. "Take it with you."

She nodded.

He stepped away.

The earthenware container was warm from his hand. She stood, wanting to say more, wanting to ask why he'd decided to be kind to her. She debated the wisdom, and finally turned back. "Mr. DeWitt?"

He said nothing, but his eyes revealed his interest.

"Thank you for everything."

"You're welcome."

Whatever his reason for seeing to her care, she appreciated it. "You really have no reason to believe who I say I am. I admit what I did was rash. I fully expected that when I explained the situation to you and gave you the money Tess left, you would understand and could send for another wife." She studied his unchanging expression. "I knew it would be an inconvenience, but I guess I wasn't thinking of what a disappointment you'd be in for."

She walked to the bedroom door. A thought occurred to her and she turned back. "You never asked me anything about her."

His deep voice came softly from across the room. "What does it matter now?"

Her hand stilled on the latch. "You deserve better."

With that, she hurried into the room.

Cooper stared at the closed door. What had she meant by that? He deserved better than Tess Cordell? Or he deserved better than being left at the altar, so to speak?

The lady was a fascinating blend of contradictions. On one hand, her poise and delicate beauty lent her an other-worldly air of sophistication and charm. Just the type of woman he'd expected—and dreaded. On the other hand, her headstrong actions and bold speech rattled him even more because of their unfamiliarity. She was educated. She was sharp and informed. She was born and bred to a life he had no capability of understanding.

The vivacious flare in her eyes and the stubborn tilt of her chin characterized an impetuous child. Her softly curved body belied that. And the more he saw of her nature, the more he didn't believe she would lie to get out of a situation she'd changed her mind about. Her determination included a healthy dose of integrity.

She was the reporter she said she was.

What, then, was he going to do with her? It had been plain to him from the first that he was stuck with her for at least two weeks, unless he took her back to the Missouri River crossing himself. That was out of the question. He had a business to run. He had lumber coming tomorrow and supply wagons the following day.

Well, she would have to earn her keep. That's why he'd sent for a woman in the first place. Wasn't it?

Cooper glanced at the wooden bar across the cabin door, unrolled his fur pallet and blew out the lantern. No sliver of light beneath the bedroom door showed him she'd doused hers, too. He slid off his moccasins and placed his rifle beside him before he lay down.

He smiled, thinking of her reluctance at putting him out of his bed. He'd made the foreign piece of furniture only two weeks ago and had yet to sleep on it. The idea for it had come to him one night before he'd finished the log house. He'd lived in the soddy behind, his dead brother's wife, Chumani, and son, Yellow Eagle, living in the soddy beside. Once he'd sent for a bride, he'd planned the cabin, but he hadn't really considered all the added things that went with it—and her.

A little at a time, he'd filled the place with the trappings of civilization. A wife from the city would need a stove; he couldn't expect her to cook over a fire. And a bed, he'd thought, much, much later. A lady would need a proper place to sleep. And so he'd built it, thinking, as he planed and fitted each piece of wood, of what Tess Cordell would be like.

Simple curiosity. It hadn't mattered that she be young or attractive. A pleasant nature, capable hands and a quick mind would have been enough. Someone to help him with his work. Someone to teach Yellow Eagle to read so he'd have a running start on the future.

He truthfully hadn't expected Tess Cordell—or Hallie Wainwright—to jump off that stage into his arms, eager to marry him. But after meeting the head-strong young woman who had arrived, the thought was appealing. What would he be doing tonight if the saucy beauty in the other room had been his intended bride? The thought unleashed the long-denied physical cravings of his body. Cooper couldn't help wondering…wishing.…

He turned over and adjusted his body in his nest of furs, banishing those dangerous thoughts. He'd see to her safety until the stage came to return her home. Until then, he'd be best off to keep his mind on business. If he didn't, he'd be in for a whole pack of trouble.

But as he fell asleep, the last images in his mind were those of gold-flecked eyes and hair as dark and shiny as a prime pelt.

Hallie awoke with a start. She sat up and blinked, orienting herself. Reassured at her surroundings, she relaxed against the warm, cozy mattress and pulled the soft blanket up to her chin. She'd slept the best she had in weeks. Her host had a comfortable bed and walls that blocked outside sounds. Anyone would be quite content here, no doubt.

Why had she thought that? Reluctantly she tossed back the covers and got out of bed. She washed her face and cleaned her teeth with the tepid water in the pan and dressed quickly, wondering if DeWitt was up.

Hesitantly she opened the door and peeked out. The man, along with his pile of furs, was gone. She wandered the scarcely furnished room and finally ventured out to use the necessary—the *privy,* he'd called it.

Finished, she opened the door and headed back. A whoop sounded beside her and she collided with a four-and-a-half-foot bundle of energy. Hallie caught her balance, but the boy sprawled in the grass. Immediately he jumped to his feet and stared at her.

Hallie stared back, heart pounding. An Indian boy!

She cast a wild glance about. Where had he come from? Were there more hiding nearby? Surely he wasn't alone. Was he lost?

Seeing no one else, she inspected him from head to foot. He wore trousers, a fringed tunic shirt like DeWitt's and moccasins. Jet black hair hung to his shoulders.

Perhaps it was a trick. Maybe the rest of his tribe was waiting to swoop down on them. Should she run for DeWitt? Or scream?

The boy, who appeared to be about ten, glared at her.

She raised her hand in what she hoped was a peaceful greeting. ''Hello,'' she said, and thought herself foolish. How was he supposed to understand?

''Who are you?'' he asked in an annoyed tone, his black eyes scouring her face and hair.

''I'm Hallie Wainwright. Who are you?''

"Are you here to marry Cooper?" he asked without replying.

Startled at his speech, she overlooked his rudeness. "No. He's letting me stay with him. Who are you?"

"I am Yellow Eagle of the *Wajaje tiyospay,*" he said proudly.

"Where are you from?"

"What does it matter to you where I come from? It isn't my home anymore because of your people."

His hostility took her aback.

"Go back where you came from," he said, and turned away.

Just then an Indian woman appeared in the doorway of one of the sod houses. She wore a slim, ankle-length dress made out of the same soft-looking leather as Mr. DeWitt's clothing. Hallie stared in fascination. How many of them were there? They lived here? She'd thought the buildings and property all belonged to DeWitt.

The raven-haired woman walked toward them on silent moccasined feet. She said something to Yellow Eagle that Hallie couldn't understand.

Annoyance laced Yellow Eagle's tone and expression as he replied in their language.

The woman spoke sharply. He turned back reluctantly. "My mother says to tell you she is Chumani," he translated. "She is honored to meet you and you must come eat."

"Oh, no, I—I couldn't possibly. Thank you, but—"

"Good, don't eat." He started to walk away.

The woman stopped him with a sharp command.

"She says Coop has already eaten and she has saved food for you."

"This morning, you mean? Mr. DeWitt ate with you this morning?"

"He always eats with us."

Confused, Hallie met the dark-skinned woman's gaze. She had prominent cheekbones and wide-set, uncertain eyes.

It seemed to Hallie as though she were waiting for either approval or rejection. She said something to Yellow Eagle.

"What did she say?" Hallie asked.

"She wants to know what you said."

Hallie relaxed. If DeWitt ate with them regularly, it must be safe. "Tell her I'm grateful for her kind invitation."

Yellow Eagle spoke to Chumani in a few hard syllables. She smiled and led the way into the sod house.

The small room was clean and orderly. Chairs on one side of the blackened fireplace were upholstered with hides. A solid table and benches sat on the other. Chumani gestured for Hallie to sit. She prepared a plate from the kettles over the fire and placed it before her. Hallie picked up a smooth bone utensil and tasted the gravylike mixture poured over biscuits.

"This is delicious."

At a grunt from his mother, Yellow Eagle translated and Chumani gave her a cup of coffee. Hallie had never cared for coffee, but she took several sips so she wouldn't offend her hostess. The woman sat across from her with a quill needle and sewed a sleeve into a leather shirt.

Hallie wondered for a moment why the woman and her son hadn't made an appearance the night before and then realized they'd probably assumed Mr. DeWitt was bringing a wife home and they had given him privacy.

How curious that these Indians were living here among the motley bunch of inhabitants in Stone Creek. Now that she thought about it rationally, she realized that most news about the tribes in different areas relayed that they'd signed treaties and were living on land allotted by the government.

"How did you come to be here?" she asked, unable to quell her curiosity.

"We are Oglala," the boy replied, as if that answered everything.

"Where is the rest of your family?"

"Most are at the reservation without enough to eat, treated like dogs."

"Is that why you're here?"

He looked at his mother before answering. "Here we have food and firewood."

"You take care of yourselves?"

"My father was murdered."

The bit of information shocked her. "How awful."

"Cooper is my father now," he said, raising his chin indignantly.

That took a few minutes to register. Hallie regarded the soft leather shirt in the Indian woman's hands. It was identical to the one Mr. DeWitt had worn yesterday. She raised her eyes to her pleasant, dark-skinned face. Chumani made his shirts?

Chumani spoke softly with her son while Hallie stared into her coffee. *"Te-wah-hay,"* she said.

"What did she say?" Hallie asked.

"We are Cooper's family," the boy said.

A spark of disappointment and anger flickered in her chest. The boy considered DeWitt his father, and the woman made him shirts. She'd heard of mountain men and trappers taking Indian wives. The idea wouldn't be disturbing by itself. She stared into her tin cup.

What really sent a jolt of annoyance sparking through her blood was the fact that he'd advertised for a wife when he already had an Indian woman hidden away back here. What kind of man was Cooper DeWitt? And why had he wanted to bring a city woman out here?

She recalled the wording of his letter. He'd needed a woman to read and write. Someone to help him with his business. She remembered his words about not expecting the bride to fall at his feet. Hallie's eyes wavered back to Chumani. Now she knew why nothing but education had been important. Cooper DeWitt already had a wife.

Chapter Four

Silently fuming, Hallie finished her breakfast and managed to drink the cup of strong black coffee with only the merest grimace. *Did* this Indian woman know Mr. DeWitt had sent for a bride? Everyone else knew. But she obviously didn't speak English; it would be easy for him to hide it from her.

A bride wouldn't be so easy to hide, however. Hallie watched Chumani intricately stitch a row of tiny beads across the front of the shirt. What did the poor woman think of Hallie spending the night in DeWitt's cabin? Hallie knew nothing of Indian customs. Perhaps bigamy was acceptable. Perhaps, no matter how uncouth the man was, it was better having him take care of her than starving on a reservation, as Yellow Eagle had pointed out.

Whatever did the woman do to keep herself busy all day? Hallie would go crazy in this cramped space with only a little sewing to occupy herself.

"Thank you for the meal," Hallie said.

Yellow Eagle translated.

Chumani gave her a soft smile.

Hallie had a hundred questions she'd like to ask. She turned to Yellow Eagle instead. "Do you know where Mr. DeWitt is now?"

He nodded.

"Can you tell me?"

"He's working."

"I only want a word with him."

"He won't like it."

"I can deal with that, thank you."

The boy snorted and stood.

Hallie nodded politely as a means of excusing herself from the table, and followed Yellow Eagle from the sod house and toward the freight building. Leading her around the side, where the sound of wood being stacked echoed, he stopped and pointed, a smirk on his youthful face.

Three bare-chested men were unloading the back of an enormous flatbed wagon. Hallie had never seen so much skin in her life! She stumbled over a clump of grass and caught her balance.

Two more wagons stood to the east of the building, bulging tarps evidence of similar loads. Two of the men, whom Hallie had never seen before, noticed her, and stopped their work to stare back, pushing their sweat-stained hats back on their heads.

The third, Cooper DeWitt, pulled a stack of lumber forward, the muscles in his broad back and shoulders flexing beneath the sun-burnished skin. When neither man picked up the other end, he became aware of their distraction and turned to the cause, studying her from beneath the brim of his hat.

A queer enchantment held Hallie motionless. It was impossible not to look. The morning sun gave his chest and shoulders a warm glow. The wind caught the thick blond rope of hair hanging down his back, and it fluttered like the tail of a wild horse.

He came to life, gave the others an aggravated glance and shoved the boards back into the stack. Speaking curtly to the men, he turned and walked toward her. Hallie made up her mind not to stare at his shocking display of flesh and muscle. He made a rapid series of gestures. Yellow Eagle replied, gave Hallie a smug grin and ran back toward the soddy.

Hallie watched his approach, appreciation and apprehension tumbling in her stomach. Determinedly, she thought of the kind Indian woman making him a shirt, and annoyance won out. "I need to speak with you."

"Stay near the house," he said, ignoring her request.

She kept her eyes on his face. "I am near the house."

"I mean, you shouldn't come here."

"Why not?"

"The house is safer."

His words managed to take off some of her cheekiness. She glanced around. "Do the grizzlies come around in the daytime?"

"Animals aren't the only danger."

Her attention wanted to flutter downward, but she steadfastly stared into his eyes. "What do you mean?"

He set his jaw, accenting his generous lips and square chin. "Men come and go here all the time."

"I was raised around men, Mr. DeWitt. I'm not intimidated." All the men she'd been raised around were gentlemen and kept their shirts on, but she wasn't going to point that out.

"The men in these parts don't see many women. Especially not young, pretty ones."

She couldn't help the flush that rose in her cheeks. He thought she was pretty? Hallie had to remind herself why she'd come out here. "I need to speak with you."

"I'll see you at mealtime."

"This is important."

"I have work to do. I'll see you at noon."

"What do you expect me to do until then?"

His assessing blue eyes flicked over her hair and face. "What did you plan to do when you came here?"

"I planned to get a story!"

"Then write a story." He turned and walked away.

Hallie's gaze dropped from his broad back to his narrow waist. She didn't let herself take note of the muscles beneath his buff-colored, fringed trousers.

Frustrated, she turned back toward the house. *Boston Girl Dies Of Boredom,* she thought humorlessly. Chumani was working beside a fire pit, so Hallie sauntered back to watch her. The top of a good-sized cylinder of tree trunk had been hollowed into a bowl shape. Chumani placed damp kernels of corn in the well and pounded them with a wooden beater.

Before Hallie's eyes, the corn was ground into meal. "That's amazing!"

Chumani glanced up from her work and smiled.

"I've never seen anything like this before. At home we shop for meal and flour at the mercantile. It's all sewn into bags when we get it."

The black-haired woman nodded and pounded.

Hallie sat on a nearby stump and watched. She ignored the echoing sound of lumber being stacked. The Indian woman really was pretty. Her black hair caught highlights in the sun and black lashes and brows complemented her sleek brown skin. She moved and worked with grace and confidence.

Hallie could see how she would appeal to a man. Besides her unassuming beauty, she was hardworking and quiet. Was that the kind of woman Cooper thought he would get from the city, too? What kind of woman would submissively sit by and allow him to dally with another woman? The thought got her hackles up again.

Hallie glanced at the pot bubbling over the fire and the rustic tools gathered nearby. Chumani had been working on this earlier, and had apparently joined Hallie inside while she ate, as a courtesy.

Yellow Eagle brought firewood, stacked it a safe distance from the cookfire and disappeared.

Growing restless after an interminable length of time, Hallie asked, "Can I help?"

Chumani tilted her head.

Hallie pointed to herself. "Me. Help?"

She made a useless gesture of busy hands, but Chumani seemed to understand. She led her to the pot over the fire where corn bubbled in blackish water. Demonstrating, she carried a wooden scoopful of corn to a piece of burlap stretched between four sticks stuck in the ground, and poured the corn onto the fabric. Next, she took a dipper of fresh water from a bucket and poured it over the kernels. The water rinsed the corn and ran through the burlap.

She handed Hallie the scoop.

"I understand," Hallie said, grateful for a task to keep her hands and mind busy. "Rinse the corn. I can do that." Energetically, she set about the task. After several scoops of corn, she raised the bucket. "Water's gone."

Chumani nodded.

Hallie studied her.

The woman pointed at the pail, at another one nearby, then behind the soddies.

Finally comprehending, Hallie muttered, "Go get more." She carried the buckets and headed in the direction indicated, discovering she was upstream on the river she'd washed in and drunk from the night before. She staggered back into the clearing. "These are a lot heavier on the way back."

Chumani's innocent smile gave her a moment's wonder, but she shrugged it off. She'd made five more trips up and down the riverbank before the corn was rinsed. Chumani's job was looking better and better all the time.

Hallie assisted her in moving the heavy kettle from the fire. Chumani ran green sticks through several sickly pale headless blobs of flesh with flopping appendages and hung them over the fire.

Hallie's stomach turned. "What are those?"

"*Gu-Que,*" Chumani replied. At Hallie's lack of comprehension, she tucked her arms in and flapped her elbows.

"Some kind of bird," Hallie said with an uncharacteristic lack of appetite.

Yellow Eagle brought several pieces of bark and placed them beside the fire. Chumani stirred together a batter using the cornmeal and poured it into the concave bark strips. She placed them before the fire.

The birds turned a golden brown and the smells actually resembled an appealing dinner cooking. The batter in the bark bowls gradually turned into crusty cornbread.

Chumani spoke to Yellow Eagle and he ran toward the freight building. Several minutes later DeWitt and the two men—all properly clothed, thank heavens—appeared, and everyone traipsed into the sod house. DeWitt stood aside and allowed Hallie to enter ahead of him. Their eyes met briefly.

"Mr. Clark," DeWitt said, indicating the middle-aged man with lank brown hair that hung to his shoulders. "And Mr. Gilman. They're freighters from up north."

The second man was younger, with shoulders as wide as DeWitt's, and gray eyes that roamed her face and hair before she lowered her gaze, unwilling to witness the rest of his perusal.

None of them pulled out a chair for her; she did it herself, pretending she hadn't noticed.

"Unusual to see a young gal like you in these parts," Mr. Clark said. "How'd you come to be here?"

"Well, I—"

"She's meeting her husband here," DeWitt interrupted from the seat he'd taken beside Chumani. Hallie noticed he'd recently washed and the hair at his temples was damp. "They'll be moving on to Colorado."

Hallie glared at him, but he ate his food placidly. She kept silent through the rest of the meal, except to ask Yellow Eagle what kind of bird they were eating.

"Pheasant," he replied curtly.

She'd eaten pheasant before, but their preparation gave the meal a whole new perspective.

The freighters thanked Chumani and headed out.

"Are you going to keep your word and speak with me?" Hallie asked DeWitt as he finished his coffee.

His blue gaze bored into her. "Go ahead."

She glanced at Chumani. "May we go outside?"

He stood and ushered her ahead of him.

Hallie stopped behind his log house and turned. "First, why did you tell those men a lie about me meeting a husband?"

"For your safety."

"What do you think you're protecting me from?"

"Men out here don't live by the civilized rules you're used to," he said. "You should've learned that from your stage trip."

The reminder of what could have happened to Olivia and the rest of them at the hands of those stage robbers squelched any other objections she may have had. Hallie rushed on to the real problem. "I'm disappointed in you."

His expression didn't change. He waited.

"I think it's deplorable that you sent for a bride when you already have a wife!"

He frowned. "Chumani?" he asked.

"You know very well that I mean Chumani. Perhaps she doesn't mind sharing a husband with another wife, but I can assure you that any wife you get from back East will have plenty of objections."

His fair brows rose, wrinkling his forehead.

"What were you thinking of?" Hallie asked, waving her hand, inspired by her topic. "If the men out here expect women to endure the hardships of the travels and this land, then they'd better start living by more civilized rules."

His expression didn't flicker.

"The first rule being one wife per man."

"She's my brother's wife, not mine."

"I really thought you were serious about wanting a wife, the way you fixed up the house and all, but—what?"

"It's the duty of a dead warrior's brother to take his wife as his own."

Hallie frowned, mulling over his words. His brother was an Indian? How could that be when he was as white as she was? The possibilities intrigued her. There was a story here, somewhere, and a fascinating one at that!

"Chumani agrees I should have a white wife. I provide for her, but she's not my wife. Not in the way that you're thinking."

Hallie's neck and cheeks grew warm. "I see."

"May I work now?" he asked.

She nodded and he walked away. She would have to break through his reticence to get to the story inside.

She helped Chumani wash the dishes in a tub outdoors, more at ease beside the woman now that she knew she and Cooper weren't...involved.

Returning to the afternoon's work, she felt a calm sense of relief seeping into her pores along with the afternoon sun. Cooper didn't have an Indian wife after all. The odd reassurance puzzled her. Why should she care?

She made it clear that she'd like to try her hand at pounding the corn. Chumani cooked more kernels in the kettle, throwing ashes into the water to give it that black color. She cooked and rinsed and carried water, and Hallie's arms and shoulders grew numb from the repetitive and painful task of grinding. By supper she could barely raise her arm to lift the bone eating utensil.

"Miss Wainwright?"

Hallie jerked her head up, realizing she'd been drifting off to sleep sitting at the table. "Yes."

"You can start earning your way," DeWitt said.

Irritation wailed from her tired muscles. "I thought I did that today."

"Did you?" Across the table he regarded her. Firelight

bounced off the golden glints in his hair and shadowed the chiseled planes of his face. His cheeks showed the barest growth of stubble, like fine-grained sandpaper, and Hallie had the surprising urge to rub her knuckles across his jaw to discover its roughness.

With concentration, she relaxed her fingers on the fork. "I helped Chumani grind the corn. I carried water and rinsed and even pounded."

"Chumani's done that alone for years."

"Well, I—I…" Unexplainably, his words hurt her. She'd failed to win his approval even though she'd learned quickly and shared a good portion of Chumani's work. Why was his approval or disapproval important?

She was trying too hard, as usual. "I thought I was helping," she said, carefully hiding her disappointment.

"You owe me. Don't forget that."

How could she forget a mistake like that?

"One of the reasons I sent for a wife was so Yellow Eagle would have someone to teach him to read and write."

She set down her fork and glanced at the boy. He stiffened immediately. The worried look he shot Cooper turned into a glare when he regarded her.

"And the other reasons?" she asked.

DeWitt took the last bite of his supper and washed it down with coffee. "My business has grown fast. I can't keep track of orders and payments and shipments like I should."

"You need a bookkeeper?"

"Yes."

She regarded Yellow Eagle. He had pursed his lips and sat defiantly, staring at his plate. "I'll need his cooperation if I'm going to teach him."

"He'll cooperate," DeWitt assured her.

Yellow Eagle said something in a tone that told her he had no intention of cooperating. DeWitt spoke back and the boy's face reddened. He refused to look at either of them.

"He will cooperate," DeWitt said pointedly.

Hallie didn't know which of them would be more difficult to work with; the contemptuous nephew or his obstinate uncle. But she'd gotten herself into this mess; she would get herself out of it. If earning her keep and being able to pay him back so that she could get home meant swallowing a little pride and adhering to his demands, she could do it.

He waited patiently.

"I'll teach him. And I'll do my best to put your books in order."

His massive shoulders seemed to relax, but it must have been the play of firelight. He gave a curt nod.

Hallie straightened her back and winced. DeWitt spoke to Chumani. She opened a few small bags and sprinkled a mixture into boiling water and placed a mug before Hallie.

"What is it?" Hallie asked, sniffing the steaming brew.

"Spignet root tea for your back," he replied.

Hallie sipped. "It's pretty good."

Chumani said something and Cooper translated. "Where are you from?"

"I'm from Boston."

They exchanged words. "Is Boston far?" Cooper asked for her.

"Yes. It's in Massachusetts, way to the east."

"The East has more white people than there are buffalo chips on the prairie," Yellow Eagle brooded.

Hallie ignored being compared to a buffalo chip. "Why do you say that?"

"So many whites have come that there are no hunting grounds left. And more come still. The East must be crowded with your kind."

Hallie glanced from Yellow Eagle to DeWitt and back. "The cities are crowded, yes. There are so many buildings that you have to look straight up to see the sky. I never saw the sky in all directions until I got here."

"After all the whites build their houses and stores, it will be like that here, too," Yellow Eagle said.

Hallie couldn't imagine there being enough people to fill up the vast open spaces of the badlands she'd seen on her journey. "Oh, I don't think so," she said. "And the people have so many exciting things to bring with them."

"We don't need anything the whites bring." Yellow Eagle's expression was scornful, DeWitt's downright provoked. Hallie felt as if they'd ganged up on her.

"What about printing presses and books?" she asked.

"The Sioux passed down history and legend long before the whites came," DeWitt commented in a flat voice.

"Tools," she added.

"They made their own." His eyes narrowed in a contemptuous expression. "Don't forget soldiers."

"Doctors," she supplied. He couldn't deny modern medicine was a benefit to mankind.

"The Sioux have their own medicine men. How's your back?"

She arched it gently, and realized with surprise that the ache had disappeared.

"Don't forget whiskey," he said. "And smallpox and cholera. As many of The People have died from your diseases as by your guns."

Hallie couldn't think of a reply. She'd been made to feel unwelcome from her very first step in this land, and every word he spoke intensified that feeling.

Chumani said something in her language and Yellow Eagle translated. "Where are your people?"

"Family," DeWitt clarified.

"In Boston. My father and brothers run *The Daily,* a newspaper. My mother…" Hallie paused, wondering how to explain her mother to these people. "My mother runs the house."

DeWitt spoke to Chumani at length. She signed back.

"Your mother taught you to cook and sew?" he asked for her.

She lowered her eyes from DeWitt's. So much of what they said, so much of their resentment toward her seemed motivated because she was white. What sense did that make? "No. We have servants who cook and our clothing is made at a dressmaker's. Mother oversees those things and does charity work."

Cooper listened to her explanation of her family without surprise. Pampered city women were sorely out of place in this land. What had he been thinking of in sending for one? Perhaps it had been for the best that Tess Cordell had changed her mind and gone to Philadelphia. He would have to think long and hard about placing a new ad. He didn't have any more choice now than he'd had then, however.

He still needed someone to teach the boy and help with his business. Maybe there would be enough time for this young woman to accomplish both of those things. He had her over a barrel, actually. She was broke and helpless, and he was her only source of help and protection.

"Are you ready for sleep?" he asked, noting her growing weariness.

She nodded and helped Chumani pick up the dishes. He had to admit she dug right in and helped with the chores and meals—part of that fierce sense of independence she waved like a banner. She didn't like being dependent on him. She would do whatever it took to get away from here.

"Come." He waited while she said good-night to Chumani and Yellow Eagle, and led her to the house. She walked close at his side in the darkness, her skirts brushing his trouser legs. The mysterious rustle of whatever she wore beneath created a foolish leap of sensation in his stomach. She was the first young white woman he'd had contact with in over twenty years. He didn't know how to talk and act around her and he didn't like the fact that he was wondering.

She meant nothing to him. She stood for everything he hated.

A coyote howled and she grasped his arm with a sharp intake of breath. The shiver of pleasure that ran across his shoulders was entirely against his will.

One hand clung to his bicep through his shirt, the other his bare forearm. Her soft breast pressed against his upper arm. He turned his face and the top of her head came just below his chin. He'd smelled her before. The day she got off the stage. The same night, when he'd ushered her into the house. But he'd never been this close, never smelled her and felt her at the same time. Her clothing was cedar scented, and she emanated a soft, powdery, flowery smell he couldn't define. Tonight those scents combined with wood smoke and woman, and he didn't like his physical response one bit.

"What was that?" she asked.

"A coyote. They only come in close if we have game hanging in the smokehouse. No need to be afraid."

She seemed to realize what she'd done, and let go quickly. "I'm not afraid."

Cooper could still feel the touch of her soft hands on his skin, the warm press of her flesh against his arm. He didn't want to have a reaction to this woman, but she was a woman after all, and he was a man. Her cultured speech and delicate white skin only proved her unsuitability to this land and to him. They didn't make her any less appealing; in fact, as long as he was being honest with himself, part of her appeal probably stemmed from that untouchable quality.

Two weeks and then she'd be gone. He hoped he could continue to deny his attraction until then.

He opened the door and she followed him into the dark room. Cooper struck a flint and lit the oil lamp on the table. He handed her the flint box, their fingers touching briefly. "Can you find the lamp in the other room?"

"I remember where it is. Thank you."

"You can start Yellow Eagle's lessons in the morning. Will half days give you enough time?"

"I don't know." Her eyes were huge and dark in the shadows. "I've never taught anyone before. I can probably teach him to read in the mornings. Perhaps we could go over the morning's lessons again before bed each night."

He didn't like the direction his thoughts took when she innocently mentioned bed each night.

"This is so very important to you?" she asked. "That he learn to read and write, I mean. So important that you wanted someone besides yourself who has only a few hours to teach him?"

Cooper was glad for the distraction. "The Sioux are being forced to sign away their land in trade for food and the meager provision of the reservations. Those who can adapt and survive in the white man's world will have a chance for a better life."

"I never knew…I mean, I never thought about what it must be like for the Indians.…"

"Few whites have, Miss Wainwright."

"The papers print stories of hostile Indian attacks and innocent women and children being killed. There are hundreds of dime novels about the renegade savages and the heroic efforts of the soldiers."

"Who writes them?" he asked.

Her level gaze faltered to his chest, then quickly returned to his face. "White men."

"There might be some truth in them," he said.

Her expression grew thoughtful, drawing his attention to the full lower lip she held between her teeth. She was lovely. And feminine. And so out of place here. "Good night, then."

She seemed to rouse herself from her thoughts, gathering her skirts and turning. "Good night, Mr. DeWitt."

She entered the bedroom. The lantern light flickered on the walls a moment later and the door closed. Cooper took his guns apart at the table, cleaned and oiled them. Time and again he found his attention wandering to the closed door. He tried to concentrate on his task, but instead imagined her removing her clothing and getting into bed. The light under the door disappeared.

He was getting what he wanted without any entanglements. She would teach Yellow Eagle to read and set his company in order.

Things could still work out for the best. He could get the help he needed and not have a city woman underfoot for good, after all. A woman like that was the last thing he needed in his life. Thank goodness he'd been able to realize it before it was too late. Tess Cordell had done him a big favor.

The sound of horses and shouts woke Hallie before dawn the next morning. She washed and dressed in a skirt and blouse, her arm and shoulder muscles screaming. They ached even more when she quickly rebraided her hair and wound it in a knot on the back of her head. The sounds were still loud as she hurried through the outer room.

She lit the lantern, discovering DeWitt's fur pallet empty, as though he'd just sprung from it. She hurried out.

Just southwest of the house, startlingly vivid in the early light, a dozen Indians sat atop horses. A few raced back and forth between the house and the gathering. All of them had long black flowing hair and wore thigh-high leggings with breechclouts. Some were bare chested, others wore quill vests, and one sported a flannel shirt.

Hallie tried to take it all in at once—the beaded bands and feathers, the assortment of muscular horses and wild men.

Running back into the house, she looked about wildly, finally noticing a revolver lying on the table. She grabbed it and ran back out.

Her attention centered on the man standing on the ground

in front of the gathering—Cooper DeWitt. He wore nothing but a scrap of leather around his hips, a flap barely covering his buttocks, exposing acres of solid flesh and muscle. His long hair, unbound, whipped in the wind. In his hand he held a rifle.

Hallie raised the gun and walked closer.

One of the Indians got off his horse, noticed Hallie and stared. His jet hair was banded across his forehead with a beaded strip of leather. A tiny buckskin pouch, no more than an inch in diameter, hung on a thong against his chest.

Several of the Indians on horseback whipped arrows into their bows and aimed.

DeWitt turned and discovered her. He raised a hand and spoke rapidly to the Indians. "Go back in," he said to her.

"But—"

"Where did you get the woman?" the broad-chested Indian in front of him asked. He was as muscular as DeWitt, the corded thighs astride the horse as thick as small trees. A leather strip strained against his powerful bicep and Hallie imagined the strength with which he could use the knife and hatchet on his belt.

Surprised at his near perfect English, Hallie answered herself. "I'm meeting my husband here and we're going on to Denver."

The self-preserving lie fell from her lips easily. Something in DeWitt's blue eyes flickered. "Give me the gun," he said, reaching toward her.

"Trade," the Indian said. "Her for the prisoner."

His assessing black eyes swept her body and Hallie suppressed a shudder at the thought of being his prisoner. She shot a questioning glance back to DeWitt, reassuring herself he wouldn't do such a primitive thing.

He met her gaze, his open palm still waiting.

For the first time, she noticed the white man slung over one of the horses, his wrists and ankles bound. Above the bandanna that distorted his cheeks and hid the lower half of his face, distressed brown eyes stared back at her.

DeWitt was still waiting for the gun.

Why didn't he let her help protect them? He merely gestured with his open palm again.

Hallie eyed the prisoner, the Indian on the ground and those with their bows and arrows ready. DeWitt had cared for her mosquito bites, had been concerned enough with her welfare to house her under his roof. He'd instructed Chumani to give her healing herbs for her back. He needed her to teach Yellow Eagle. He would not turn her over to this Indian.

Left without a choice, she handed him the gun.

The Indians chuckled among themselves, placing their arrows back in their quivers. The one in front of DeWitt spoke, and he answered.

"Cut him down and come eat," DeWitt said.

The Indian gestured, and two braves cut the prisoner down. Immediately the man reached up and yanked the bandanna from his mouth. He rubbed his wrists and stumbled forward as though the circulation in his feet had gone. "I thought I was a dead man," he said.

"I'm sorry," DeWitt said, and reached to steady him. "I apologize for my brother. Last Horse doesn't trust strangers."

Hallie comprehended his words slowly. His brother? His brother? DeWitt turned fully toward her for the first time, and her confused gaze lowered to his broad chest. He too, was wearing a tiny pouch on a leather thong, which lay against his smooth brown skin.

Without reservation she allowed her gaze to drop to the scanty leather covering, down to his bare feet and back. Up past those thick bare thighs and smooth hips, almost expecting to see scalps hanging on his belt. Up beyond his chest to the wild mane of hair that hung over his shoulders

and down his back. For the first time she realized who he
was—what he was.

He was one of them.

Beneath that sun-burnished tan, his skin was as white as
hers. But he was one of them. The things he'd said that
made no sense before were perfectly plain now. He'd slept
on the ground most of his life. He resented the encroach-
ment of civilization. He resented her. He spoke the Indians'
language and made their signs.

He was one of them.

Chapter Five

The tall man with the chafed wrists composed himself and nodded at Hallie. "Wiley Kincaid, ma'am. I'd tip my hat, but one of them's got it."

DeWitt shouted something above the Indians' laughter. A brave on a brown-and-white-spotted pony rode forward, swept off a black hat and smashed it down on Mr. Kincaid's head. The others laughed and the brave galloped back into the gathering.

Wiley Kincaid yanked the hat off and looked it over, working dents from the crown, brushing at the fine felt. As though satisfied that no real damage had been done, he placed it on his head, only to remove it immediately and bow. "It's a pleasure to meet you, Mrs.—"

"Lincoln," Hallie said, concentrating to keep the corner of her lip from twitching.

"Mrs. Lincoln," he replied. "Any relation to the Lincoln practicing law in the States?"

Hallie waved her hand. "On my husband's father's side somewhere," she said dismissively. "Such a mess this war with Mexico, isn't it?"

DeWitt's irritated expression nearly made her laugh aloud. "My husband is quite a bit older than myself, the dear sweet man," she cooed. "I'm afraid he keeps awfully busy setting up camps and ordering detachments about, you know, all those positively achingly dull things." She slipped her arm through Kincaid's and flashed him her most radiant smile. "And what is it you do, sir?"

"I was a tanner for several years. Not so many pelts anymore, so I'm making harnesses and saddles."

"A tanner. Now, doesn't that sound fascinating! You will have to tell me all about it."

He flushed, succumbing to her charm. "Yes, ma'am."

"Where's your rig?" DeWitt interrupted.

"They came up on me about fifteen miles from the station. My horses and wagon are back there."

"After breakfast I'll ride out with you," DeWitt offered. Hallie had to pull her stubbornly disobedient gaze from his nearly naked body. He entered the house briefly and returned clothed.

She realized Last Horse was following them around the log house and scurried ahead, shooting into the soddy ahead of them. "Mr. DeWitt is bringing company to breakfast," she told Chumani. "And one of them is an Indian!"

After the foolish words were out of her mouth, she was glad Chumani couldn't understand her. Hallie grabbed tin plates and hurriedly placed them around the table.

The men entered the soddy. Last Horse stared at Hallie, his black eyes raking her body from head to foot. With a predatory glitter, his gaze rested openly on the front of her shirtwaist. Heat seared her neck and cheeks. She'd never been ogled openly and in such a rude manner until she'd reached this godforsaken country. Neither had she known men could be so crude. She'd read stories about savages carrying off women settlers, and realized even DeWitt's attempt at protecting her with a fictitious husband would be no deterrent to a lawless man.

Discreetly, DeWitt placed himself between her and the Indian.

Mr. Kincaid pulled out her chair. She gave Last Horse

her haughtiest rebuff and sat, DeWitt taking the seat beside her.

Chumani served fried bread with potatoes she had pulled from the fire and peeled blackened cornhusks from. It was obvious that she was used to visitors. Kincaid received her usual gracious smile.

Kincaid cast Last Horse wary glances as they ate, but the Indian ignored everyone and wolfed down his food without using the bone utensils. Chumani, too, gave Last Horse careful consideration.

"Looking for a place to start a harness shop?" Cooper asked.

"Might be. Are there logs available?" Mr. Kincaid asked.

"Just received a shipment of debarked lumber," DeWitt replied. "Costs more, but you'd have your building before winter."

"Sounds good. Spending the winter in a tent doesn't have much appeal," Mr. Kincaid said.

"You're staying?" Hallie asked.

"Looks like a good spot," he replied, then turned to DeWitt. "Do you trap?"

DeWitt shook his head. "Not anymore."

"Do you buy hides?" Last Horse asked.

Hallie stared at the Indian in surprise. Kincaid nodded.

"I'll sell you hides," the Indian said, and stood. Chumani handed him a bundle of food she'd wrapped.

"Being around him feels like standin' naked in a nest of rattlers," Mr. Kincaid said after Last Horse had gone.

"Stay on your toes," DeWitt replied.

"For heaven's sake, why do you just let that savage come right in and make himself at home at your table? He could have killed Mr. Kincaid!" Hallie said. "He's obviously dangerous."

DeWitt brushed his palms together and stood. "He's my brother."

Their gazes met and held.

"And it's my table."

What had she gotten herself into? she wondered for the hundredth time. The person she was depending on to pay her wages and get her home, the only person she could place an ounce of trust in, considered himself brother to a leering savage! Last Horse looked at her as if she was dinner after a long, hard day of killing and looting. Yellow Eagle outright hated her, and now this person thought she was married to an ancient army officer. Chumani couldn't understand a word Hallie said, which was probably for the best or she'd have made another enemy by now.

It was all too much. Hallie excused herself and ran to the house.

Cooper delivered Yellow Eagle to the log house directly after breakfast the next morning. He set a crate on the floor near the table and straightened.

"Where did you get all these?" Hallie asked, withdrawing slates and primers and stacking them on the sturdy table.

"I ordered them as soon as I planned to send for someone. Yellow Eagle knows what is expected of him. If he doesn't cooperate he'll be punished."

Hallie gave the Indian boy a hesitant glance.

"After the noon meal he's to help his mother."

Hallie nodded and Cooper exited the house. She dragged her gaze from the closed door to the churlish boy facing her. "Well, have a seat. We'll see what we have here."

She sorted through the books and placed two slates on the table.

Yellow Eagle remained standing.

She ignored him for a few minutes, then straightened and finally cast him an exasperated look. "Look," she said, hands on hips. "I know you don't like me. I know you don't like this whole arrangement."

His ebony eyes bored into hers.

"I don't like it, either. You think I want to be stuck out

here lugging water from the river, chucking buffalo chips into the stove and having every filthy, flea-bitten, tobacco-chewing man from here to wherever gawking at me like I'm a two-headed calf in a carnival? Well, I don't,'' she assured him, working up a head of steam. ''I'd just as soon be home taking a bath in a copper-lined tub or being served tea in the afternoon and then watching a play at the theater. But whining about it or giving dirty looks isn't going to make it happen. I have to teach you to read before I can go home, so by God, you're going to sit in that chair and learn to read.''

Yellow Eagle slid into the chair across from her.

''We start with the letters. Once you remember them and the sounds they make, you'll be able to read.''

Hallie tried to recall how she'd learned. She printed one letter at a time on her slate, had him trace over it, then make his own on his slate. She told him all the words that she could think of for each letter.

By the time morning had passed, they'd reached the letter *g*. Sitting at Chumani's table, Hallie felt as if she'd earned her dinner in the fashion DeWitt expected.

''How did the lesson go?'' he asked.

''Considering he'd rather scalp me than learn the alphabet? Quite well, actually.''

''Good.'' He accepted a cup of coffee from Chumani. ''You can keep busy at the house this afternoon. In a day or two I'll have more time to show you what needs to be done at the freight company.''

She nodded, accustomed to men telling her what to do, while not convinced they knew what was any better for her than she did. She excused herself.

Back at the house, she brought her writing supplies into the big room, pulled the heavy table in front of the window and set about writing her stage-robbery story. Before long she was caught up in the excitement of her true-life adventure, certain any number of eastern publications would snap up the story. Perhaps she could write her own dime novel!

Cooper chewed the last bite of his stew and washed it down with the cold coffee in the bottom of his cup, wondering what Hallie was up to. Chumani had sent Yellow Eagle for her, but she'd told the boy she wasn't hungry.

He thanked his sister-in-law and made his way to the house. Near the window, in the waning light, Hallie was concentrating on putting letters on a page. A neat stack of neatly penned papers sat near her elbow. She didn't notice his presence until he lit a flint and lifted the chimney on the lantern.

"Oh! You're back!" She glanced up and blinked. An ink smudge streaked the side of her nose, two more dotting her jaw, as though she'd sat with her chin in her hands thinking.

He lit the lamp and pushed the tin plate he'd brought for her across the table. "You feel okay?"

"Oh, yes, I'm fine." She looked down at the plate with surprise. "I just didn't want to lose my train of thought at the time Yellow Eagle came for me. I do that sometimes…forget to eat when I'm caught up in a story."

"No wonder you're so skinny."

The firelight caught the flecks of gold in her eyes and reflected them as angry sparks. "It's fashionable to have a tiny waist."

"Seems a man'd rather have a woman who doesn't look like a good gust of wind would carry her to Denver."

She removed the cloth from the plate and got herself a fork. "I'm not going to be baited, Mr. DeWitt."

"You might as well call me Cooper."

"I don't think that would be appropriate."

He shrugged.

She tried the fish and sweet potatoes. "Would you like to read it?"

"What?"

''My story about the stage holdup?''

He glanced at the stack of papers and back at her eager expression. ''No.''

The excitement vanished from her face and she picked at the remaining food on the plate. ''Why not?''

''I know what happened.''

She shook her head in disgust. ''I should have known better than to extend an offer of friendship where you're concerned.''

''Is that what that was? I thought you just wanted me to see how good you are.''

She capped her bottle of ink. ''That too, maybe.''

He glanced at the cold stove. ''Would you like some coffee?''

''No, thank you, I...''

''What?''

''Well, I don't like coffee. I only drink it because Chumani gives it to me.''

''Why didn't you just say so?''

''I tried to be polite,'' she said, irritation lacing her tone. ''She's very kind to me.'' She carried the plate to the basin.

He built a fire in the stove, anyway. Thinking of the supplies he had stored, he made a trip to the freight building and returned several minutes later with fresh water. He set a tin and a new metal cup before her.

''What's this?'' she asked.

''You city women like tea, don't you?'' He dipped water into the coffeepot and placed it on the stove. ''I don't have a teapot.'' He poured more into a pan and set it at the back where it would warm for her to wash with later.

She watched him, her ink-stained fingers resting on the shiny tin. He turned away.

''You don't like me,'' she said from behind.

He remained facing the stove and didn't comment.

''But you made a special trip to bring me tea from the other building.''

He didn't want her digging into the reasonings for why he'd done it. He wasn't sure himself. "Do you like tea or not?"

"You're a narrow-minded man, Mr. DeWitt."

That did it. He turned and faced her. "Am I?"

"You don't like me because I'm white. Which is ridiculous because you're white."

He held her steady, gold-flecked gaze. A silken tendril of dark hair had fallen and lay along the ivory column of her neck and the heavy lace collar of her blouse. Her shoulders were slender, but she held herself with confidence and grace, giving the impression that she was stronger than she looked.

"Or is it because I'm from the East?" she asked.

She was not a full-breasted woman, but the swells beneath the crisp white fabric intrigued him all the same. On each sleeve an inch of lace lay ruffled against her delicate wrists.

"I'm accustomed to not being accepted," she said. "You can't discourage me."

Why on earth wasn't she accepted in her society? She was beautiful, feminine, obviously educated and talented.

Behind him the water boiled. He removed the pot and placed in on an iron trivet on the table. Hallie struggled with the tin. Cooper brushed her fingers aside and popped the lid off with a thumb.

She stared at his weather-browned hands for a moment, then glanced away, getting up and returning with one of the bone spoons. She scooped tea into the water and dropped the lid on the pot. "We'll just let it steep a few minutes. Do you want some, too?"

He'd never tasted tea in his life. Never cared to. He'd been hooked on coffee since an old trapper had introduced him to it at the age of ten, but some self-destructive inclination deep inside made him agree. "Sure."

She reached for another cup, his old dented one, and sat

back down. She didn't meet his eyes this time but let her gaze wander the room.

Cooper observed the same things she studied: the walls he'd plastered and limed, the open shelving beside the stove, the planked floor. What must she think of this place? Of him? She came from an elegant home with servants and lavish furnishings. Out here, this house was a mansion. Where she came from, it was little better than a shed.

She sat with her back straight, her hands folded primly in her lap, a princess in his crude, pathetic castle.

"Why aren't you accepted?" he asked, amazed at his lack of self-control. What did he care?

Her gray-gold eyes came back to his face. He wanted to reach over and wipe the stain from her nose. "I was born the wrong gender to amount to much in this world," she said, trying to sound matter-of-fact, but a trace of hurt came through. "I'm a nuisance. I don't wear pants, so I can't aspire to be anything more than a bauble for some man's mantel. And since that prospect doesn't appeal to me, I'm not valued too highly."

Any man would want her, that was obvious. It wasn't that she was unappealing or unfeminine. She said she'd grown up in a household of men. Cooper could almost understand their frustration with her. But, for some abstract reason, he could see her dissatisfaction, too.

"I suppose you see men's and women's roles all laid out neatly, too," she said.

"Women are revered by the Oglala," he replied.

"Because of their child-bearing capabilities?"

He shrugged. "I suppose so."

"Have you ever heard of Margaret Fuller?"

Another one of her lessons? How she stored so many names and events in that head, he'd never know. "No," he said on a deep sigh.

"She holds seminars regularly and attracts all the Boston luminaries. She's in Europe right now, but she's written a book, *Woman in the Nineteenth Century.* The book's open-ing a few eyes as to how women are treated.''

"Not your father's, though, huh?''

She looked away and he knew he'd touched a vulnerable spot. "No. Not his eyes.'' She rose from her chair to peer into the pot. "I think it's ready. Do you have any sugar?''

He found a small bag; she poured and they sweetened their tea. Hallie sipped hers with closed eyes and an engag-ing smile. "Mmm. Perfect.''

Cooper tasted the sweet brew and actually agreed.

She licked her lips, her pink tongue tracing a moist line over the soft-looking skin. An involuntary shaft of desire plunged in his abdomen. "I haven't had tea since…''

He welcomed the distraction. "Since when?''

"Since I met with Tess Cordell.''

"It's best she didn't come,'' he said. He didn't want her to feel sorry for him, and that was the impression he got whenever they'd spoken of the woman.

"Yes,'' she agreed.

She'd said that he deserved better. What had she meant by that? "It didn't matter to me what kind of woman she was,'' he said, reaffirming the fact to both of them.

"She was pretty,'' Hallie said.

He would never have asked. He would never have let her think it mattered. Did she sense that it did?

"Blond,'' she continued. "Blue eyes and a sweet face. A good gust of wind wouldn't have carried her to Denver.''

He hid a smile behind his cup. Maybe he shouldn't have made a reference to Hallie's lack of endowments.

"Young,'' she added.

He pictured the woman, but somehow the description didn't appeal to him.

"She wouldn't have been happy here,'' Hallie speculated. "She would have missed the clothes and parties and such.''

He knew that. He'd always known that. He'd just gotten

a little too lonely and let that need override his good judgment. It wouldn't happen again. "Like you," he said.

She shrugged.

They savored a second cup of tea. Cooper studied the neat stack of papers. She'd meant well in telling him about the Cordell woman. She'd even managed to leave his pride intact. "Why don't you read it to me?" he suggested.

Her eyes widened in surprise. "You mean, try it out on you?" She picked up the papers. "All right."

Cooper listened in fascination as she began the tale of the white girl's journey into forbidden territory. She had a spellbinding manner of using just the right colors and descriptions until he smelled the wind and tasted the dirt on his own tongue. Her interpretation of their encounter with the stage robbers had his heart pounding, and for the first time he understood her terror and sense of loss. Not only the loss of her money and valuables, but the loss of something less tangible. The experience had invaded her person and stolen more than a little innocence and self-confidence.

When she regaled him with the remainder of the ride to Stone Creek, the women's reactions, Ferlie's colorful speech and her exasperation with all of them, he laughed out loud.

Hallie lowered the last page and studied him with a new expression of interest and surprise. Her attention dropped to the smile that lingered at the corner of his mouth. "You liked it?" she asked.

"The Sioux have passed their stories down from generation to generation since the beginning of time," he said. "Storytellers are an important part of any heritage."

"Does that mean you like it?"

His approval was important to her in some unaccountable way. "You're very good."

A smug little smile graced her lips.

"For a woman," he couldn't resist adding.

Her eyes widened and she cast him a calculating glance. He thought he saw amusement flicker behind her eyes before she stood and cleared the table. "Maybe sometime you'll tell me an Oglala story."

He stood. "Maybe sometime."

She picked up the papers, ink and pen.

Cooper turned and picked up the other pan of warm water. "I'll carry this to your room for you."

He followed her through the doorway and poured the water into the crockery bowl he'd placed in her room for a washbasin.

She set the items in her hands down and lit the lantern. "Is there enough warm water left for you?"

He shook his head. "I'll go down to the river."

Her slim, dark eyebrows rose in wonder. "To wash?"

"To bathe."

She looked away. In the glow from the lantern, a blush crept up her cheeks. "It must be cold."

"Not as cold as it will be in a few more months."

"And you bathe in the river all year round?"

A city woman wouldn't understand, not a female accustomed to having water carried and warmed for her, probably even scented and oiled. He couldn't offer a woman luxuries like that. "Pretty primitive for your tastes, I'm certain."

"Well, I—I just never thought of it."

"Let me know if you want to try it," he teased, knowing she'd be mortified. "I'll stand guard for you."

Silence ticked away in the room. He could hear her breath. He could hear his own.

After a long minute Hallie raised her chin and stared him in the eye. The lace at the base of her throat pulsed with each heartbeat. "I want to try it," she said, accepting his challenge. "I've wanted a bath ever since I got here."

"Now?" he asked.

"Why not?"

She was a feisty one, all right. Full of surprises. "Bring whatever you need. I'll get flannel to dry with."

Cooper half expected her to back out, to change her mind

before they left the house. But she didn't. She met him at the door, her wrapper over her arm, a bar of soap and a comb in her grasp. She'd brushed out her shiny hair, and the sable length draped over one shoulder in a midnight wave.

This had been a crazy idea. The thought of her unclothed only twenty feet from him would drive him out of his mind. He shook himself. He was stronger than that. He'd been without a woman too long if the thought of a naked reporter had him tied in knots.

She stayed close, and he let her take his arm to steady and reassure herself in the darkness. "Who's first?" she asked.

"You go first. That way you'll have time to dry while I'm in."

"Okay." They'd reached the bank and she laid her things down. "Turn around."

He obeyed and crossed his arms over his chest. He pretended to listen to the wind overhead and the crickets in the grass, but all he heard was the rustle of her baffling clothing, the ripple of water and her quick intake of breath.

"I won't step on anything, will I?"

He imagined her slender body outlined on the river's edge in the moonlight. "This is the cleanest spot. I've cleared away all the stones and sticks."

"I mean something alive."

Water sounded as though she'd stepped farther out. "Like fish?"

"Fish!" she squeaked.

"They'll swim away from you. They wouldn't be so hard to catch if they came right up for a kiss, would they?"

"Turn back, turn back," she ordered, and he realized he'd been inching his chin over his shoulder to speak to her. He stared at the back of the soddies.

"Does Chumani do this?" she asked.

"I'm sure she does."

"God, it's cold."

"Just jump all the way in and get it over."

A second later a splash sounded and her gasp echoed across the water. Cooper chuckled to himself. The girl had pluck.

Water splashed and dripped and rippled and he imagined her washing her hair and body. A thunk sounded on the ground behind him. "What was that?"

"My soap."

"You done?"

"Not quite." Water splashed again. "This feels wonderful!" The splashing sounds receded.

Cooper didn't like the difference, and turned. The crazy woman had swum away from the edge. "Come back here! It's too dangerous out there!"

"I can still reach the bottom."

"All the fish are in the middle!"

She shrieked.

"Grizzly fish!"

"Now I don't believe you."

"Come back or I'll come get you!"

"All right, all right." She paddled back toward the bank. "Turn around."

He faced away.

Grass rustled as she climbed the bank behind him. He counted stars while she dried.

"All right," she said.

He turned. Her wrapper clung to her damp body. She worked at drying her hair with a length of flannel.

"Now I wait for you?" she asked.

He didn't really want her to see the fiery effect she had on his body. "Sounds fair."

She found a flat stone and seated herself with her back turned to him. Behind her, Hallie listened to DeWitt undress and plunge into the water. Impatiently she worked tangles from her wet hair. No wonder he liked to bathe out here.

The water had been invigorating. Swimming naked under the stars had given her a feeling of freedom and wholeness she'd never experienced before.

Her mother would turn purple if she knew.

Unable to resist the temptation, Hallie shifted on the rock and peered behind her. He soaped himself in thigh-high water, the moon illuminating the planes and curves of his muscled body. She'd seen his body that morning and had been too timid to look. Or maybe she hadn't wanted him to see her looking. In any case, she looked now, appreciating how marvelously he was made, wishing the moon was a little brighter or that she was a little closer.

He was a mystery, a marvel of sinew and muscle wrapped in sleek, smooth skin. He was everything she resented and everything she envied. How could she find him so fascinating? Why did looking upon him gratify her in some delightful way?

Hallie discovered her breath gusting in tight little pants between her parted lips. She placed her palms over her quivering stomach and forced herself to turn back. Men were men. Water splashed behind her. Weren't they?

She heard him leave the water and approach. He appeared at her side in the scrap of leather he'd worn that morning, his damp flannel toweling slung over his shoulder. Again Hallie marveled at the length of his tangled hair. She offered her comb. "Can we do this again?"

He nodded. With a careful expression he accepted the comb and ran it through the tangles. He handed it back. "Ready?"

She stood and followed him, less closely this time, more aware of him as a man and herself as a woman. As they climbed the bank, the wind returned and dried their hair. DeWitt opened the door and ushered her into the house.

She stopped in the doorway to her room and asked, "You never looked?"

He shook his head solemnly. "I never looked."

"You're a real gentleman, DeWitt."

"I try."

"For a savage," she added, teasing.

He raised one brow in unmistakable amusement. Quickly she shut the door. She leaned against the back, closing her eyes and seeing still the moonlit image of his glistening body. "A real gentleman."

Chapter Six

Two days later DeWitt finally had time in the afternoon to take Hallie to the freight building with the purpose of going over the record situation. They passed Jack, untangling a pile of harnesses and leads. He grinned at her, stretching one suspender out a foot with his thumb and all but rocking on his heels. "Howdy, missy."

"Hello, Jack."

As though proud she'd remembered his name, his gap-toothed grin split his face wider. He watched her walk into the back room.

"You weren't exaggerating," Hallie said softly.

DeWitt raised a questioning brow.

"About the men not being used to seeing women. You could probably sit me in one of those stalls out here and charge admission to gawk."

"Pity I didn't think of it."

"Might earn my way home faster."

Their eyes met and amusement passed between them. DeWitt gestured to the room. "This is what I've set up."

Hallie held her skirts aside and swept past him. A heavy desk sat beneath a window; behind it shelves and a flat working space had been built along the wall. She touched the desk's bare, unblemished oak surface, a pang of homesickness fluttering in her chest. The desks at *The Daily* were scarred and stained, littered with blocks of lead type and enough paperwork to fill all the empty shelves behind her. For an instant she could almost smell her father's cigar smoke.

In all likelihood, her letter to him could take weeks to arrive. For all he knew, she'd been kidnapped or killed somewhere en route. Hallie sat up a little straighter. Maybe she was making headlines back in Boston. Wainwright Girl Still Missing.

Lord, if Indians or stage robbers or grizzlies didn't get her first, her father was going to kill her.

"I ordered a lamp with a milk glass shade," DeWitt said, and gained her attention again. "Should arrive in a week or two."

Hallie sat in the straight-backed chair. "Okay, where are the books?"

DeWitt stepped beside her, opened a drawer and withdrew two ledgers. He placed them on the desk.

Hallie opened the first one and discovered the pages blank. She set it aside and opened the other. Nothing. "These ledgers are blank."

"They're new," he agreed.

She glanced aside and back in confusion. "Well, where are the records?"

Slowly he raised his hand and tapped his temple with one blunt finger.

Realization snapping her last slim hope for the job in half, Hallie cocked her head and looked at him out of the corner of her eye. "It's all in your head," she said.

He nodded.

"All the figures, all the sales, all the merchants."

He nodded.

She closed her eyes against the seemingly insurmountable task. Had he been so busy he couldn't have jotted them down? Silence stretched between them.

"That's the other reason I sent for a wife," he said. "I told you—I need help."

"I've never been an accountant. I don't know the first thing about freighting." No, that was no way to look at this. She opened her eyes and studied the books in front of her. If a man could do it, she could. "Most women haven't had any experience with this type of thing," she said, thinking out loud. "Even though they teach a little bookkeeping at Miss Abernathy's."

"Who's?"

"That's where Tess was from." He was darned lucky she wasn't a simpering female like most of the girls she knew. He could have ended up with someone who couldn't add a postscript. "But you know," she said, glancing up, "there is the Wesleyan Female College in Georgia. The Methodists are quite modern. Women get to study the same things men learn in other institutions."

Cooper nodded without comment.

"I suggested once that my father send me there."

"And what did he say?"

"A lot about men letting their wives and daughters run wild, but it all boiled down to him burning in hell first."

"Ah."

He'd given her a little more freedom to pacify her after that, though, so the suggestion had been beneficial. "I've had access to *The Daily*'s ledger books, so I've seen how it's done. I'll be able to figure it out."

He brought another chair from near the door, sat it backward alongside the desk and straddled it. "Let's work, then."

Hallie drew her pen and ink from a deep pocket in her skirt and opened the first book with a sigh. "Where do we start?"

DeWitt amazed her with his vivid recall of facts and figures. He knew shipment dates, amounts due and amounts received, even locations and names as if he was reading from a list inside his head.

By the time Yellow Eagle shouted for Cooper and appeared in the doorway, they had quite a bit accomplished. Yellow Eagle spoke to DeWitt, gesturing at the same time.

DeWitt replied.

"What did you both say?" Hallie asked with a frown.

DeWitt spoke to the child again. The boy cupped his hand upside down and moved it downward before his mouth a few times.

"Eat!" Hallie exclaimed proudly.

DeWitt pointed to her and then drew his hand, palm up, in front of his stomach in a sawing motion. Hallie shook her head. "What?"

"Are you hungry?" he asked.

"Yes!" Her smile vanished. "How do I say yes?"

DeWitt pointed his index finger up then quickly down. "Yes."

Hallie repeated the gesture.

He did it again, pointed to himself, then made the sawing motion in front of his stomach. "Yes, I hungry."

Hallie copied him. Between the freight building and the soddy he showed her the signs for walk, sun, river, house and wind. Inside, Hallie signed to Chumani that she was hungry.

Chumani laughed, pointed to her chair and made a downward motion with her fist.

"I'll bet that means sit."

After they finished and DeWitt left, Hallie helped Chumani with the dishes, then walked to the house.

She opened the door, surprised to find DeWitt and another man standing inside.

"Mrs. Lincoln," Wiley Kincaid said, stepping forward, the recovered hat in hand.

"Why, hello, Mr. Kincaid. How nice to see you."

"I'm pretty tired of my own company," he said. "Didn't

have anyone but my mules to talk to all the way from Duluth.''

She smiled. ''Would you care for a cup of tea?''

''That'd be nice,'' he replied.

''You two have a seat and I'll make it.'' She stopped in the process of picking up the tin coffeepot and stared at the stove for a long minute. ''Mr. DeWitt, may I see you for a moment?'' she asked in a sugary voice.

He stood and walked toward her, his broad-shouldered form blocking out the man in the room beyond.

''How do you light this thing?'' she whispered.

Without comment he opened the door, built a pile of kindling, placed a few dried disks on top and struck a match underneath.

''What are those things?'' she asked.

He put the index finger of each hand to his forehead, pointed outward, and made another quick motion.

''What's that?''

''Buffalo chips.'' He smiled and walked away.

Flustered, Hallie turned and took stock of the situation. The water buckets were empty.

Mr. Kincaid had taken a seat facing away from her. She held the empty bucket up high so DeWitt could see it and turned it over. He made a discreet motion with his hands. She understood perfectly well. *River.*

She pointed to him, but he deliberately ignored her, listening instead to something Mr. Kincaid was saying. Hallie grabbed the buckets and left, mincing her way toward the river in the dark. If there had been any real danger, he wouldn't have let her go alone. She hoped.

From the night before, she knew the spot where the bank was free of debris, and she made her way down the slope and filled the buckets.

The night was cool and the wind not as harsh as usual. She remembered her bath and imagined what anyone would think if they knew. Mr. Kincaid would think her a woman of loose character. Her mother would faint of mortification. Her father would—she didn't even want to consider what her father would do. DeWitt was the only person who knew. And did she particularly care what he thought of her?

Hallie lugged the buckets back, sloshing water on the floor as she tried to close the door behind her. She cleaned it up, heated the water, and much, much later served Mr. Kincaid and DeWitt cups of sweetened tea. She seated herself on the clean wide hearth and held her tin cup, realizing she'd given herself the new one DeWitt had brought for her.

As though he noticed, too, he met her eyes with his cool blue stare.

"When did you say your husband is coming, Mrs. Lincoln?" Kincaid asked.

"Well, I—did I say?" She glanced at DeWitt and back. Her mind raced, trying to remember what she'd said. "Actually, I'm not quite sure how long it will take."

"What's your business here?" The question was polite, but obviously undershot with burning curiosity. How was she going to explain staying with DeWitt?

"Mr. DeWitt is my cousin. On my mother's side. Aren't you, Coop? He's lending me his hospitality while my husband is afield."

"Wasn't there someone back East for you to stay with?" Kincaid asked. "It would have been a lot safer than out here."

DeWitt's penetrating stare burned into the side of Hallie's face. "I had to get away from the city," she said, the story coming more and more easily, and looked away sadly.

"Oh." Kincaid's round brown eyes were sympathetic. The air in the room crackled with expectancy.

"I lost a child, you see."

"Oh, dear," Kincaid clucked.

"Oh, dear," DeWitt echoed.

"The city—the entire East, for that matter, since we moved around so much, you know—was full of painful memories,'' she lamented as convincingly as she could. ''I needed time away. Time alone.''

She wouldn't look at DeWitt. She couldn't. From the corner of her eye she saw him twist his upper body away from her and run his hand over his face.

''I'm sorry,'' Kincaid said.

''Thank you.''

DeWitt's chair creaked and she let herself glance over. Arms crossed over his broad chest, his mouth twisted to the side, he was studying a spot on the ceiling with rapt concentration.

''Well, I'd better call it a night,'' Kincaid said, handing her his cup.

''Do you have to leave already?'' It seemed as if she'd just sat down. Hallie blinked. She *had* just sat down.

''Don't wanna wear out my welcome,'' he replied. ''There aren't too many folks to visit.''

''Where are you staying?''

''Set up a tent southwest a bit. I'm puttin' up my building beside it. Your cousin offered to gather up a few fellas and help me.''

''My who? My—oh, yes. Coop's such a considerate fellow. Always willing to help out. Come again. Good night.''

DeWitt walked outside with him and returned a minute later. Hallie turned from rinsing the cups.

He dropped the bar across the door into the brackets and looked at her.

''That went well, don't you think?'' she asked. Without waiting for a reply, she busied herself drying the cups and placing them back on the shelf, then blew out the lantern and headed for the bedroom.

He had rolled out his furs and extinguished the other lamp. His low voice came from the darkness behind her and sent a shiver up her spine. ''Night, cousin.''

''Good night. Oh.'' She paused with her fingers resting on the handle. ''Wake me up if Mr. Lincoln arrives.'' Hallie shut the door softly and undressed. She scampered into bed and buried her head under the covers. And then, after she was certain he couldn't hear her, she laughed.

Cooper didn't want to like Hallie Wainwright. He didn't want to hear about her family's lack of appreciation. He didn't want to experience the slightest scrap of understanding as to why a foolish young woman from a good family would take an outrageous risk and endanger herself by traveling alone in this harsh land. She was impetuous and irritating. She was naive and foolhardy and full of herself.

And she drove him crazy.

A week passed in which he didn't think about Tess Cordell's rejection. Neither did he think of sending a new letter and placing another advertisement. He spent a lot of time concentrating hard on not thinking about Hallie Wainwright.

He started to look forward to their afternoons—only because he was finally getting the company pulled together in the businesslike manner he'd craved for a long time. She was the means to an end, and he meant to see that the project was finished before she left. It had begun to bother him what would become of the bookwork after she'd gone.

At their scheduled time he found her in the office, staring out the window at the cloudy gray day. Wind buffeted the puttied pane of glass. She didn't hear him approach, pointing out her defenselessness and affirming his opinion. She lacked the skills to survive in this country.

Some devilish inspiration spurred him to pick up one of her writing pens lying on the desk. With his usual stealth, he moved directly behind her and placed the slender wood against her back. She didn't give him a chance to speak.

Instead of the shriek he expected, she spun and sharply kicked him in the knee. In both surprise and pain, he bent over at the same time she recognized him and moved forward with a regretful expression of horror. Their heads

butted so hard, Cooper saw stars. His knees buckled and he
knelt on the plank floor, the pen falling away.

"Oh, Cooper!" Hallie said, and his vision cleared enough
to see her grope for his shoulder and lower herself. Her hand
cupped the side of her forehead. She plopped beside him
with a rustling flurry of skirts, her feminine scent rising to
his nostrils and clearing his head.

Blinking, he focused on her. Her eyes watered and she
rubbed her head. Her startled gaze met his, more gold than
green or gray today, and her fingers slipped down to cover
her mouth.

Too deceived by her girlish frame and lack of experience,
he'd forgotten Ferlie's account of Hallie taking on the stage
robbers. He was the one who was too soft!

"Oh, get it over with," he said.

She dropped her hand, threw back her head and laughed
out loud.

He wanted to feel humiliated that a skinny city girl had
dropped him to his knees, but the absurdity of the situation
got the best of him and a chuckle erupted from a long-
untapped reservoir deep in his chest. His knee throbbed and
his ears rang, but he couldn't remember ever thinking that
anything was so hilarious. He laughed. He laughed until he
lost his breath. He laughed until the sound came from a
newly discovered place deep inside him.

Hallie tried to compose herself, but every time another
gale burst from him, she joined in. His eyes watered and
his cheek muscles ached.

Gradually their laughter subsided. Hallie sighed aloud.
Tears sparkled on her black lashes and winked from the
outer corners of her eyes.

He hadn't planned to do it. He raised his arm and her
eyes closed as, with his thumb, he brushed the glistening
drops from the lashes of one eye and then the other. His
thumb looked huge against her fragile cheekbone, his hand
dark and coarse in comparison to her delicate ivory skin.

Beside her face, he rubbed his wet thumb against his fore-finger.

Her dark-lashed eyes fluttered open and she stared at him, her expression a little curious, a little expectant. Her smile had waned and her rosy lips parted in a manner that was innocent yet tempting.

Thunder rolled overhead and rattled the windowpane.

He couldn't let himself think of why he didn't just leave her alone in the first place, why he hadn't given her the choice of sleeping with Chumani, or why he found reasons to keep her in his sight and under his care.

Right now he wasn't thinking of anything but the evocative sight of her dewy lips, the clean womanly scent that drifted from her clothing and her skin, and the driving pulse that chugged in the back of his brain.

Her breath caught and an answering heat spread through his loins. Without thought to the consequences, he leaned forward and touched his lips to hers. They were every bit as soft and warm as he'd imagined. He inched away. Her eyes had darkened and she watched him through lowered lashes. Her lids closed completely and she stayed where she was—waiting.

Cooper kissed her again, tentatively gauging her reaction, his own reaction and the shocking first awareness of their joined lips.

Raising his hands, he held her uptilted face between his palms. With as much gentleness as he could muster, he drew the kiss out, knowing she wasn't breathing, encouraging her to relax and share the splendid sensations.

He eased away for mere seconds at a time, making the kisses shorter, less intense. She breathed then, the warm air rushing against his cheek.

He wanted to pull her against him, wanted to taste her fully and delve his fingers into her fragrant hair. But he didn't.

He kissed each corner of her full mouth, and she returned

the velvet kisses. Her palm, warm but trembling, touched his upper arm through his shirt.

Cooper pulled away, tenderly holding her face near his. He read the new question in her eyes—they no longer asked what was he going to do, but why had he done it? Drawing a shaky breath, she said, "Mr. Lincoln is going to be highly upset with you when I tell him about this development."

He grinned self-consciously. With the tension defused, Cooper released her and got to his feet. The room had grown dim and rain beat in earnest against the roof. "Maybe you'd better not tell him."

She accepted his assistance and stood, brushing her skirts. "It'll cost you."

"Oh?" Kissing her had been reckless. Dangerous. He had better instincts than that. The whole episode was going to cost him. Dearly. He lit the lantern on the desk. "What's your price?"

Composed, she sat and drew the ledgers from the drawer. "Oh. How about a stage ticket to the ferry? I know you have connections."

Her ready words reminded him of how badly she wanted away from here. He'd already given considerable thought to paying her way back to Boston. He could put her on the stage—hell, he could take a few days to see her as far as the steamer, and then be done with her. Her father would even pay him back. Part of him kept holding out. Some crazy, self-destructive part.

Yellow Eagle needed the skills she could teach him. The People needed the service she was providing for the freight company. More planning, more profit; more profit, more food and supplies.

Lightning briefly illuminated one side of her face and clothing. Thunder echoed. "Sorry," he said. "I guess you'll just have to tell him."

Her guarded expression didn't reveal her disappointment. Cooper wouldn't let himself feel guilty. In a few more days the stage would come through for the mail. Her family would get her letter and know she was safe. She admitted they didn't need her back there. What would a few more weeks hurt?

The rain hadn't let up by the time they'd finished for the day. Cooper held a tarp above their heads and they ran to the soddy for supper, and later to the house for the night.

Wicked thoughts ran through Hallie's head as she lay in bed listening to the storm that night. If she set her mind to it, she could probably find where Cooper kept his cash. With enough determination she could pry open a strongbox. She could pay him back when she reached home. It wouldn't really be stealing; it would only be borrowing.

If he were any kind of a gentleman he'd simply loan her the money and see to it she got home. If he were a gentleman, he wouldn't have kissed her the way he had.... No, that was wrong. She couldn't delude herself. He hadn't forced himself on her. He hadn't been coarse or rude or pushy. He'd been tender. Uncertain.

He'd been a gentleman.

And she'd wanted it.

Her heart fluttered into her throat at the remembrance. She'd been perfunctorily kissed at her doorstep a few times. Once she'd been kissed in a carriage, and had practically had to leap out onto the brick pavement to get away.

But Cooper DeWitt's kiss had been something entirely different. Something entirely warm and disturbing that turned her insides to warm honey yet exhilarated her at the same time. His kiss revealed an undiscovered part of Hallie Wainwright that she wasn't prepared to look at. His kiss made her afraid of herself.

A light knock sounded on the door and she jumped beneath the covers. "Yes?"

"Were you asleep?" His voice came through the door, caressing her like provocative dark fingers.

She perched on the side of the bed, her senses tuned to

the darkness and the man on the other side of the door. "No."

"I wonder…if I could talk to you for a few minutes."

Her heart pounded like a silly schoolgirl's. "Just a minute."

She pulled her wrapper over her nightdress and tied it snugly at her waist. He waited, fully clothed, at the table in the other room, the lantern light gilding his hair and firm jaw. Hallie slid out a chair and sat across from him.

He glanced up. "Want tea?"

She shook her head. "No, thanks."

Several minutes passed while the only sound was the patter on the roof. "I couldn't sleep," he said finally. "We have to figure this thing out before the stage comes."

Was he going to mention the kiss? Had that been keeping him awake, too? It was a cool evening, but warmth flooded her cheeks.

"I've been using you," he said.

Uncomprehending, she could only wait.

"It's not fair of me to try to keep you here against your will." He studied his long-fingered hands, flattened on the table. "I can afford to send you home."

Listening, she felt hope rise in her chest.

"I could even take a few days and see you safely to the steamer." At last he looked up. "I wouldn't let you go alone."

His concern for her safety touched her. "You would help me get home?"

He nodded. "I will. Understand, I will." He looked at his hands again. "But I want to ask you something."

"What?"

It took him several seconds to form the words. "It's important for Yellow Eagle to learn to read and write. You haven't had much time with him and I know he's being difficult, but he's learning."

"He's a bright boy."

"I've changed my mind about…about a wife. It wasn't a good idea. This is no place to expect a woman to live unless she's been here her whole life and doesn't know anything else."

Hallie knew Tess Cordell's rejection had bothered him, but he could send for someone else. Sure, she'd thought Tess was out of her mind to consider marrying a frontier man sight unseen, but that had been before she'd met him. Before she'd seen for herself. Any of those girls at Miss Abernathy's would swoon at the sight of Cooper DeWitt. Any of them would leap at the chance to live with him, work with him…sleep with him.

A crazy pattering in her chest matched the staccato beat of rain against the roof.

"But I need somebody for the boy," he went on, "and I don't know how I'll find a teacher."

His meaning sank in. "You…you want me to stay and teach him?"

"Teach him," he agreed. "And keep the books."

Bewildered, Hallie sat thinking.

"I need you to work for me," he said. "But I'll get you home if you want to go."

Hallie was used to men telling her what to do, used to them ignoring her wishes and thinking they knew what was best for her. She was used to being patronized and cajoled and scoffed at.

She wasn't used to anyone giving her a choice.

She studied his enormous hands spread on the table. Her gaze took in the mane of hair loosened and flowing across one shoulder and down his back. She appreciated his strong, straight nose, his wide jaw and determined chin. She responded to his words in a vulnerable way he couldn't have been aware of, a way he couldn't have planned.

She had a choice.

She could go home.

She had a choice.

He needed her.

For once she had a choice.

"I will work for you." It was more a question than a statement.

"Yes."

"And you will pay me."

"Yes. And I will see that you travel free on my stage line."

"I'd rather you put the money in my hand each week and when I have enough I'll buy my own ticket."

"If that's what you want."

"That's what I want."

"All right."

"Did I tell you about the Lowell Mills in Massachusetts?"

He cast her a patient glance. "No."

"The women go on strike from time to time for better wages and working conditions."

"What does strike mean?"

"They quit working until their demands are met."

"Hallie, what does that have to do with us?"

She shrugged one shoulder, already feeling a little foolish for bringing it up. "I want you to know women are gaining respect as employees. I deserve the same wages as a man."

He didn't mention these weren't factory conditions. He didn't point out all she had to do was get on the stage and go home if she didn't like it. All he did was say tolerantly, "I don't think you'll have to strike."

Of course she wouldn't. He'd already been more than fair. "I'll stay."

His expression flattened in surprise. "Like that? Just like that, you'll stay?"

"I'll stay."

"Well." He straightened in his chair and threaded his fingers through the hair at one temple. "When you're ready, I'll see that you get home safe."

She nodded and stood. "All right, then."

"Hallie."

She looked back at him.

"Thank you."

She gave a nod and moved toward her room. "You're welcome."

A pounding on the door startled Hallie. She emitted a little squeak and stared wide-eyed at Cooper.

He grabbed a rifle from beside his bedroll and gestured for her to go into the other room. She did so, holding her wrapper closed at her throat, and leaving the door open so she could stand just inside and listen.

"Who's there?"

A muffled shout met her ears.

"Ferlie!" Wood scraped as the bar lifted. "What's wrong?"

"It's those dad-blamed, menacin' outlaws again!" he growled. "Ain't doin' a lick o' good to try to get people or mail b'tween here and nowhere 'cuz them sonsabitches come outa nowhere and pick us clean."

Hallie rushed back out into the other room. "Mr. Tubbs! Are you all right?"

The gray-bearded man's eyes widened and he doffed his dripping, battered hat. "Yes'm. I'm jest fine." He cackled. "Shoulda had you with me. Whoo-ee! Maybe we coulda saved the mail."

"Sit down over there," she invited, pointing to the hearth. "Mr. DeWitt, why don't you start a fire so he can dry out? I'll make you some nice hot coffee."

"Well, that would be *right* nice," he replied, and exchanged a look with Cooper. Cooper nodded, taking Ferlie's slicker and hanging it on the antler rack by the door.

"You're early," Cooper said, crouching to build a fire.

"Woulda been here this mornin'. Made good time outa Dog Flats. Then those sonsabitches ran me down. Pulled me off the hard-packed trail and the wheels sunk over the hubs. It's gonna take a day to dig that rig out.''

''At least you're okay.''

''Romney busted a leg and I had to shoot him.''

''Damn!'' Cooper's jaw hardened and he pounded a fist on his knee.

''Who did you shoot?'' Hallie asked in mortification.

''One of the horses,'' Cooper explained tersely.

''Oh.'' She sighed, feeling relieved but foolish.

''I rode Theo and led the others back. Roused ol' Jack and he's seein' to 'em.''

The men talked and Hallie waited for the water to boil. Finally she carried them each a steaming cup.

''You bed down here,'' Cooper said. ''First light, we'll take the team and go dig the coach out.''

''What if it's still raining?'' Hallie asked.

They both looked at her as if she'd asked if the sky was still blue.

''Hadn't you better wait until it clears?''

''That could be another day,'' Cooper responded. ''I can't leave the stage unguarded that long. Something worse could happen to it.''

''That's a fine-sprung Concord, miss,'' Ferlie said. ''Coop has himself a heap o' money sunk into that beauty.''

''Oh,'' she said. ''Of course.'' She met Cooper's fair gaze, reassured over her decision to stay a while longer. She certainly didn't want to take any chances on running into those stage robbers again. It was a miracle Ferlie had survived each time. ''How many times have you been robbed?''

''I lost a couple of freight wagons earlier this year,'' Cooper explained. ''And each of my two coaches has been held up half a dozen times.''

''I can see why the freight wagons, but is robbing stages profitable?'' she asked, trying to understand.

''Well, they get a little jewelry, some cash each time.''

"Scattered the mail to hell and back in the mud this time," Ferlie said in disgust. "Beggin' your pardon, ma'am," he added, and blew on his coffee.

"Why would they care about the mail?" Hallie asked.

Cooper shook his head in frustration.

"Are there any gold or cash shipments?" she asked.

"No. Hasn't been anything valuable for months."

"Then they're just malicious," she continued. "There's no gain in that."

"They're mean, all right," Ferlie agreed.

"It sounds like they're deliberately out to get you, Mr. DeWitt," Hallie said.

Cooper frowned. "What do you mean?"

"Has anyone been killed?"

"Not yet."

"Everyone is frightened. The mail is lost. Somebody wants to stop you or hurt your business."

"You read too much."

"Think about it!" She reached across and placed her hand on his arm.

"I'm thinkin', I'm thinkin'." He glanced at her fingers.

She pulled them away quickly.

"Who would want to do me harm?" he asked thoughtfully.

Who indeed? she wondered. Whoever it was, if that's what this was really all about, had targeted Cooper or his stage line. They'd come close to doing personal harm to her and the brides. One of Cooper's horses was dead and his valuable stage was stuck in the mud somewhere in this wasteland. Somebody was out to cause trouble, and she was stuck right in the middle of the situation.

Even if she hadn't given her word to stay and work for him, it wouldn't be safe to leave now. She was stuck in the badlands, unless a miracle happened.

Chapter Seven

"Let me go with you." Her tone forceful, she steeled herself for the following argument.

"Everyone will go." His matter-of-fact statement surprised her. "It's not going to be easy digging that stage out. The more hands the better. You and Yellow Eagle can keep watch."

Gratified, Hallie agreed.

"We need to rest now," he said.

She wished them good-night and hurried to the other room.

It wasn't even light yet when a rap on the door awakened her. "Time to head out," Cooper called from the other side.

Feeling as if she'd barely slept, Hallie groaned and rolled out of bed, washing and dressing quickly.

She entered the outer room, blinking against the lantern light. Wearing a wet slicker, Cooper jammed supplies into saddlebags. Two rifles lay across the table. "Chumani's got breakfast on."

She marveled at his energy. "It's too early to eat."

"Have to. Might be late before we get back, and all we'll have with us is some jerky. Don't you have a pair of boots?" He raised a doubtful brow at her soft kid footwear.

"These are my boots."

He took several extra minutes to locate a pair of knee-high moccasins. "Put 'em on right over the top of your shoes. They'll keep your feet dry."

He turned away politely. The moccasins fit easily over her boots, the laces tying above her knees. He handed her a slicker and picked up the bags. "Come."

Used to his curt command, Hallie followed him to the soddy, careful of the precarious footing in the slippery mud. Golden light filled the little house, the rich smells of bacon and coffee more appealing than she'd have imagined. The warmth of the tiny room, the common goal they shared and life going on despite the elements outside gave Hallie a sense of belonging she was unaccustomed to.

After eating, they gathered in the barn. "Open your slicker," Cooper ordered.

Hallie glanced dubiously at the gun and holster in his hands, but obeyed.

He hesitated. "You'll never be able to hold this up."

"Too skinny, right?" she asked wryly.

"Here. Take the slicker off for a minute and let's cross it from one shoulder over your chest. Won't be very comfortable, but you'll be able to reach it and it won't get wet."

"It makes me nervous," she said, but she followed directions. His massive arms reached around her effortlessly and her attention focused on his fingers fastening the buckle over her breasts.

"I know you can shoot it," he said, pointedly ignoring their physical closeness. "Somebody somewhere has a bullet hole you put there."

"Am I going to need it?"

His blue eyes met her gaze. "I don't know, Hallie. I'm giving it to you for your protection, as well as ours. That's the way it is out here. We look out for each other."

She studied the grim line of his lips, stern but sensual, and her thoughts inconveniently slid to the kiss they'd shared. "Okay," she said.

He looked up and caught her expression. Did he know what she'd been thinking? She thought so, because he finished the task quickly and with deliberate care.

Jack and Cooper had placed sideboards on one of the wagons and stretched a tarp to shield the bed. Hallie climbed in beside shovels, ropes and buckets and made room for Chumani, Yellow Eagle and Jack. Ferlie and Cooper rode on the seat above.

The wagon groaned, the harnesses clinked and they were on their way. It took longer than she expected to reach the sunken Concord. Hallie peered from beneath the protection of the tarp. As Ferlie had related, the coach sat up to its hubs in mud.

Cooper appeared at the back of the wagon, his expression unreadable. He shrugged out of the slicker, tossed it in on the floor and stripped his buckskin shirt over his head. In seconds he wore nothing but the leather flap that revealed his muscular buttocks. He reached for the shovels and gestured to Hallie.

No one else paid any mind to the fact that he'd stripped, so Hallie avoided staring at his body and followed him through the pelting rain.

"You stand watch over there," he said, pointing to a rise a few hundred feet from the wagon. "But don't stand near the grove of trees." Already his wet body glistened in the gray dawn light.

"Why not?"

"Lightning."

"Oh."

The rain darkened his hair. "If you see anyone in any direction, don't shoot, just run back."

"All right."

He walked away and she forced herself not to stare. How logical, she thought. Rather than waste the effort of trying to keep clothing dry, he'd removed it.

Day arrived, but Hallie wasn't sure how much time had

passed. There was no sun to judge by, and the progress on digging the slippery mud away from the stage was painstakingly slow. Jack had stripped to his trousers and Ferlie had cast aside his slicker. The three men dug. Chumani carried the heavy pails away and dumped them. Sometimes Ferlie or Jack stopped digging to help her.

Hallie scanned the horizon, the butte to her right, and the grove of trees. Even beneath the low-hanging gray sky the land possessed a haunting beauty all its own. Its magnitude was still as overwhelming as the first time she'd seen it.

With that realization came another, ultimately more disturbing. Two weeks had slipped past and she hadn't contacted the brides even once! That's why she'd come in the first place! Cooper would have every right to doubt her credibility. Fine day to think of it, she scoffed at herself. When the weather cleared, she'd have to make time to do her interviews and work on the story.

For a few minutes she watched Chumani lugging full buckets.

They'd been at the job for hours. She slipped and fell, and Hallie ran to help her. "Let me do this for a while." Hallie insisted, and pointed to her post. "You go watch."

Gratefully, Chumani turned and headed away.

"Wait, you need the gun." Hallie opened her slicker.

Chumani opened hers to reveal a holster on her hip.

"Oh." She gave the woman an encouraging smile. "Okay. You go rest awhile." She made the sign for sit. Chumani nodded and hurried away.

The mud grabbed at Hallie's feet with loud sucking sounds, pulling her into its depths and making walking a challenge. Hallie managed to pick up two buckets.

"Hallie?" Cooper paused in his digging and leaned on the shovel handle. He stood in the knee-high hole he'd dug around the wheel, his hair plastered to his head and back, his massive chest heaving with exertion. He was covered in mud from his feet to his lean thighs, and as he paused, rivulets ran downward over corded muscle. Hallie raised her eyes. The unceasing downpour had kept his shoulders and back clean. He blinked moisture from clear blue eyes.

"Chumani needed a break." She pointed to the rise. "She's watching."

Something like approval flickered in his expression. "Another hour or so and we'll stop a few minutes to eat. Glad you ate this morning?"

"Am I ever." Slipping and sliding, she hauled the buckets away. Every time she returned more had been filled. The slicker made her progress slow and the gun lay like an anvil against her ribs. Ferlie, buckskin shirt and pants plastered to his bowlegged frame, paused in his digging to help her haul.

Finally Cooper called a break, and they sat huddled beneath the tarp, chewing stringy beef jerky and damp bread.

"Soon as we get back out there and scrape the pits out fresh," Cooper said, "we'll hitch the team up and pull her out. Ferlie, you take the team. Jack, watch the holes for slides, and you—" he turned to Chumani, his nephew and Hallie "—will push from behind with me."

"Us?" Hallie squeaked.

"It's not one person's strength that matters," he said. "It's all of us together."

"Who will keep watch if we're all at the stage?" she asked.

"We'll scan the area before we start," he said.

The others made themselves comfortable for the few minutes of rest.

"Don't you have a story you'd like to point out to me now?" he asked, leaning back against the side of the wagon. He raised one knee and Hallie had to deliberately resist looking at the damp flesh revealed by his pose. Wasn't the rough wagon bed uncomfortable against his bare skin?

She forced herself to sound natural. "What do you mean?"

"You usually have a story to compare with."

"Oh, well, not for this one." She hadn't thought he'd ever been listening. He wasn't really, he just thought she was silly and was making fun of her. She glanced at the others, but they were absorbed in eating or resting. "I didn't think you paid any attention."

"I pay attention." His eyes telegraphed a message she didn't understand, and then darted over the gray landscape. "I'd better go have a look around. Then we'll get started again."

Hallie focused on the pile of rope and not on him as he walked away. She raised her gaze to Chumani. A speculative smile hovered on the woman's lips. They exchanged a grin.

"Damned rain'll probably wash us all to Mexico if'n we don't get out there and haul that Concord outa them gullies we dug." Having caught his second wind, Ferlie led them from the wagon.

The men positioned the mules ahead of the coach and fastened them into their traces, all the while talking to them, touching them and running their hands over their rain-dark coats. Thunder rumbled, and the men calmed the skittish animals.

Hallie and Yellow Eagle carried as many sticks and rocks as they could find and placed them behind the stage for solid footing.

Everyone took their places, Ferlie on the high seat, Jack watching the wheels with a shovel in hand, and the rest of them behind the boot. Cooper stationed himself in the center, his back and shoulders to the rig, his hands cupping the bottom. "When I give the call, shove for all you're worth," he instructed.

Hallie took a place between Cooper and Yellow Eagle. What would they do if this didn't work? They'd spent the whole day digging. She supposed they could stand guard over the coach until the rain stopped and the ground dried up. But who knew how long that would take?

"H'yah!" Cooper shouted, startling Hallie. She recognized the sound of the whip, and Ferlie's colorful admonitions rang out. The coach creaked and she leaned into it with all her weight.

Beside her, Cooper used his powerful leg muscles to push. The veins in his neck stuck out, his shoulders and arms bulged with the strain. The stage inched upward. Without letting go, he turned and continued to lean his weight into the effort with a shoulder.

Hallie's own arms ached, and she scrambled for footing on the slippery rocks. Breathless grunts and straining growls broke the monotonous sound of rain on the ground. The whip cracked again, followed by a chain of curses and the braying of a mule.

At last the coach lunged away, and Hallie fell face first into the slippery ooze. The cold caught her by surprise and she inhaled quickly, choking on the mouthful of mud. She spat and sat on her heels to wipe her eyes. Lengths of hair, fallen from her chignon during the day's struggle, lay sodden against her neck and face.

Ferlie led the team to higher ground. Jack ran ahead and steadied the mules. Cooper staggered to a halt.

Cold and wet, covered with mud from head to toe and her bladder near to bursting, Hallie thought of her comfortable home back in Boston, the nice warm newspaper office and the meals served to her on primrose china. Maybe she could have tried a little harder to earn her father's respect. Or maybe she should have accepted Evan Hunter with a grain of salt and gone on the way she always had. Maybe she could have swallowed her pride and given a second look at one of those pale, boring young men her father pushed at her.

Ferlie jumped down and caught sight of Hallie.

''Whoo-ee, missy!'' His amused cackle rang out across the countryside.

Beside her, panting with exertion, Chumani and Yellow Eagle giggled.

Cooper turned, and his eyes widened. His obvious attempt not to laugh struck Hallie as funny.

Though shivering and filthy, she saw the humor in her ungraceful position and her whole situation. She could only imagine what she must look like. Wobbling to stand, she laughed at herself, and the others joined in.

The men harnessed horses to the wagon they'd brought and Chumani gathered the shovels and buckets. Hallie sluiced mud from her face and slicker while already the rain had begun to rinse her clean.

Miserable, she glanced around. She wouldn't be able to endure the bumpy ride home without relieving herself. Glancing over her shoulder, she headed for the stand of gnarled trees that grew beside a windswept butte. No one would notice if she left for just a minute.

Hallie made certain she wasn't visible from the wagon and tended to her need. As she arranged her clothing, a new sound arrested her attention. Twigs snapped and heavy breathing met her ears.

Mortified that someone should have seen her at such an indelicate task, she scrambled to pull her soggy clothes in place. Her heart pounded. She'd sat watch all day and when they least expected it, when she hadn't been watching, the outlaws showed up. It was her fault that their lives were now in danger. Her soaked pantaloons bunched at her thighs and wouldn't pull up.

The breathing and peculiar grunts grew louder. Panicked, Hallie fumbled with her wet slicker and drew the heavy weapon from the holster. Cooper had told her not to shoot, just to run for him, but that had been in the case that she saw them from a distance. Now they were right on top of her! As clumsy as she was in this mud, and with her drawers halfway up, she would never outrun them.

An enormous dark shape lumbered into view several feet away. Hallie's heart stopped altogether. Her ears hummed with sheer fright. The animal sat back on its haunches and sniffed the air with a pointed black snout.

A grizzly!

Paralyzed, Hallie wasted valuable seconds quaking where she stood. Her heart chugged to life, hammering against her breast like a wild thing. A scream shaped itself in her throat and lanced the air in a shrill, pulsating shriek of pure terror.

The bear swung his ponderous head and stood on hind feet, pawing the air. Hallie saw eight feet of wet brown fur, long talonlike claws and more jagged, snarling teeth than she could count.

The animal's snout twisted from side to side, and a soul-chilling roar effectively sliced off her frantic screams. Hallie finally remembered the gun in her hand and raised it. The weapon trembled in her grip, but self-preservation forced her to aim it at the growling animal. It took two hands to steady the barrel and squeeze the trigger.

The shot reverberated off the surrounding countryside and jerked her off-balance.

Enraged, the animal dropped to the ground and lumbered toward her. Hellfire! Hallie didn't know whether to shoot again or attempt to run. She was dead either way. She stood her ground and pulled the trigger.

Another shot echoed seconds behind hers. The bear stopped in its tracks and stumbled to a halt.

A third shot rang out from behind her, and the bear lay motionless.

Quivering, Hallie turned. Cooper lowered his rifle and walked toward her, rain sluicing over his sleek body.

She looked back at the dead animal and nausea rose in her throat. Black spots floated in front of her eyes and she weaved where she stood.

Cooper caught her effortlessly before she fell. He sat her on the ground and forced her head between her knees, which wasn't easy with soggy petticoats and drawers bunched there. The revolver was removed from her limp fingers and she stayed that way for a few minutes, resting until her breath came easily. She raised her head and he caught her hood before it exposed her to the rain. Her eyes were huge and luminous, the gray-rimmed irises reflecting her dismay.

Her earsplitting screams had raised the hair on his neck. He was grateful for the screams. Grateful for enough warning to grab his rifle and get there before it had been too late. His heart had pounded when he'd seen the maddened grizzly ready to pounce on her slight form in the oversize slicker.

But, true to her remarkable character, she'd plugged at least one bullet into the beast's hide. That had only made it madder, but at least she'd done something. If he hadn't arrived when he had, she'd have been ripped to shreds. The alarm he experienced over that thought distressed him as much as the thought itself.

"Whoo-ee!" Ferlie cackled, stomping up behind them. "Whatcha gonna do with your bear, missy? We gonna have steaks tonight?"

Her eyes widened even farther. "My—my bear?"

"Your bear," Cooper confirmed. "We'll clean him for you, of course. Make a nice rug for her parlor, won't he, Ferlie?"

"Could hang 'im on your bedroom wall and wake up to 'im ever' mornin'," Ferlie suggested, picking up on Cooper's teasing.

Hallie, face streaked and hair caked with mud, narrowed her lovely eyes at them.

Chumani moved forward, knife in hand, and approached the animal.

"What's she going to do?" Hallie asked, her lips turning white.

"Leave his innards here," Cooper explained. "Coyotes won't follow us home if we leave 'em dinner."

"Oh, my…" She rose and staggered.

"Come on." He lifted her into his arms and walked toward the coach and wagon. "You wait in the stage for us."

"In the stage?"

"Yes. Unless you think we ought to let the bear ride there."

"Oh, no. I didn't think…"

He paused for her to twist the handle and deposited her inside the Concord.

"Cooper?"

"What?"

"Thank you. For saving my life, I mean. I'd be dead if you hadn't shot that bear."

"You're welcome, but Hallie?"

"What?"

"Please tell someone before you traipse off from now on."

"Oh. Sure." Sheepishly, she settled back on the leather seat. "I'm dripping all over the upholstery."

"Better you than the bear." She looked up and he winked. "It'll clean up." He handed the revolver back to her and closed the door.

"Cooper?"

He peered through the window.

"Could I borrow your knife, too?"

"What for?"

"Just loan me your knife."

He pulled it from its sheath at his waist. "It's sharp."

She took it, handle first, yanked her skirts up, sliced her pantaloons off and tossed them through the window into the mud. Handing the knife back, she said, "Thank you."

Cooper took it and glanced from her to the garment on the ground. "Always thought all those clothes were more trouble than necessary."

"Next time I think I might come face-to-face with a grizzly, I'll leave my underclothing at home." She leaned back against the leather seat and covered her face with her hands. "My mother would absolutely die."

He chuckled and walked away.

Everyone's good mood was contagious. Their trip had been successful, and along with bringing the Concord back, they had a good supply of meat for the coming winter. But the best part, Hallie noted, was that Yellow Eagle ignored her with a bit more respect.

Missing was the usual sneer or rolling of eyes when someone spoke to her or about her. He even assisted Cooper in hauling a half barrel into the house and placing it beside the kitchen stove.

"What's this?" Hallie asked.

"Thought you could use a warm bath after today," Cooper replied. The two left several times and returned with water.

The thought of settling into a warm tub revived her and she eagerly heated the water on the stove.

"What about you?" she asked Cooper after Yellow Eagle left. "You could use a hot bath, too."

"I'm used to the weather," he replied.

She dipped her fingers in the tub and let the water trickle back. "It feels go-od," she said in a singsongy voice of temptation.

He glanced pointedly at the tub. "I wouldn't fit in that barrel."

She looked over her shoulder. "Oh. So you wouldn't."

He took a step away.

"You could stand in it and lather up, then rinse off using one of the pans," she suggested.

"It would make an awful mess."

"It'll clean up," she said, echoing his words about the coach.

"We'll see." He headed for the door. "Call me when you're finished."

"Where will you be? Will you hear me?"

"I'll wait outside."

"That's silly. It's still pouring out there."

"I've been in the rain all day, Hallie. What's a few drops more?"

"Well, it's cooling down now. You'll catch cold."

"I've never had a cold in my life." He exited the door, closing it firmly behind him.

Hallie stripped wet clothing from skin covered with gooseflesh and lowered herself into the steaming water. It felt wonderful. River bathing was nice in fair weather, but Cooper didn't know what he was missing. The hot water soothed her aching muscles and relaxed her. She closed her eyes and sank deeper into the tub, enjoying the warmth.

Remembering Cooper waiting out in the elements, she washed her hair, soaped, rinsed and dried herself. Dressed in her wrapper, she dipped two buckets from the tub and opened the door to throw the contents out.

Glancing to the side, she caught sight of Cooper beneath the corner eave of the house where the rain funneled down. He stood beneath the downpour, his face turned upward, foam rinsing from his hair and nearly naked body. The light from the doorway illuminated the curves and indents of his muscular form.

He sputtered and shook his head, and the light caught his attention. He turned toward her, but Hallie was the one who froze as if she'd been caught nearly naked.

She'd never thought a man could be beautiful. The closest thing she'd ever seen to a male form had been in the paintings at the Dageford Museum. She'd studied the likenesses a time or two, curious but not altogether taken. But Cooper was flesh and blood, light and shadows, sinew and muscle, and she could study him from now until forever and never tire of his masculine grace and beauty.

Hallie shook herself from her reverie and dumped the pails. "Come warm up now."

She poured hot water from the stove into the barrel and carried her things into the bedroom without looking at him again. Closing the door tightly, she combed the snarls from her hair and dressed.

The sound of splashing water ceased, and minutes later he called to her. "I'm building a fire. Come get dry."

She stepped out and sat on a chair near the fireplace. Cooper, wearing his buckskin pants and shirt, fed a few blocks of peat into the fire he'd started.

"Did it feel good?" she asked.

He turned, and his blue eyes were backlit by an internal flame. "Yes."

His hair left a wet patch on the back of his shirt.

"Oh, here." She left and returned with dry toweling and her comb and brush. Cooper accepted the flannel and dried his hair. He took the comb and impatiently worked at the length over his shoulder.

Hallie brushed his hands aside and took the comb. A unique woodsy scent drifted to her nostrils. "What did you wash with?"

"Yucca."

"What's that?"

"A root."

She worked the thick mass free of tangles. "You're the first man I've known to have long hair."

"It's troublesome. I've thought about cutting it."

"But you haven't."

"I am what I am. Cutting my hair won't make me any more white or any less red."

Hallie slipped away and brushed her own drying hair in front of the fire. He sat on the floor, his wrists resting loosely on his knees, and observed her.

"How did you come to be brothers with Last Horse?" she asked.

"Is this the reporter asking?"

"No. I just wondered."

"I've lived with the Oglala since I was about eight."

Hallie brushed her hair and listened.

"My own father was a trapper, part French. He married my mother and took her up north. She was never happy. She was from the city."

His hair had begun to dry and the fire ignited highlights in its length. He turned his back to the hearth and stretched out his long legs.

"When I was born, he moved her to the territory, closer to civilization. My father lived in peace with the Oglala. They were our friends, the only family I ever knew. But my mother was miserable, so we moved farther and farther east, and eventually my father cut himself off from his livelihood. Once there was nothing left, she left him. He went east after her, leaving me with a family who ran a trading post."

Hallie tried to comprehend the kind of life he spoke of, but couldn't.

"He didn't come back, so I ran away to the land and the people I knew. Running Elk took me in as his own son, gave me shelter and taught me to hunt and trap. I grew to manhood among The People."

"But you didn't stay with them."

"I stayed with them until the whites drove them from their homes and hunting grounds," he said, anger lacing his tone. "I stayed with them until they were penned on a reservation like dogs."

She turned from his contemptuous glare and regarded the crackling yellow and orange flames.

"I can do more good for them here," he said more gently. "I claimed a land grant and sold years' worth of furs to start this company. From here I can provide food and clothing for them."

"I didn't realize," she said.

Their eyes met in the flickering firelight. "I can take them supplies and see to it they're warm in the winter,'' he went on, his tone now carefully devoid of emotion. ''But what I can't give them, what they need as much as any of those things, is their dignity.''

A responding sadness left Hallie bereft. The abandoned child he spoke of had grown into this capable, caring adult. This man of physical strength and determination possessed an overwhelming sense of loyalty that she could only hope to aspire to.

No wonder he had no particular fondness for whites. No wonder he'd changed his mind about a city woman for a wife. No wonder she'd grown to appreciate the man she'd glimpsed deep inside. Even though she'd had a few minutes of doubt that day, Hallie didn't regret leaving the comfort and safety of her oppressive life back East. No longer was she merely *reporting* on life, she was *living* it. She wasn't experiencing exciting situations vicariously through words on a page, she was seeing them in living color!

He stared into the shadowy room as though unaware of how much he'd revealed about himself.

''I'll bet you have a lot of interesting stories,'' she said, to draw him out of his mood. ''We could come up with some tales that would set the folks back East on their ears.''

''Your stories are better than mine,'' he amended. '''Hallie and the Grizzly.'''

'''Hallie and the Stone Creek Stage Robbers,''' she added, enjoying their warm camaraderie, and then thought of her earlier decision. ''Cooper, I have to interview the brides. Can you take me to see them?''

''I suppose so. They were something, weren't they?'' He grinned as if remembering that day. ''How about 'Life Among the Border Ruffians'? That's what the red-haired one called 'em.''

Thunder rumbled overhead. ''How about 'Forty Days and Forty Nights'?'' Hallie asked.

''What's that?''

"The rain." She laughed. "You've never heard of Noah?"

"No."

"Well, have I got a story for you."

The following day the rain let up, but the wind grew cold. During lesson time, DeWitt showed up wearing a fur-lined jacket and slammed the door behind him.

He ruffled Yellow Eagle's hair and contemplated Hallie. "Ferlie's heading out today."

"Oh?"

"This is your last chance."

"What do you mean?"

"I can't let him go alone. I'm riding with the stage as far as the Mississippi. You can pack up and come along if you want. I'll see that you get home."

Surprised, she set down the slate she held. "I thought this was already decided," she said, glancing at Yellow Eagle.

Assessingly, the boy watched her with wide ebony eyes.

"You deserve a last chance," Cooper said. "It's getting colder every day. Looks like we'll have an early winter, and with all the moisture we've had, it could be a rough one."

"I'll be inside by the fire, won't I? You're not going to toss me out in a drift."

"What I'm saying is that this is it, Hallie. Last chance. Once winter sets in, you're here for good."

She looked from Yellow Eagle's interested expression to Cooper's carefully bland one. "Well, we'll have Yellow Eagle reading and writing by spring. Just make sure you get the mail through so my father knows I'm all right."

He didn't let it show, but she knew her words pleased him. His blue gaze touched her face with warmth. "I will."

"How long will you be gone?"

"A few days. I'd feel better if you stayed with Chumani while I was gone."

She raised a brow in question.

"Come." He gestured and led her outside the door with one hand on her upper arm. "There are the other men, Hallie. Once they know you're alone at night…"

She saw the picture. Remembering the way they'd ogled her at the trading post, and the manner in which Last Horse had raked her with his lecherous eyes, she didn't need any more convincing. "I'll take a few things and stay with Chumani."

"Thank you."

The warmth of his hand burned through her sleeve. "Thank you," she said. "You always think of my safety."

His eyes dropped to her mouth and she caught her breath at the heat she read in their depths. His other hand bracketed her chin and raised her face to his.

Hallie's heart set up a flutter. "What—?"

"You could talk a man blind, Hallie."

Her eyes widened and his face lowered.

"I don't think—"

"I don't care if you think or not. Just don't talk."

Chapter Eight

His lips claimed hers in a kiss that elicited sensations she wasn't prepared to deal with. She smelled the earthy yucca root in his hair and on his skin, tasted the man and felt the gentle kneading of his fingers on her arm. This time the kiss was more than an accident, more than a test: there was purpose behind it. Purpose…and fire.

Curiously, she was sorry he was leaving—not because she'd be afraid, but because she didn't want to be left behind without him.

An odd rush of loneliness enveloped her and she found herself returning the kiss, not caring if she shocked him or if she'd perhaps be sorry later, caring only that he'd be gone and this was what she'd have to remember.

Her hand crept to his chest and she encountered the pouch he wore beneath his shirt. "What's in here?" she asked against his lips.

"*Sicun,*" he replied.

"What?"

"My spirit stone."

"What—"

He stopped the question with his mouth. She loved the warm, firm feel of his lips against hers. *What would his cheek feel like if I reached up and touched it?* She indulged herself, framing his lean jaw and delighting in the delicate scrape against her palm, aligning their mouths, holding him to her.

He wrapped an arm around her back, easing her against him until her breasts flattened on the hard plane of his chest. Against them, his heart thrummed a steady beat.

His tongue drew a line across the barrier of her lips. *What would he taste like if I...?* and she parted them, allowing him to penetrate her mouth the way his warmth and scent filled her senses. A curl of fire licked inside her.

He made a sound deep in his throat and she didn't want to know what it meant. She didn't want to surrender this feeling. She didn't want to have this moment end and see uncertainty or regret pool in his eyes.

Behind him the wind rose and fluttered a length of his hair against her cheek. She tucked it behind his ear, and he ended the kiss.

The wind cooled her damp lips and she became aware of how warm and sensitive her skin had grown. All over her body she recognized the touch of her clothing against her tingling flesh. He held her shoulders gently between his strong hands.

Another gust of wind flattened her skirts and whipped a long tress of her hair across her face. With masculine awkwardness, he brushed it aside. "If you have a problem, send Yellow Eagle for Lowell Heckman."

"Who?"

"The smithy. I trust him."

She remembered the black-haired man at the livery the day she'd arrived. He'd been surprised to see her, but not rude or leering like the others. She agreed.

He took a few steps back.

"Bye, Cooper."

"Goodbye, Mrs. Lincoln."

She couldn't resist a crooked smile.

He plunged toward her, circled her waist with both hard

hands and pressed a last spontaneous kiss against her lips. Seconds later she watched him cross the distance to the freight building and flipped a halfhearted wave at his back.

Shaken to her toes, Hallie let herself into the house. With a curious expression, Yellow Eagle watched her cross the room. "Where were we?" she asked, trying to keep her voice from sounding as breathless as she felt.

"We were doing *s* sounds."

"Yes." She settled onto her chair.

He had a dozen *s*'s neatly chalked on his slate. "I know one."

"What is it?"

"Stupid." His black eyes met hers with a challenge.

Undaunted by the contempt she'd come to expect, she returned, "Strong."

"Sssss-snake," Yellow Eagle hissed, with as much venom as he could manage lacing his tone.

She grinned in spite of herself. "Savor."

He leaned toward her. "Spit."

"Spellbinding." She didn't hear his next word, because her thoughts returned to the sultry kiss, Cooper's smoldering eyes and the sensations still shimmering inside. Her pulse had staggered and her heart had soared. These new feelings astonished her. She hadn't wanted him to go. But what did she want? What was there to want?

He needed her to help him. And after that…

Hallie turned back to Yellow Eagle. She wouldn't think about after that.

Wiley Kincaid called on them at the soddy the next night. Hesitantly, Hallie opened the door. Even though he'd always been a perfect gentleman, the thought of having him here with Cooper gone unsettled her. She couldn't very well tell him that they were alone, however. "Come in for tea." Hallie invited.

"Cooper working?" he asked, glancing around.

She met Yellow Eagle's eyes briefly. "Yes."

Kincaid took the seat she offered. "I have a brother who's thinking about coming out here."

"Oh?" She headed for the stove, but Chumani waved her back.

"I sent a missive with the stage, explaining there's land available. I expect he might look it over come spring."

"That would be nice."

They sat awkwardly for a few minutes until Chumani brought the tea. Hallie poured, Chumani and Yellow Eagle took seats by the fire and she served them.

"He has a family," Kincaid explained. "Missus and young 'uns and all."

"My," she said, sitting across from him. "What would he do?"

"Teaming earns ten dollars a day," he said.

"What's that?"

"Teaming. Hauling freight."

"What Cooper does."

"That's right."

"Would Cooper hire him?"

"I expect so."

"Got enough whites in the territory," Yellow Eagle said in a condemning tone. "Soon we won't be able to see the sky."

Kincaid frowned at the boy, but Hallie offered support, replying, "Does seem that way, doesn't it?"

"Rain set me behind in getting my building started," Wiley said, changing the subject.

"We have had our share, haven't we?" Their recent day in the rain was vivid in her memory. "By the way, I shot a bear."

Kincaid's brown eyes widened and his cup stopped halfway to his lips. "You what?"

"I shot a bear." She felt a little more secure having him think her capable.

His disbelief showed in the way his forehead puckered
between his brows. He looked to Yellow Eagle for confir-
mation.

The boy nodded.

Hallie regaled him with the story, leaving out the part
about why she'd been at the base of the butte and how
Cooper had actually fired the deadly shots.

Yellow Eagle grinned and turned away to poke the fire
with an iron tool.

"Where's the hide?" Kincaid asked.

"I'm not sure."

"Can I prepare it for you?"

"Well, Chumani can show me—"

"Oh, please let me. I'd like to."

"Well…" She looked to Chumani, but the woman only
nodded tolerantly. "All right."

He set his cup down. "I'd best be headin' home. Thanks
again."

Hallie saw him off and picked up their cups. "Let's go
over your letters before bed," she said to Yellow Eagle.
"You've done so well with letters and sounds that we'll
start putting words together next week."

"And then I'll be able to read?"

"In a very short time," she agreed, carrying their slates
and handing him one. "I have more books in my trunk for
this winter."

"I'll still be an Oglala," he said, looking up at her, a
belligerent scowl on his young face.

Hallie glanced between Yellow Eagle and his mother and
dropped to her knees on the rug. "Of course you will," she
said softly. "No one is trying to make you a white person."

From his doubtful expression, she had to wonder if he
believed her.

"Your uncle only wants you to be able to meet the whites
on their own ground," she explained. "They place much

value on the written word, and successful men need the power it gives them.''

''Power?''

''Yes,'' she said with enthusiasm. ''Power!'' She fully understood Cooper's strategy now. ''Many of the treaties have been broken,'' she went on. ''Your people can't read what they're signing. The agents hardly care and if they do they have little control. But if the Indians themselves can read, well…'' Her mind raced ahead. ''They'd know what they were signing. They could communicate with President Polk. Why…'' She looked up in surprise. ''What if some could have college educations and become *lawyers?*''

''Power,'' Yellow Eagle repeated thoughtfully, then picked up his slate. ''Let's get on with it.''

The office in the freight building seemed enormous without Cooper there. Wanting to have the account books finished when he returned, Hallie had spent every spare minute on them. She added up the last column of figures and double-checked her work. A sixth sense alerted her to another presence, and she glanced up.

An Indian in leggings and a quill vest stood in the doorway. *Last Horse.* All the stories she'd read came to mind and Hallie's heart beat a little faster. ''May I help you?''

On silent feet he slipped into the room.

''Cooper isn't here.'' As soon as the words were out of her mouth, she regretted them. Rationally, she told herself he already knew Cooper wasn't there, and that's why he'd been bold enough to approach her.

He stood at the corner of the desk without reply.

She laid down her pen. ''What do you want?''

He stepped closer and she considered getting up and darting away, but knew he'd be faster.

His calculating coal black eyes pored over her hair and clothing and Hallie cringed inwardly. Beneath the beautifully crafted quill vest his broad chest was bronzed and sleek. His arms were as big around as Cooper's, strips of leather banding his biceps. A long, bone-handled knife lay sheathed at his hip. Hallie tore her gaze from it and refused to show him her fear.

He moved stealthily until he stood behind her, out of her line of vision. She concentrated on breathing normally. What had he come for? What would he do to her?

"What do you want?" she asked again, more angrily this time. He spoke English—let him say what he wanted.

He touched the back of her hair and Hallie damned herself for jumping. With a nightmarish vision of being scalped, she reached back, only to encounter his hand and yank hers back.

Hallie sat frozen while he found the pins that held her chignon in place and dropped them on the floor. Her hair spilled down her back. He lifted it and inhaled. He moved around her side.

She stared ahead, heart pounding erratically. Jack was out there somewhere, wasn't he? Would he hear her if she screamed? Or would that only end up getting him hurt?

With an agile movement Last Horse leaned over her. She locked her gaze on his chiseled face. He leaned forward and smelled her hair again, the pouch around his neck swinging before her nose. One side of his hair fell forward. Hallie could smell him—a trace of the yucca plant, but more horse and musk, an unpleasant smell that she would forever associate with fear.

Moving back slightly, he ran a hard finger over her cheek, traced her eyebrow and caught her earlobe between his thumb and forefinger.

She turned her head, pulling away from his touch, and made a move to get up out of the chair. If he had wicked plans for her, she wasn't going to sit passively and make it easy for him.

Last Horse gripped her upper arms and held her fast. "Don't move."

She glared at him then, anger sparking to life.

He bent toward her and put his nose right against her jaw. His tongue flicked out and he tasted her.

"I have many horses," he said, his breath touching her neck.

She pulled away and stared at him.

"I will make a gift of them to your father."

What was he talking about? "My father wouldn't know what to do with your horses," she said. "He doesn't want them."

He looked surprised. "Blankets? Furs? What does he value?"

"What does it matter what my father likes? He's not here."

"I would make a trade," he said.

"For what?"

"You."

Indignation swelling in her every fiber, she stared at him. Her neck and face grew uncomfortably warm, and her heart thumped frantically. Did he think she was a trinket that could be bartered for? "Well, I don't want to be traded. I'm not a horse or a blanket. No deal."

With little effort on his part, he pulled her out of the chair, still holding her arms, and placed his face inches from hers. "Your father might say different. He might be glad to have you gone."

"No, he wouldn't. My father loves me."

"If that's true, why are you here?"

"He didn't know I left."

Those merciless black eyes bored into her. "No one knows you're here."

Oh, God, she'd made a mess of it now! Fear got the best of her. "Yes! Yes, they do!" She hated the tremor that had crept into her voice, hated that he would hear her fear. "Cooper took a letter to my father. He knows I'm here."

Last Horse let go, and she stood on her own. He didn't

move away. "Anything could happen to you. Bad things happen to white women."

He was right. She cursed her foolishness. "Cooper sees that I'm safe from harm."

"He's not here." He stalked her in a tight circle, the warmth from his hard-muscled body tangible through her clothing. "I want to see you without your dress."

Horrified, Hallie spun away from him and clenched her hands before her breasts. Immediately she felt silly and dropped her arms. Her strength was no match for his. Whatever happened now depended on her using her wits.

Though he could have stopped her, captured her in an instant, he allowed her to put some space between them. She faced him squarely. "I'm not breeding stock. I won't be stared at and poked. This is not the way it's done with my people. You've had your fun, now leave."

An appreciative glimmer blazed in his dark eyes. "You have a strong heart."

He wouldn't think so if he could feel it ready to explode from her chest.

"I'll go," he said.

Hallie didn't allow her gaze to falter.

"You will see me again." He walked around her, their gazes locked until she had to turn and swing her head to the other side to watch him move from behind her and approach the door.

As silently as he'd entered, he was gone. She could still smell him. Still taste the fear on her tongue. She had no doubt that he'd keep his word and she would see him again. What should she do? What would Cooper do if she told him?

Her heart slowing back to its normal rhythm, she closed the ledger and capped her ink. It wasn't exactly flattering to be considered for trade like a saddle or a bushel of corn. Was there a culture anywhere in which women were equals? She would love to see it.

Pausing in the doorway and glancing about, she thought of the heavy gun Cooper had given her to carry the day they'd dug out the stage. She didn't like looking in every corner and shadow and wondering when Last Horse would show up again. Perhaps carrying a gun was the answer.

A few months ago she would never have thought she could aim a gun at a man and pull the trigger, no matter what he had planned for her. She'd done it once when her life and the lives of the other brides had been endangered; she could do it again. She wouldn't remain vulnerable.

Hallie hurried to the sod house.

Cooper rode hard the last several miles, eager to get back. He was obviously getting soft. Three meals a day and a roof over his head every night had spoiled him. He remembered a time when sleeping, eating and working outdoors were his life. He still slept lightly, attuned not only to each sound from outside, but now to those from the other room.

Having Hallie so close was a distraction from sleep and work.

He had realized the day Last Horse brought in Wiley Kincaid slung over a horse that the sight of himself dressed in only a breechclout had shocked her. She'd probably never seen a man—or another woman, for that matter—in a state of undress. Civilized people thought differently. They were embarrassed about natural things like nudity and mating.

He'd respected her background and tried to act civilized around her. He couldn't have worked all day in the rain in those clumsy clothes, though. She would just have to accept that this was a different land. City customs had no place in the face of survival.

And she was a city girl to the bone.

Kissing her once had been a mistake. Kissing her a second time had been stupid. What had he imagined would come of it? She was as white and citified as only a girl from Boston could be. He'd never even seen the inside of a real house or been to a school. He'd dressed in buckskin since the day he'd been born and he had more in common with the trappers and Indians than he did with her kind.

What must she think of him? He wasn't certain why she'd consented to stay on when he'd given her every opportunity to leave this time. Maybe her reporter's curiosity drove her to finish the stories. Maybe his difference fascinated her.

Fascinated and yet repelled. A ripple of unease slid through his chest. Maybe she just wanted to take a firsthand story home to win the approval she craved from her father.

He was a story.

Cooper's horse stepped over a gully and he rocked with the nimble motion. The weathered stage station came into view. He nudged the horse into a trot.

Angus saw him from a distance and met him. "Any problems?"

"Didn't see any holdup men," Cooper replied. They spoke for a few minutes and Angus said, "Coop, why don't you bring the Wainwright girl over?"

Cooper studied the man's uneasy stance. "She'll be wanting to do that. She's writing a story, you know."

"Yeah. Well, I don't know about the story, but Evelyn is...well..."

"What?"

"I dunno. It's hard for her bein' out here with no other womenfolk to talk with."

There it was. The first sprout of dissatisfaction. Cooper didn't want to tell him it would grow huge and eat them both alive. "Yes. I'll mention it to Hallie. I'm sure she'll want to come."

"Good." Angus patted the horse's neck and watched Cooper ride on.

After rubbing his horse down with fistfuls of straw, he turned him into the corral and spotted Kincaid's horse tethered to an outside rail. Cooper found Jack oiling harnesses in the doorway. They talked briefly, and Cooper walked to the soddy. It was nearly suppertime, but no smoke drifted from the chimney. His stomach rumbled; in his hurry to get back, he hadn't eaten.

No one was in the sod house. The fireplace and stove were cold. Nearing the house, he discovered where everyone was. Laughter rang from inside.

Cooper pushed open the door and stepped in. They sat before the fireplace—Hallie, Chumani, Yellow Eagle and Wiley Kincaid.

"Coop!" Yellow Eagle shot up and barreled into Cooper's chest. Cooper caught him and gave the boy a fierce hug. Chumani, wearing a fancy green shawl, greeted him softly.

"Where'd you get that?" he asked.

"Hallie," she replied.

Cooper turned to Hallie.

"She said my name!" Hallie said in surprise. Chumani smiled at her. "She made me moccasins, see?" Hallie lifted the hem of her wool skirt and showed him the moccasins with Chumani's distinctive quill pattern across the toes.

What had been going on in his absence? His Oglala sister-in-law was wearing a store-bought shawl, Hallie wore deer hide footwear, and Wiley Kincaid had made himself right at home among them.

Kincaid stood. "You've been working long hours."

Cooper glanced from one face to the other, understanding they hadn't told the man he'd been gone. Kincaid could have figured it out on his own, though. "Yes," he agreed. "And I haven't eaten all day."

"Oh!" Hallie jumped up and hurried to the other end of the room. "It will only take a few minutes."

Chumani joined her.

"I'm going to bathe." Cooper brought clean clothes from the other room.

"I'd better be goin'," Kincaid said.

"You might as well stay and eat with us," Hallie called.

Kincaid looked to Cooper.

"Stay," Cooper said. "We'll make plans to put that building up in the next few days."

"All right. Much obliged." He sat back down.

Cooper washed in the river, wondering why Kincaid visiting while he was gone disturbed him. The man treated the women with respect and had done business with Cooper in a forthright manner.

The smell of cooking met him when he returned. The women had fried salt pork, thin and crispy, with smooth and creamy brown gravy. There were even johnnycakes and hot maple syrup.

"We made an applesauce cake earlier," Hallie said, clearing the table and presenting the golden brown confection.

Cooper looked at her in surprise. He didn't know if he'd ever tasted an applesauce cake.

"Mr. Kincaid found me a cookbook at the trading post," she said with a bashful smile. "At home we always have dessert after a special meal."

What made this meal special? Company? Cooper accepted the spicy-smelling slice she handed him. He sampled a bite. It tasted wonderful. "What are these spices?"

"Cinnamon and nutmeg mostly," she answered. "You're not familiar with them?"

"I knew they were in one of the last shipments."

"Now you know why Magellan and Cortez got rich," she said.

"Who?"

"The explorers who sailed across oceans to bring spices from faraway lands."

"Oh." How did she always manage to make him feel inadequate? Her head must be full of knowledge.

"Certain foods are traditional with different cultures," she said, "but people are always eager for a new taste experience."

"I'll have to remember to offer spices for mining camps and settlements," he said, thinking aloud.

"You could be onto something there," Kincaid said. "'Course, settlers don't have much to spend on anything other than the necessities."

"But the mining camps will pay any price for supplies," Cooper said. "I've been able to take over supplying a lot of the camps because I charge them a fair price."

"You mean other freighters take advantage of them?" Hallie asked.

"All of 'em," Cooper replied. "They figure the miners are horning in on the land and water. If they're foolish enough to leave families behind in the hopes of getting rich, they're foolish enough to pay unfair prices. And they do."

"But *you* don't," Hallie said after a moment. "Even though you don't like them on the land."

"I've made my way without stealing anything from anybody," he said.

She looked up at him, the gold centers of her eyes bright with unvoiced questions. Had she taken his words with more than one meaning? Of course, he meant the whites encroaching on Sioux land, but had he also been thinking of his money and stage ticket she'd used without permission? He had no reason to trust this woman, and plenty of reasons not to. Everything he knew about her pointed out how inappropriate her presence was. He'd be a fool to let things go any further than they already had.

When Kincaid suggested they go out for a smoke, Cooper drew his long pipe and tobacco from his bag and left with him. They walked from the house. Kincaid lit a cigar. Cooper tamped tobacco into the bowl of his pipe and lit it. For the first night in days, the cloud cover had disappeared and a half-moon hung against the night sky.

"Seems peculiar that any husband would leave a woman like that out here in the territory," Kincaid commented finally.

Cooper remained silent.

"This isn't exactly a stopover on the way to Mexico, if that's really where Mr. Lincoln is."

"What are you sayin'?" Cooper asked.

"I'm just saying a husband would have left her in the East where she'd be safe." He puffed on his cigar, and the tip glowed orange in the darkness. "Only women out here are runnin' away from something or don't have any means of support except doing what men will pay for."

Cooper jerked his attention to the man's face in the moonlight. "You're thinking wrong if you're thinking that. She's a respectable woman from a good family."

"Seems that way."

"It is that way."

"Don't get riled, DeWitt. I have good intentions."

"Like what?"

"Like every other man in the badlands. I want a wife."

Cooper absorbed the words calmly, rationally.

"I don't think you're her cousin. And I don't think there's a Mr. Lincoln," Kincaid stated. "But I understand why you all made him up." He turned to face Cooper. "If there's something between you and her, say the word and I'll back off."

Chapter Nine

Something between them? Like those kisses? Like the things he'd shared with her by the fire that night? Something between them?

No, there couldn't be anything between them. They were from different worlds.

"If not," Kincaid went on, "I'm interested myself."

"There's nothing between us," Cooper said flatly. "She'll be going back to Boston in the spring."

"Maybe," Kincaid said. "Maybe not."

"That'd be up to her," Cooper said.

Kincaid ground out his cigar beneath his heel and stuck out his hand. "Thanks for the meal."

Cooper shook his hand. "Give me a day to get the men lined up and we'll be out to put up your building."

"Much obliged."

They walked to the corral. Kincaid mounted his horse and rode off.

Cooper knocked his pipe against a corral post and scraped the barrel clean. He tucked it into its bag and touched the pouch around his neck that held his spirit stone. His was a particularly powerful stone, found near an anthill, having been pushed from beneath the earth.

He didn't know what to ask his guardian spirit for. He

only knew that Wiley wanting to marry Hallie disturbed him when it shouldn't. There was no reason for him to care. The only thing that mattered was that she teach Yellow Eagle the skills he needed. And she was doing that.

Whether she went home to her rich father or married Kincaid meant nothing to him. He only knew he wouldn't hang around and watch her dissatisfaction bloom and ruin them both.

Cooper released the stone and headed back to the house. He needed a good night's rest.

The following morning Yellow Eagle was back to his churlish self. The favor Hallie had won in her face-off with the bear had worn thin. He was silent and uncooperative, and Hallie was glad for lesson time to end.

During Cooper's absence, she and Chumani had spent evenings together, and Hallie had hoped the woman's son had grown more accepting of her, but his ambivalent attitude matched that of his uncle's.

She hadn't had an opportunity to mention Last Horse's visit and didn't want to bring it up in front of the others. Earlier, the ponderous sounds of mule teams and heavy wagons had reached the house. Glad to see a sunny day and grateful to have Cooper back, Hallie crossed the yard to the freight building. She found him stacking crates against an inside wall.

"Hi," she called.

Cooper turned and wiped his sleeve across his forehead. "Hi."

"Get a shipment today?"

"Yep. Got the lamp. Go look at it on the desk."

She went to look at the lamp he'd ordered. It was rather ordinary, like lamps she'd seen a hundred times. She wandered back. "Almost done there?"

"A few more."

She watched him finish the chore. "Can I show you a few things?"

He nodded and followed her through the doorway.

"Here's what I wanted you to see." She flipped open one of the ledgers and pointed.

"Do you like the lamp?"

She looked at it and back, realizing it held some significance for him. Had he bought it to please her? So her eyes wouldn't tire? Hallie glanced again at the milk glass shade and recognized that the lamp was an extravagance out here where practicality meant survival. "It should give off a lot of light."

Her finger remained on the figures.

His gaze didn't drop to the book.

"Look," she said.

"What is it?"

"Read it." She held the open page out to him.

He took the ledger and stared at it. A muscle jumped in his jaw.

"Well?" she said.

His face reddened. "Well, what?"

"You've been losing a few cents on lanterns and canvas from St. Paul. You'll either have to buy somewhere else or charge more."

He shoved the book back into her hands.

"Well, wait a minute," she said, trying to hand it back. "I wanted you to see—" Losing the struggle, she held the ledger to her breast, awareness thrusting itself into her head. He avoided her eyes, his square jaw taut. "You can't read, can you?"

He didn't reply.

"I don't know why you didn't just tell me."

"Well, you know now. Tell me whatever is so important."

She did, pointing out the few inconsistencies in the record

keeping. "Now that I know, it's even more amazing to me that you kept track as well as you did. How do you count?"

"My father taught me to keep track of pelts by making nicks on a stick. I figured out a system. The Oglala do the same thing with stones or twigs."

"Incredible," she said.

"Not really." He headed for the door.

"Wait a minute, I really had something else to tell you." He stopped and turned back.

Being alone in this room with Cooper evoked feelings in sharp contrast to those of being alone with Last Horse. She trusted Cooper, maybe more than was wise, but her heart told her to confide in him. "I had a visitor while you were gone."

"I know. Kincaid is catching on."

"He is?" She blinked with surprise. "Darn. Well, he's not the one I meant."

Cooper's brows rose. "Someone else?"

"Last Horse."

His expression darkened perceptibly.

"He came here yesterday."

"Here?"

"Here. To this room."

"What did he want?"

"Well..." She glanced to the side. "Cooper, do you think he would hurt me? Is he really dangerous?"

"I don't know. He hates whites, but he deals with them because of the whiskey they trade."

"What about you? You're white."

"His father adopted me and treated me like his own son. Last Horse resents that, but he puts up with me because of our father's status. He and his band are barely tolerated by The People. If he did anything to me, The People would banish him."

"Does he live on the reservation?"

"He has a woman there."

"But he doesn't stay there?"

Cooper shook his head. "It's a touchy situation. Last Horse is like a rattlesnake coiled to strike."

"So he would hurt me?"

"I wouldn't put it past him. Tell me what happened."

"He wanted to give my father some horses or blankets or something in trade for me. I told him that was ridiculous, that I wasn't a piece of livestock."

A muscle jumped in Cooper's jaw. "And he accepted that?"

"He seemed to. He told me I'd see him again, but he left. Cooper, should I carry a gun?"

He looked at her as if he were considering the same thing. "Anything else?"

Yeah, he suggested I take my clothes off so he could get a better look. "He's not a gentleman, Cooper. I was scared and I didn't like the feeling one bit. No one's ever made me feel like that before."

"Like what?"

"Like…like I did when he looked at me. Like a possession there for the taking."

"Did he touch you?" he asked, his voice gruff.

Heat seared her cheeks.

"Where?"

"My hair. My face."

"That's all?"

"That's more than enough without an invitation!"

"I'll get you a gun." He headed for the door once again.

"You can join Yellow Eagle tonight," she said, her words stopping him.

"What do you mean?"

"I mean, I've seen you watching us when we do letters and numbers in the evenings. You might as well work with us."

"We'll see."

She tilted her chin and looked him in the eye. "Yes, we will."

He turned and left.

"No letters tonight," Hallie announced to Yellow Eagle that evening.

He followed her away from their usual spot at the table and remained standing while she sat on the rug before the fireplace.

"Come on," she coaxed, patting the spot beside her.

Reluctantly he sat cross-legged, propped his cheeks on his fists and frowned at his lap.

"Tonight we read." She waited for a reaction.

After a few minutes he looked up.

She revealed the book she'd hidden in the folds of her skirt.

"You're going to read to me?" he asked.

"No."

He frowned and stared at his knees again.

"You're going to read to me."

His head jerked up. "I can't read!"

"Of course you can. What do you think you've been doing with all those letters?"

"Those are just sounds."

"And words. Remember bird and rock and snake?"

"Yeah, but there are lots more words than those in your books."

"And you will know those, too," she insisted. "Now, let's start." She opened to the first page and scooted beside him, holding the book open. "What's this word?"

He looked at the first word on the page where her finger pointed. *"In."*

"Good. And this one?"

"A."

"And this one?"

"Pla—plack," he pronounced.

"Place," she corrected.

"Place."

She moved her finger.

"Wh—ere."

"Where. Good."

"M-an," he sounded out, and her finger moved to the next one. "That's it?" he said, raising puzzled black eyes. "That's all there is to it? I'm reading?"

Hallie smiled. "You're reading, Yellow Eagle."

He stumbled through the first sentence, then the first paragraph, needing her help only a few times by the end of the page.

Cooper entered and picked up his pipe pouch.

"Sit with us," Hallie invited.

"I was going to go smoke," he said.

"Stay. It'll remind me of my father."

"He smokes a pipe?"

"Cigars."

He settled in a chair and packed tobacco in the bowl.

"I'm reading," Yellow Eagle announced to his uncle.

"Read that page over," Hallie whispered near Yellow Eagle's ear.

He started at the beginning, and the words flowed more easily this time. He'd only forgotten one that Hallie needed to help him with. Cooper lit his pipe with a stick from the fireplace and his fragrant tobacco lent a cozy atmosphere to the evening and the warm room. In his youthful voice, Yellow Eagle read to the end of the page.

"I'm very proud of you," Hallie told him truthfully.

He ignored her praise.

"I'm proud of you both," Cooper stated. "Miss Wainwright has given you a gift, Yellow Eagle, a gift that will make you a better man. A gift that will help your people. Wherever you go for the rest of your life, you'll take her gift with you."

Yellow Eagle looked at his uncle thoughtfully, but refused to meet Hallie's eyes.

"You'd better be thinking of the gift you'll give her in return. It needs to be something just as valuable."

"That's not necessary," Hallie objected. "It's part of our—"

"Yes," Cooper interrupted. "It is necessary. Among The People, gifts are like trades. To accept it, Yellow Eagle must give one of his own."

"I'll think on it," Yellow Eagle said, and stood.

"No lessons tomorrow morning to give you time to plan." Cooper declared.

"Can I take this with me just for tonight?" the boy asked, still holding the book open to the page he'd read and avoiding her face.

"You certainly may." Though he wasn't letting it show, she knew he was proud of his accomplishment. He grabbed his fur-lined coat and left.

"I have something for you." Laying down his pipe, Cooper opened a chest near the door and removed a roll of soft leather.

She watched with uncertainty. "For me?"

He nodded and returned, unwrapping the bundle on his knees. She'd asked him about the wisdom of a gun, but they hadn't discussed it any further, so the weapon he revealed took her by surprise. The gun was so small it fit in the palm he extended. "It's not loaded."

Hesitantly, Hallie picked it up. It was surprisingly heavy and beautifully crafted from dark wood, the handle curving into and under a metal barrel that was only about an inch and a half long. The weapon was small enough to hide in her reticule or a pocket.

"These are the shells. It only holds two." The small box he held revealed the metal cylinders. He showed her how to load it. "This derringer is only good up close. You wouldn't stand a chance against a bear.'' His blue eyes reflected a hint of humor.

"I'll remember that," she said, then sobered. "I'll pay you back."

He shook his head. "I bought it from a teamer. It's not new."

"But still, I owe you—"

"It's a gift," he said abruptly, cutting off her objection.

Hallie took the gun and the bullets into her room and returned. "Then I'll have to give you a gift of equal value."

Cooper bit the stem of his pipe and regarded her with apprehension expanding in his chest. Anything she had to offer wasn't meant for him.

She brought slates and chalk from the table. "A gift like teaching you to read. Would you say that's equal to seeing to my safety?"

"I would, but I don't—"

"You mean it's not as valuable as your gift?"

"Of course, but—"

"Then no objections." She settled herself on the rug, her full skirt billowing around her in a bewitchingly feminine display. How could he sit with her each night, listen to her gentle voice, see her ready smile and not fall into something that would be a big mistake?

"I already owe you, remember?" she said. "And you need to be able to keep the books after I'm gone."

He couldn't argue. He didn't. He simply felt like a callow boy. He switched his pipe to the other hand and awkwardly accepted the chalk she pressed into his fingers.

"You will copy everything I do," Hallie instructed. Beneath her tailored white blouse, her breasts were softly curved. Her hair held a silky sheen in the firelight. He remembered watching her dry it before the fire. He remembered everything about her, and his body responded with a surge of heat and unbidden desire.

She made a partial circle on the slate and drew a stick alongside it. "*A*," she said.

He copied it.

"*A*," she repeated. "Say it."

He wanted to push her down on the rug and show her he was a man, not a child. "*A*," he said.

"Now I'm going to tell you words that start with *a*, and we'll see if you can think of some. Listen to the sound." She repeated the letter a few more times. "*Apple. Arm. Apron. Arithmetic.*"

He wanted to shut her up with a crushing kiss and run his hands over her until she was weak and pliant. He looked at the letter on his slate.

"*A* is a vowel," she continued. "And vowels are either long or short." She gave him both sounds. He wanted to ease her city-made clothes off and see her slender body in the glow of the fire. Her words weren't making sense. He'd have been better off if she'd never discovered his inability to read or write. At least then she wouldn't make him feel like a child or an idiot.

"Army," she said. "Afraid. Ant."

He stood, let the slate clatter to the floor and knocked his pipe clean against the fireplace. "This is stupid."

She grinned up at him, not the least bit daunted. "That's exactly what Yellow Eagle said a few weeks ago. And you just heard him read."

He set the pipe on the hearth and yanked his shirt off over his head. "I'm going to sleep. Leave or stay."

The amusement on her face vanished, and her gaze darted from his bare chest to the furs he'd begun to roll out.

Without a backward glance she disappeared into her room.

Undressed, he stretched out on his pallet, the warmth of the fire caressing his skin and adding to his frustration. Before she'd come, he'd been a capable, independent man. But she'd pointed out all his inadequacies and turned him into an intimidating hulk. He didn't like how he behaved around her.

He didn't much like Cooper DeWitt.

Which only served to prove that she couldn't like him, either. And he wanted to keep it that way.

"Do you ride?" Cooper asked at breakfast.

"Ride," she said, chewing a slice of the bread she'd helped Chumani toast in the oven. "Like in a carriage?"

"On a horse," he replied.

She'd never been on a horse in her life. "I can ride."

"Good." He finished his breakfast and stood. "Come to the barn as soon as you're ready. It won't take us long to get to the Hallstroms'."

Excited about seeing Evelyn, she agreed.

"You do have riding clothes?" he asked. "We don't have a ladies' saddle."

Hallie shook her head. "I didn't bring any."

"You came west without riding clothes," he stated.

She shrugged noncommittally.

"Come with me."

Shooting Chumani a questioning glance, she excused herself and followed. At least he seemed in a better mood than the night before. The abrupt dismissal had kept her puzzled half the night. "Where do the Hallstroms live?"

"Not far from the stage station." He led the way into the house and strode into the other bedroom. Never having been in the room, Hallie preferred waiting outside the door. "Here," he said, returning and stuffing a kid-soft piece of clothing into her hands.

"What is it?" she asked.

"Trousers."

Warmth crept up Hallie's cheeks. She'd never heard the word said aloud before. Her family called them "nether garments."

"Put 'em on under your dress," he said.

Heat radiated through her upper body. She had to be blushing wildly now. "Why?"

"When you get up on that horse, do you want me staring at your legs the whole ride?"

She was momentarily taken aback by the fact that he'd obviously considered her exposed person, but more so by the way he'd spoken to her. Even her mother had never spoken the word *legs* to her—it was definitely considered a naughty term.

"Oh. No." She held the trousers up and looked them over dubiously. Her mother would have had a fit of the vapors over this situation.

"They're too big," he agreed without her saying anything. "Just lace the middle up tight."

Mortified, she turned away. "Okay."

Ten minutes later she met him before the barn, where he and Jack had two horses saddled and waiting. His glance flicked from her black kid boots, across her wool skirt and tailored jacket to the narrow-brimmed straw hat with ribbons trailing off the back. It felt positively decadent wearing something he had worn. Was he thinking of her legs in his trousers?

"Do you have it?" he asked.

"Have it?"

"The gun."

She patted the derringer in the pocket of her skirt.

He nodded his approval, then gestured to the horses.

She glanced at Jack and back. "Which one is for me?"

"The mare," Cooper replied.

The mare? Hallie looked both horses over. How was she supposed to tell which was the mare? One was a dappled gray with black spots spattered across its shiny hide. The massive animal's mane and tail were a charcoal gray. The other bore copper-colored specks on a predominantly white coat. Its mane and tail were pure white. The white hair over its forehead appeared more feminine to Hallie. She pointed. "This one?"

"That's a gelding, Hallie," Cooper corrected. "This one's the mare."

How did he expect her to know? Certainly not—! Cheeks flaming, she couldn't keep her eyes from scanning the mysterious underbellies of both horses. Why, there was a difference!

Hallie stepped beside the steely gray mare.

"These 'uns are Coop's animals, miss," Jack said in a warning tone.

Standing this close, the horse was huge! She swallowed hard. "Yes?"

"They're Injun broke. You gotta mount 'em from the left."

"Of course." She started to walk behind the horse.

"No!" Jack moved toward her.

"What?"

"Don't never walk back of a horse. Go 'round front where they can see you and won't kick."

"I forgot." She veered around the animal's head, staring up into one wide-set eye at a time. The mare nodded her head and took a step forward, nostrils flaring.

Hallie jumped back.

"She just wants to get to know you," Cooper said. "Talk to her. Touch her."

Hallie stared up into the enormous dark eye and frowned. "Hello, there," she said, then glancing over her shoulder. "What's her name?"

"She doesn't have a name," Cooper said.

"Why not?"

He didn't reply, and she looked over her shoulder again. He and Jack exchanged a look.

"Most Injuns don't name their horses," Jack said.

"Well, I think she needs a name. How can I get to know her if I can't call her something?"

"Call her anything you like," Cooper said impatiently. "Just get on her."

She glanced around, and couldn't begin to figure how she was supposed to get on the beast's back.

Cooper stepped up and showed her where to grab the saddle. "Put your foot here," he said, holding the stirrup in place.

Hallie, balancing herself on his arm to raise her foot that high, experienced exceeding gratefulness for the trousers beneath her skirts.

"Pull yourself up," he said matter-of-factly.

She tried, but only succeeded in flinging herself across the saddle on her belly. She stared down at the dangling stirrup on the other side. The mare sidestepped, and Cooper grabbed her thigh to keep her from plummeting off the other side on her face.

"Whoa, girl," Cooper said, gentling the gray with his soothing voice. With strong but respectful hands he lowered Hallie back to the ground. "Okay, again," he said to her.

This time he flattened a broad hand across her backside and, before Hallie could register surprise or embarrassment, lifted her onto the saddle. The imprint of his invasive touch barely had time to register. From up here the ground looked a long way down. She gripped the knob protruding from the saddle and hung on.

He offered her the reins.

She let go with one hand long enough to take them from him.

He placed a moccasined foot into his stirrup and, with a creak of leather, effortlessly lifted himself astride the massive gelding.

"Tap your heels against her flanks," he said.

Flanks? She glanced over, saw how Cooper nudged his horse and did the same. The mare started forward. Hallie stifled a squeak, immediately caught up in trying to stay seated for the jostling ride. Her teeth jarred and her buttocks slammed repeatedly against the hard saddle, and instinctively she tried to steady herself with the reins.

The horse drew up short, flinging its head back and snorting.

"Hang on to the pommel, Hallie, not the reins!" Cooper ordered.

Sorting out his instruction and swallowing her panic, she let loose of the reins. The animal turned in a tight circle.

Cooper sidled his mount up beside hers and steadied the mare.

"Thanks," she said.

"My horses are touchy," he said. "If you pull on the reins they stop. If you pull to the right, they turn right. If you pull to the left, they turn left. I should have told you."

"That's okay."

He put some distance between them and they moved out once again. She'd never imagined riding a horse would be this difficult! However did men do it for days and days? She was already praying the Hallstroms' place was only a few more feet.

Cooper didn't seem to have any difficulty, and she observed the casual way he sat the animal. She discovered that bracing some of her weight against the stirrups as they crossed gullies helped ease the jarring.

They traveled at a moderate pace, Cooper riding close. Finally, assured she wouldn't be flung to the ground and trampled at any moment, she relaxed and beheld the countryside.

As they traveled west, the landscape was more picturesque than the endless sky, unbroken by cliffs or conifers, meeting the horizon in all directions. Here the erosive power of nature had eaten away the outer skin of the prairie, exposing a panorama of color and clay forms.

A deer darted from a cottonwood gully and Hallie pointed in fascination.

"Whitetail," Cooper said.

"Isn't this just the most breathtaking scenery? Oh, look! What are those?"

"Pronghorn," he replied. "Antelope to you."

"Antelope starts with an *a*," she said.

He ignored her.

"So does Angus."

No reply. The small herd grazed until one of the antelope caught sight of the horses, and gracefully, like dancers in a synchronized ballet, the animals turned, revealing bright rings around their rumps, and ran out of sight. Disappointed, Hallie sighed.

"The cabin's just ahead," Cooper said.

"Why isn't Angus at the station?"

"He doesn't work for me all the time," Cooper answered. "He farms this land, too."

They passed a field of stubble, then the cabin and a low, slant-roofed structure for housing animals came into view. Several chickens pecked in the dirt beside the door. Angus came from the animal shelter and met them. "Coop! Miss Wainwright! You came!"

Cooper slid from his horse in a graceful dismount and turned to Hallie. Thighs trembling, she stood in the stirrups, freed one foot and swung the leg over the horse's rump. Cooper caught her before she fell in a heap in the dirt. "These Dakota horses must be taller than the ones back home, eh?" he asked, settling her and stepping back.

"Much," she replied. "Must be all this fresh air that grows them so big."

Evelyn, a calico apron covering her gray dress, appeared in the doorway with a hesitant smile. "Miss Wainwright?"

"It's Hallie," she said, moving around Cooper on wobbly legs.

"Hallie." Evelyn gave her an awkward hug and immediately stepped back. "Mr. DeWitt."

"Ma'am." Cooper tipped his hat. Pulling a tin from a

saddlebag, he pushed it into Hallie's hands without ceremony and turned with Angus, walking the horses away.

Carrying the tin she recognized as tea, Hallie followed
Evelyn into the dim interior of the tiny cabin.

"For you," she said, and placed the metal container on
the plank table.

"Tea?" Evelyn's plain face lit up momentarily. "How
thoughtful." She frowned immediately and her glance
darted around the rustic little room. "I don't have a teapot."

"No worry," Hallie said. "Just boil water in your coffeepot. That's what we do." She found the word *we* disturbing in some betraying manner she chose to ignore.

While Evelyn fumbled with the water bucket and metal
coffeepot, Hallie glanced around the room. Open shelving
held tins and dishes. Pans and utensils hung from the low
ceiling. At the other end of the room, a lumpy bed covered
with a patchwork quilt took up more room than anything
else. Hallie glanced back and met Evelyn's timorous gray
eyes.

Evelyn's pale complexion reddened, giving Hallie cause
to wonder. None of the women who'd come west with her
had been prepared for the fates that awaited them. The brief
descriptions in the advertisements and letters had painted
only a sketchy picture, leaving their imaginations to fill in
the details. Their own limited experiences had colored the
vista with inaccuracies and wishful thinking.

"Will you answer questions for my story?" Hallie asked.

Evelyn placed a few sticks in the stove and ineffectively
tried to light them. "I'd probably talk to the devil right
about now, just to have some company." She jerked her
head around and blanched. "I didn't mean that you're—
that—"

Hallie waved off Evelyn's embarrassment. "Here, let me
show you how."

"Angus keeps trying to show me, but I just can't seem
to get it right."

Hallie brushed her aside, built the fire and placed the pot on the stove. "What were your first reactions to the Dakotas when you got here?" she asked.

"Pretty much what they are now," the woman said, sinking tiredly onto a chair. "I wondered what I was doing here. I didn't know how to do anything. Everything I learned at Miss Abernathy's is useless."

Hallie nodded with growing understanding. "What are your days like?"

Evelyn's thinly lidded eyes turned to her. "I've ruined most of my clothing trying to do my own laundry. The rest gets torn on nails or ripped on bushes. I mend a lot. I read. Angus, well, he tries to help me with things as much as he can, but he's awfully busy with the farm. Everything has to be ready for winter."

Hallie had been having such a grand adventure herself, she finally stopped to recognize what a hardship this life was for the women who'd come west. "Are you lonely?" Hallie ventured to ask.

Evelyn's pained expression was one of guilt. Tears formed in her eyes and her lower lip trembled. "You're the first person I've talked to besides Angus." She blinked and straightened. "Tell me what your life has been like."

"Well!" Hallie launched into detailed accounts of the Indians, the bear, and her teaching and accounting experiences. Evelyn actually laughed and asked her to go on. They'd drunk several cups of tea by the time the men walked through the doorway.

Evelyn started at their arrival.

"Did you ladies have a good morning?" Angus asked.

His wife smiled nervously and nodded. And then as if realizing he'd mentioned the morning was gone, she stood and looked around with a lost expression. "We need something to eat," she said.

Cooper watched the woman flutter uselessly. He glanced

at Hallie and she, too, watched her with a frown. Evelyn looked in a few canisters, took a pan down and opened the stove door, forgetting a rag and burning her fingers.

Without prelude, the woman burst into tears.

Chapter Ten

Cooper, having no experience with crying women, had the singular urge to get up and run. He and Angus exchanged looks of embarrassment and confusion.

Hallie moved to Evelyn's side and tenderly wrapped an arm around her shoulders. She handed her a square piece of rough toweling to dry her tears and fed a log into the fire. "Do you have some salve?" she asked Angus.

He handed her a tiny round tin and she dabbed a little of the substance on Evelyn's palm. "There, now. Do you have salt pork? Flour? Here, find me a bowl."

Within minutes Hallie had organized ingredients and was showing Evelyn how to prepare a simple meal.

Cooper hated to see this happening to his friend. Angus had burdened himself with a useless city woman and worse, if the look on his face was any sign, he cared about her. He'd looked relieved to see them arrive that morning. He'd come up with chores for Cooper to help him with just to stay away from the cabin. Cooper had seen through his ruse, but had gone along. Maybe the women needed some time alone. They'd probably commiserated together.

Would visiting the brides satisfy Hallie? Or would being around women raised as she was point out how crude her surroundings were? Would she regret not taking advantage of her last opportunity to go east before winter set in?

"I got a good wheat crop in just before the rain started," Angus mentioned, drawing Cooper's attention. They discussed the fishing that year, and before he knew it, Evelyn set the table and Hallie served the food.

Angus ate the meal appreciatively and encouraged Hallie to talk about her article. As soon as they'd finished eating, she scraped the plates and heated wash water. She bustled about efficiently, and Angus turned to Cooper with a raised brow.

Cooper glanced from the station manager to Evelyn. She stared at Hallie with a lost expression, from time to time glancing at Angus as if she hoped he didn't notice her inadequacy.

Cooper couldn't wait to leave. By early afternoon he had the horses ready and called Hallie from the cabin. She wished Evelyn and Angus a gracious goodbye, thanking them for their hospitality, and this time mounted the gray a little more gracefully.

Why hadn't she just told him she'd never ridden before? He suppressed a grin every time he remembered her approaching the beast with apprehension in her wide, expressive eyes. She wasn't a very good liar. By that night her heedless pride would earn her the sore backside she deserved.

Was he pushing her to make himself feel superior because she'd made him feel like a child the night before?

"Oh! What are those?" She pointed to a bank of cascading red and white wildflowers.

"Wild rose. Prickly pear over there."

"Aren't they beautiful?"

He'd always thought so. Hearing her agree surprised him for some reason. "The first flowers had no seeds and couldn't reproduce themselves," he said.

"How do you know?"

"Do you want to hear or not?"

She nodded silently.

"The first plants had only stems and green leaves," he said, relating the ancient tale. "But Unk, the god of passion and rain, was jealous of their beauty. Gnas, the demon of schemes and plots, taunted her about their beauty until she breathed on the plants and withered them and they all died."

"What happened then?"

"Skan, The Most Holy, saw the destruction and made plants with buds to bear seeds so the plants could make more of themselves. Wohpe, the goddess of beauty and happiness, gave the plants flowers to cover them and colors to make them beautiful."

"That's a wonderful story," she said.

They rode a few miles in silence.

A thundering sound reached them. Beside him, Hallie glanced up at the sky.

Cooper reached an arm out. She reined her horse in and they sat side by side. "It's not thunder," he said. "Wait."

The sound grew louder.

He motioned for her to follow, and walked their mounts to a small rise. On the plain to the west ran a herd of wild horses, their manes and tails streaking in the wind.

Hallie wore an expression of fascination and he turned to see the herd through her eyes. The animals were magnificent, wild and beautiful. He would come back for a few to replenish his stock.

"I was wrong," Hallie said at last.

He glanced at her in surprise. The golden centers of her irises were bright rays in the sunlight. "About what?"

"When I said all the things the whites brought made it better out here."

He remembered her optimism on the subject. And his sarcasm.

"It's lovely just the way it is," she said. "I wish it didn't have to change."

"It will."

She nodded sadly. "Yes, it will. But with men like you… and Yellow Eagle…the change won't all be bad."

Absorbing her words, he led them down the rise and toward Stone Creek. She understood. Somehow, she understood his intent for The People and his nephew. He couldn't have put it into words, but with her he didn't have to.

The more he learned of her, the more time they spent together, the harder it was to accept that he wasn't good enough for her. She recognized that he was a man of the land, a brother to The People. But even though she didn't necessarily look down her nose at him, there was a significant difference between them.

And she would be going back.

Cooper hadn't known much fear in his life. Enemies didn't frighten him. Animals and snakebites and bad weather didn't frighten him.

Death didn't frighten him.

"I think I'll call her Wild Rose."

He turned from the dramatic fall grasses and clay formations to observe the young woman riding beside him. "Who?"

"The horse. You said I could call her anything. I like Wild Rose."

Her silly bonnet, buffeted by the wind, was not doing a thing to protect her from sun or wind, and the afternoon sun shot rays of fire through her disheveled hair. Hallie Claire Wainwright, small and naive and too proud and stubborn for her own good, who talked too much and thought too quickly and had been to school. This unfamiliar creature with pale white skin and delicate bone structure, this city girl who named horses after flowers and had dreams and expectations as big as his own, scared him to death.

And he didn't have the first idea how to handle the fear.

Or the woman.

* * *

The next day a commotion from the other side of the freight building snatched Hallie's and Yellow Eagle's attention from their studies. Wincing, Hallie grabbed a coat and limped behind Yellow Eagle across the distance to the corrals.

"Wild horses!" he shouted with excitement.

Several lathered horses ran in a pack around and around the inside of the corral. Most were white with large patterns of color. Cooper lashed the gate closed and led his panting, copper-speckled gelding toward the barn.

"You gonna break 'em for riding?" the boy asked as Cooper neared.

Cooper's face and hair glistened with perspiration. "Yes." He drew his leather sleeve across his eyes. "And for the teams. I have enough now to breed and sell."

"Do they bring good money?" Hallie asked.

He glanced at her.

"I'm sorry," she said quickly. "That was none of my business."

"They bring excellent money," he answered. "Enough for a big profit next year."

They stood alongside the fence and watched the tiring animals. The horses blew through their noses and slowed their run. A few fell behind and walked.

"They're beautiful," Hallie breathed in admiration.

"They're tobinos," Cooper said.

She turned her face up.

"Like he's roan or red speckled," he explained, nodding at his gelding. "Wild Rose is a dapple gray."

Hallie grinned at his use of the name she'd given the horse.

"That's a dun or a claybank." He nodded to the animal the color of dirty canvas that Jack led toward the barn.

"Did you know all that?" she asked Yellow Eagle.

He nodded.

"No studies for a few days," Cooper said.

Hallie drew her brows up in question. ''What do you mean?''

''We'll be working on Kincaid's building from sunup on. You and Yellow Eagle will be needed.''

''What can I do?''

''Our neighbors will be there. You can either help the women cook or help with another job.''

''You mean the brides? The brides will be there?'' she asked eagerly.

''I knew that would interest you.''

''Of course! I can get the rest of my interviews for my articles.''

He leaned toward her. ''I could swear I smell horse liniment.''

She drew her jacket around her protectively and looked away.

He led his horse toward the barn.

The next morning Hallie chose to ride with Chumani in the wagon Jack drove. Her sit-down-upon muscles still hadn't recovered from her horseback riding, but she refused to use the liniment Chumani had given her if Cooper thought it made her smell like a horse. Cooper and Yellow Eagle rode ahead and led them to Wiley's tent, which flapped in the wind. Beside it, an enormous pile of wood had been stacked, and a short distance away, a mound of rocks had been gathered.

Hallie helped Chumani establish a cooking area, constructing an open-fronted canvas tent to break the wind, and collecting stones for the fires. Before long more wagons arrived. Vernon Forbes, wearing a freshly pressed shirt beneath his overalls, assisted Zinnia down from a wagon.

Hallie waved.

''Miss Wainwright?'' The wind struck Zinnia in the face and she pressed her hat to her head, grasped her basket and lumbered toward the shelter, her enormous bosom jostling beneath her shiny green dress. Without stopping to set the basket down, she enfolded Hallie in a fleshy, sachet-scented hug. "Oh, Lord, it's so good to see a familiar face!" she said, and tears leaked from the corners of her wind-reddened eyes.

"Zinnia, this is Chumani," Hallie said, prying the basket from her side and introducing the women.

Chumani smiled and made the sign for good morning.

Zinnia looked her over and turned back dismissively. "I'm surprised you're still here."

Hallie glanced from Zinnia to Chumani. Expressionless, the Indian woman unpacked a crate. "I haven't interviewed all of you brides yet. And I made a deal with Mr. DeWitt."

"Oh?" Zinnia's eyes flashed curiously.

"I'm teaching his nephew to read and write. He hired me to put his accounts in order, as well. It'll probably take me most of the winter. I'll head back to Boston in the spring."

"Oh." Zinnia finally set her basket down. "Where are you staying?"

"I've taken a room," Hallie said, making her living arrangements sound more like a boardinghouse than Mr. DeWitt's home. "It's quite nice. I get meals, too."

A creaking wagon lumbered near. Zinnia stayed beneath the shelter, but Hallie ran to greet the arrivals. Tall and just as scrawny as the last time she'd seen him, Stuart Waring set the brake handle and helped his wife down.

Olivia saw Hallie and ran and took her hand. "There's that dear, brave girl," she said with a smile. "I've mentioned you every night in my prayers."

"Why, thank you," Hallie said with surprise. "Perhaps that's how I survived the bear."

"What!" Olivia saw Zinnia at that moment and ran forward. Zinnia enfolded the lanky woman as she had Hallie. "Now, what's this about a bear?" Olivia asked.

Evelyn came next and joined in the reunion, followed by a small woman named Nellie Kell, who had two youngsters in tow. Nellie and Chumani took over the food preparation.

Hallie asked Zinnia and Olivia all about their first weeks in the territory and took notes. Both women were mildly homesick, but both seemed to have adapted better than Evelyn. Olivia acted happy, at times speaking of Stuart as though they were a love match. She blushed profusely at one point and whispered, "I haven't had my time since I've been here. I think I'm going to have a baby."

Hallie surveyed the other women's reactions. Zinnia giggled. Evelyn picked at a thread on her sleeve and refused to look up.

"That's wonderful, Olivia," Hallie said.

After she'd heard more about their new lives than she cared to, Hallie wandered away from the women to see what the men were doing. Cooper, Jack and Angus worked on turning the pile of rocks into a fireplace. Yellow Eagle carried water and stirred the mixture that they used as mortar to hold the rocks in place.

Cooper stopped to talk to her for a moment, pointing to the ends of Yellow Eagle's black hair accidentally stiffened with mortar. They shared an intimate smile of familiarity and enjoyment. Hallie remembered Olivia's pronouncement about her baby and wondered if this was what it felt like to be a parent.

Of course, the child would have to like the parent better than Yellow Eagle liked her, she reasoned, feeling silly for even having the thought.

Cooper's gaze flicked over her and her cheeks burned.

"Why are you turning pink?" he asked.

She turned her face away.

He took her chin and turned her head back. "Usually I've said something coarse to embarrass you. This time I haven't."

The thought of sharing intimacies with Cooper left her speechless. She had a pretty good idea of what it took to have a baby, and just imagining participating in such an indelicate act with this man overwhelmed her. His fingers scorched her skin and she pulled away.

His burning blue gaze followed. "What are you thinking, Hallie?"

The wind cooled her skin. She ignored him and wandered to where Stuart, Vernon, Wiley and a man she assumed was Nellie's husband had started footings for the corners of the house.

"Howdy, Miss Wainwright," Stuart called.

She met Wiley's eyes. Cooper had said he was catching on that she wasn't married. He'd know for sure now, but he made no comment.

"Hi, Stuart," she replied.

The bearded man turned and nodded. "Victor Kell, ma'am."

"Pleased to meet you." She stuck out her hand. "Hallie Wainwright."

He removed his glove to shake her hand, then returned to his work.

Wiley stepped closer and she waited for a question about her name. "Sure was good of all these folks to show up to work today."

"Many hands make light work," she said with a sheepish smile.

"Sounds like an Indian saying," he commented.

"No, my mother used to say it. Though how she knew, I'm not certain. She's never done a day's work in her life."

"No?"

"Well, charity work, you know, things like that. Mostly she plays bridge and arranges flowers. I did see her hit a croquet ball once."

Wiley laughed aloud. "You're somethin', Hallie. I've never met anyone like you before."

She grinned. "Is that good or bad?"

The smile faded. "All good."

His brown eyes had grown far too serious. Hallie glanced around. "You've chosen a lovely spot."

"I can make a good living here," he replied. "Stone Creek will grow in the next few years."

"That's what Cooper says," she agreed.

"It's a good place to settle down."

She nodded. "I'd better get back and help the women."

Cooper eyed her as she passed. She flipped him a wave.

Back under the canvas enclosure, the wives had clustered near the fire. Chumani sat apart from them, shaping biscuits and placing them in a greased skillet.

Hallie left the others to their conversation and sat beside her friend. "I'm getting hungry," she said, signing the words at the same time. "Everything smells good."

Chumani signed that Yellow Eagle had already been by to snitch food.

They shared a smile.

Chumani baked three pans of biscuits and they called the men to eat. Everyone had brought their own plates, cups and utensils, and once finished, Hallie hauled water from a barrel on the side of a wagon and heated it.

Nellie and Chumani washed the dishes and Hallie dried. Nellie laid her children down on blankets and they took naps.

Preparations began all over again as evening approached. Unexpected hoofbeats sounded, followed by shrill cries and whoops. Hallie peered out from beneath the overhang and watched the small band of Indians approach.

"Oh, my God!" Zinnia's face had turned white as a lily and she weaved where she stood. "An Indian attack!"

Olivia hurried to steady her and helped her sit on one of the blankets.

The weather had turned cooler and most of the braves wore shirts and leggings. Last Horse rode in front on what Hallie now knew was a tobino, this one white with patches of black and red.

Unconsciously, her hand slid to the side of her skirt. The weight of the derringer against her thigh assured her. The men stopped work and met the riders. Unerringly, she spotted Cooper's hat and broad-shouldered frame, adding to her confidence that she was not alone or helpless this time.

Dismounting, several of the Indians peered into the backs of the wagons, obviously making the men nervous.

"My braves are hungry," Last Horse called. "Will you share your food?"

One of the men cursed. Hallie heard another say they were going to lose daylight. Cooper moved up, and Hallie knew he felt responsible for Last Horse's interference.

"We'll fix your braves something," she said, stepping forward and flicking a hand at the workers. "You go back to work until the meal's ready."

Last Horse turned and spoke in his guttural syllables and two Indians approached Hallie with headless skinned animals dangling from leather thongs. Her stomach lurched, but she swallowed her disgust; instead, she met them and accepted the heavy game.

She caught Cooper's taut-jawed expression and his almost nonexistent nod of approval before he turned and led the others back to their jobs. Carrying the bloody meat toward the fire, she met Chumani's black eyes. "I hope you know what to do with these."

Chumani nodded and took the carcasses.

"Girls," Hallie said, spinning to the others, "we're going to need more water heated and more biscuits. I'll go for the water, and Evelyn, you heat it in those pans. Zinnia, you take the ingredients Chumani gives you and stir up more dough. Olivia, feed those sticks into the fire."

Hallie exited the enclosure carrying the empty pails. "Last Horse!" she called.

He turned.

"We're going to need more firewood. Will you send a few of your men to bring us some, please?"

He looked startled. However, he spoke to two young Indians nearby. They argued, but he silenced them with a stern look and pointed.

Grumbling, they wandered away from the camp.

Last Horse followed her to the water barrels. Hallie dipped one pail at a time, secure with the concealed gun in her skirt. She remembered how close he'd been to her that day in the freight building, the way he'd touched her hair and sniffed at her. She wouldn't allow him to intimidate her again.

The second bucket full, she reached to pick up the first and found his moccasined foot in front of it. Slowly she straightened and met his indomitable black stare.

"How do your people take wives?" he asked.

His offer of horses and blankets came to mind. "The gentleman asks the lady to marry him," she replied. "Politely. With a declaration of love."

"How does he prove his worth?" he asked.

"Well…" she said, her voice trailing off. How could she answer his questions in a way he'd understand? She had no reply. She shook her head.

The wind caught his hair, secured only by a red-and-black band across his forehead.

He turned his head toward the wind to free his vision and, seizing the opportunity, she stepped around him for the bucket. He trailed her back, ducking under the awning behind her.

Zinnia gasped at his entrance, but Olivia patted her arm and urged her to stir her bowl of dough.

Last Horse seated himself near Hallie and watched her. Refusing to allow him to daunt her, she went about the work, pretending he wasn't there. Chumani skewered the carcasses and propped them over the fire. Hallie steeled herself and helped. That done, they washed and sliced turnips Nellie had brought and fried them in a skillet.

Nellie made coffee, and eventually the biscuits were

baked and the meat and vegetables tender. Chumani and
Hallie scraped together pans, tins, anything they could use
for extra plates, and called the men.

The women didn't have much appetite, though between
the workers and the Oglala there was just enough to go
around. The Indians licked their fingers and grunted, making
comments to one another. They hooted and snickered.

Two of the braves reached for the last piece of meat at
the same time, ending up in a scuffle. Exasperated, Hallie
reached across with the wooden spoon she held and
smacked each of them on the back of the hand. They winced
and withdrew, staring at her with wide eyes. Hallie tore the
meat from the roasted thigh and gave half to each of them.

She turned and found Last Horse standing behind her. She
met his arrogant black eyes without cringing. He stared
back, and the air crackled between them. What had she
done? Insulted them? Would he give a command and have
them all scalped?

Finally, tearing his gaze from hers, he spoke to his
friends, who then ran toward their horses.

Last Horse said something to Cooper, and Cooper replied.
The Indian joined the others and they rode off.

Tiredly, Hallie surveyed the mess left behind. At least
they still had their hair.

Zinnia drew an accordion-pleated fan from her basket and
fanned herself.

Jack started to chuckle.

Hallie turned toward the sound.

"I don't know what it is about you," Jack snickered.
"It's a disgrace for Indian males to do manual labor, and
there they was, gatherin' firewood."

"Is that true?" Hallie asked.

Beside Jack, Cooper sat with his lips twitching. He nodded.

She stared hard at him. Did he think this whole thing was
funny?

Angus and Victor Kell sputtered, suppressing their laughter.

"Did you see their faces when she hit 'em with the spoon?" Jack asked on a full-fledged chortle.

"They needed a lesson in manners," Olivia said defensively. "They ate like savages."

Hallie waited for Cooper's reaction to that one. He surprised her by setting his plate down and laughing out loud.

The others joined in, and Hallie couldn't help herself. The humor released the tension that had built since the Indians' arrival.

"Good meal," Wiley said. "Thank you, ladies."

The others concurred, and the men went back to finish what they could before the light waned.

"Let us finish up," Olivia offered, stepping between Hallie and the dirty dishes scattered across the area.

"Yes," Evelyn agreed. "You did more than your share."

Hallie didn't mind the break. "Okay," she agreed, and left the tent.

The wind had grown chilly. Hallie pulled her collar around her ears and watched the men. Occasionally she handed them tools or offered a hand. When it came time to clean up, she pitched in.

"Where do these go?" she asked Wiley, following him with a trowel and bucket.

"Here," he said. He ducked inside his tent and returned to take the items from her. "Thanks, Hallie. Hallie?"

She'd started to leave, but turned back.

"I have your hide for you."

"My...?"

"Your bear." He disappeared inside the tent and carried the enormous fur out.

Hallie stared at the shaggy mound of animal hair with the huge head on top, its snarling teeth gaping at her. Stifling a shudder, she wondered what she was going to do with it.

"Th-thank you."

"It was my pleasure."

She accepted the fur, learning its staggering weight with awe. A living creature had dwelled inside this skin for years and years.

"I've been waiting for a chance to speak with you alone," he said, his brown eyes solemn.

"You know I'm not really married." She glanced aside. It hadn't been nice to try to fool him. If she'd known what a respectable fellow he was, she wouldn't have resorted to the crazy story for protection. "I'm sorry, Wiley."

"It's okay," he said. "I think I know why you did it."

"No hard feelings, then?" she asked hopefully.

"None."

She flashed him a friendly smile.

"Hallie, I…"

"What?"

"I'm gonna have a nice house here when we're finished. I decided on a house and the shop separate."

"That'll be nice."

"I want to start a family."

She nodded, adjusting the fur in her arms and deliberately not looking at the head too near her chin. So many of the men out here had hopes for the future. Plans for businesses and farms and dreams that included wives. She understood now why they sent for women from back East. "You could…" She glanced up and, discovering his enamored gaze, realized what he was thinking. "Oh, Wiley, no…"

"I'd like you to marry me, Hallie."

Chapter Eleven

"**I**'d make a good husband," Wiley assured her. "I'll have a successful operation going in a year or two. You've heard us talk about more and more settlers moving here."

"It's not that I think you wouldn't be a good choice," she said quickly. "It's just that I'm not staying. I'm a reporter from *The Daily,* a paper back East. I came out here to get a follow-up story on the brides. Unfortunately all my money and valuables were stolen, or I'd have been back home by now."

"Is there someone back there?"

"Someone...?"

"A man."

"No!"

"Then stay."

"I'm not *looking* for a husband," she objected.

"Why not? What will you do?"

"I'll write stories," she said, riled now. "I'll have a perfectly good life and I won't wither up and die because I haven't yoked myself with a man."

"It's DeWitt, isn't it?"

"What?"

"You and him. He got to you first."

"Oh, really!" She turned away, then thinking better of

it, spun back, hands on hips. ''You're just like every other man I ever laid eyes on. You don't think a woman has a shred of value on her own. Well, mister, if you want to change my mind about how women should behave, you'll have to get in line!''

''Hallie!''

She heard him, but she was already marching away at full tilt. Ignoring the curious stares of the other men, she stomped past them and placed her hideous bearskin in the back of Cooper's wagon. Entering the cooking tent, she vented her frustration, slamming supplies into the crates and carrying them out.

Cooper secured the lids on the water barrels, glancing back as Hallie climbed into the back of the wagon beside Chumani. ''Men!'' he overheard her say to his sister-in-law. ''They're all a bunch of overbearing, egotistical, rutting dogs!''

He glanced back at Kincaid, who was waving the men off, and wondered what he'd said or done to get her in such a state. Whatever it was, he'd be darn careful not to make the same mistake. Climbing up on the seat beside Jack, he shook out the reins and led the horses toward home.

The following days went more smoothly without the interruption of the Oglala. Once again, Hallie made herself indispensable, organizing meals, arranging supplies and befriending the women. She steered clear of Wiley Kincaid, and Cooper found her avoidance obvious.

''What did you say to her?'' he asked Kincaid while they hammered shingles on the roof.

''Who?''

''Hallie.''

Wiley pushed his hat back on his head and confessed, ''I asked her to marry me.''

''That's why she's avoiding you like a pile of—''

''You noticed, huh?''

Cooper nodded without answering and grabbed a handful of nails.

"If you and her are...you know...you should have told me when I asked you about her."

He thought of the kiss they'd shared and dismissively denied anything between them. "She doesn't think any better of me than she does of you."

"I don't know if that's any comfort." Wiley wiped his forehead with the back of a hand.

"She tries so hard," Cooper said thoughtfully, resting on his heels for a moment. Her whole purpose in coming out here in the first place had been to gain favor with her father and bolster her position at the newspaper. What kind of need drove a young woman to prove herself in such a risky way? She could have been killed a dozen times over by now. Killed...or worse. What impelled her?

Pride. She had plenty of that. But enough to base her crazy scheme on? He didn't think so.

Love. Did she love her implacable father so much she would do anything to please him? Maybe.

Ambition. Were recognition and position the goals she strove for? Somehow they didn't suit what he knew of her personality.

All of those were possibilities, but some inner sense told him that there was something more, some soul-stirring need that he couldn't quite recognize because of his ignorance.

And the worst thing was...he'd started to care.

Wiley's house was completed just as the weather turned cold. Hallie hadn't gone inside once it was finished. She didn't want him to get the idea that she was in any way interested. She felt badly about avoiding him; his company and friendship had been pleasant—but that's where it ended.

The women parted tearfully on the last day of the house raising, knowing it could be months before they saw one another again. Hallie wished them well, glad she had Chumani, Yellow Eagle and Cooper to winter with.

During their evening lessons one night the following week, Yellow Eagle made an announcement.

"I thought up a gift for Hallie."

Cooper looked up from the boots he drew laces through and gave his nephew an encouraging nod.

"It isn't a gift I made or bought, because her gift to me wasn't made or bought. It's something she'll carry with her always, like my reading and writing, and it will make her life better, just like her gift to me."

"You've thought this out carefully, haven't you?" Cooper said.

Hallie listened with growing interest. Yellow Eagle never missed an opportunity to display his resentment, but he would do anything to please his uncle.

"I've thought of it every day," the boy replied.

"What is it?" Cooper asked.

Yellow Eagle's flashing dark eyes darted from his uncle to Hallie. "A *sicun*."

Hallie remembered the word from the time she'd asked Cooper what was in the pouch he wore on a thong around his neck. A spirit stone.

A thoughtful expression softened Cooper's handsomely rugged face. "At first you didn't want to accept Hallie's gift, did you?"

Shamefacedly, Yellow Eagle shook his head. "I didn't know how important it was. I do now."

Hallie heard his admission with surprise.

"Maybe Hallie won't be ready to accept your gift, either," Cooper said. "Not until she understands how important it is."

Yellow Eagle absorbed that and grinned. "The gifts are equal then, aren't they?"

Cooper lit his pipe and puffed. "And…" He looked over at Hallie.

"What?" she asked skeptically.

"Yellow Eagle had to work to receive his gift. You will, too."

"What do you mean?"

"No one can give you the stone. You have to find it yourself."

"Well, I can do that," she said, gesturing toward the door. "There are rocks all over out there."

Cooper shook his head. "This has to be a special stone. A pure stone. From a riverbed or from inside the earth."

Was it Yellow Eagle's plan to have her drown or freeze swimming in the river? Not excited about the implication, she said, "I either swim or dig."

The three of them exchanged glances.

Hallie rejected the first idea immediately. "That river's got to be awfully cold by now."

Uncle and nephew agreed.

Excitedly, Yellow Eagle spread both palms out flat and then rapidly poked two fingers on his right hand forward and pulled them back.

Cooper's broad smile divulged how brilliant he thought the suggestion.

Not understanding the sign, Hallie stared at them in exasperation. "What are you talking about?"

"There's hundreds of prairie dogs out toward Standing Rock," Yellow Eagle explained.

"And…?" she prompted, leaning forward.

"They push stones up from their burrows and tunnels."

"Oh." She sat back. "So we ride out there and I pick out a rock."

They nodded.

"Then I put it in a pouch and wear it."

They shook their heads.

"There's more?"

"You take the stone to the Yuwipi man," Yellow Eagle explained.

"The who-what-i?"

"The Yuwipi man," the boy repeated. "He does the sacred naming ritual so the spirits enter the stone."

Was this sacred stone thing really important to him? Was this a sincere gesture? If so, he'd no doubt be insulted if she refused, and she didn't want to ruin the first bit of progress she'd made toward gaining his acceptance. Hallie bit her nail. Imagining the bizarre activity with more than a little hesitation, a fortuitous thought came to her. Her gaze slid to Cooper.

He raised a dubious brow as though wary of her thoughts.

A sacred Indian ritual! She would be one of the few whites to ever participate in such a thing! Her father would jump at this story. "Where's this Yuwipi man?" she asked in excitement.

"At the reservation," Cooper replied.

"When can we get the stone?"

He shrugged. "Tomorrow?"

Hallie clapped her hands. "I can't wait!"

He studied her curiously, finally turning to Yellow Eagle. "That took a lot of thought," he said. "I'm proud of you."

Yellow Eagle's chest swelled.

"Close your book now," he said. "We'll get an early start."

The boy obeyed and wished them good-night, slipping into his coat and leaving.

Cooper made tea, and surprised her by carrying the slates to her. The other evenings after Yellow Eagle was gone, she'd had to coerce him into doing letters. "You've decided it's not so bad?" she asked.

He sat cross-legged beside her and handed her a piece of chalk. Their fingers brushed. "I've decided you were right. I do need to learn to do the books after you're gone."

"Cooper."

He tilted his head.

"There's something I've been wondering about."

"That's no surprise. You ask more questions than anyone I ever knew."

She shrugged.

"Okay, what is it?"

"Who wrote the letter to Tess Cordell?"

He looked at his blank slate. "Mrs. Kell."

"Nellie Kell?" She imagined him asking the woman to write the letter for him. Had he been embarrassed? Nellie was so down-to-earth and practical, she would have been easy to approach with the favor. "Well, I'll be," she murmured, then turned her attention to their lesson. "Where were we?"

"We finished and we were going to start over."

"Oh, yes. With capitals this time," she said. She drew the *a* he remembered and added another symbol beside it that looked like a tepee with a bar across the center. "Lowercase *a,* capital *A,*" she said, pointing.

Cooper drew the same symbols. "Why two that mean the same thing?" he asked.

"Names start with capitals, names of people and cities and countries."

"Why?"

"Because they're important."

"And other things are not important?"

"The first word in a sentence starts with a capital letter, too," she added.

"Why?"

"So you can tell it's the beginning of the sentence when you're reading, I guess. Are you trying to pay me back for all the questions?"

He shook his head. "Words and thoughts on paper are amazing."

Hallie turned and observed the chiseled line of his jaw in

the firelight. "You're right. It is amazing. I've taken it for granted my whole life."

He looked up and met her eyes. "You probably think I'm ignorant."

"Not at all," she replied. "Communicating *without* writing, now that's hard," she said. "I've learned more from you and Yellow Eagle and Chumani than I ever knew before."

"Like what?"

"Oh, like how to dye quills and fabric, and how to survive on my own cooking, and what to do for a snakebite—or mosquito bites."

They shared an irrepressible smile.

"Practical things," she said. "Things about life." She was quiet for several minutes. "You know what one of my greatest fears has always been?"

He shook his head.

She brushed a strand of hair from her face and left a streak of chalk on her cheek. "That I'd end up like my mother."

"Would that be so bad?" he asked softly.

"It would be awful," she whispered. "Once her years of producing children were over, she became like an expensive but ugly gift that no one knows quite what to do with. You keep it around because it would be unthinkable to get rid of it, but everyone's uncomfortable having to look at it."

"Doesn't your father…" His voice trailed off. "Don't they have a…good relationship?"

"It's good for him," Hallie said, and heard the resentment lacing her tone. "He has a comfortable, well-ordered home and someone to entertain guests. She could have been anyone—anyone capable of giving him sons."

"You wouldn't be like her, Hallie." His deep-strung voice was low and reassuring.

"I would be if I gave my father his way."

"And what is that?"

"Forget the paper. Marry one of the fine young men he and my brothers parade before me."

"But you won't do that."

"No." She adjusted her skirts and their knees bumped.

"What's wrong with the men?"

She shrugged. "Nothing. They're just—men."

"Egotistical, rutting dogs?"

She blushed and snuck a glance at him from beneath her lashes. "You heard that, huh?"

"I didn't take it personally."

"Why not?"

"Should I have?"

"No!"

Graciously, he let it go. "*A* is a vowel," he said.

Mildly surprised, she nodded. "And how does it sound?"

"Ay and ahh," he said, making the letter sound like an expression of pleasure.

She grinned. "Now give me words that start with *a*."

"Alive."

"Anxious," she said.

"Ache," he said.

She looked at his hands on the slate and her heart beat a little faster.

"Alone." He looked up, and his clear blue eyes drew her into their depths. "Amazing," he whispered.

They leaned toward one another until their lips were inches from touching. "Admit," she said.

Blue fire burned in the depths of his eyes before Hallie closed hers against the pounding of her heart and the expectation quivering in every pore. Their lips touched briefly, his warm and unassuming, hers hesitant…guileless.

Hallie pulled back and he made no move to stop her. She looked at the seductive lips she'd just kissed and instinctively reached up to touch them, running a finger across the pliant flesh, two fingers down the cleft in his chin, and flattened her palm against his rough cheek.

Releasing the slate, she leaned toward him and used both hands to trace the strong line of his brow and thread the hair away from his temples. She drew a line down his nose and paused, bracketing his mouth with both thumbs, her fingers lying along his jaw.

His passivity lent her freedom to enjoy the feel of his skin beneath her hands. His very difference from her own skin and hair infused her with an ardent desire to learn more. Satiating her curiosity, she skimmed his muscled neck to his shoulders. Beneath the leather shirt he was broad and solid. For a brief moment Hallie considered the impropriety of touching him this way.

But she was a questioner at heart and all the answers to the mystery that made up this man were beneath her fingertips, so she availed herself without a second thought. Had he returned the caress, had he done anything but sit pliantly beneath her exploration, he would have broken the wondrous trust that allowed her shameless awakening.

She discovered his muscled chest and the eloquent beating of his heart beneath the shirt. She fingered the mysterious stone that rested upon his breastbone and ran her palms down and back up his rock-hard sides. She met his blazing eyes and saw the muscle in his jaw twitch.

Her hands couldn't circle even half of his bulging biceps. She wished he wasn't wearing the shirt, so she could touch his smooth dark skin and see the play of firelight over his body.

"Would you..." she heard herself asking in a voice not at all like her own, "take your shirt off?"

His expression didn't change. Slowly he set his slate aside and unlaced the front of the shirt. With a graceful motion, he pulled it off over his head and sat back.

Hallie moved directly in front of him. He was even bigger and broader without the shirt. She hesitated.

"Shall I put it back on?"

"No." Her hand stopped in the air between them.

Cooper raised his palm against it. His long fingers dwarfed hers. She examined the calluses on his palm and laced her fingers with his briefly before dropping his hand and splaying both hands against his chest.

His skin jumped at the first touch.

She flattened her hands and ran them across his warm, silky skin, his flat brown nipples puckering at the contact.

He closed his eyes and breathed through his flared nostrils.

Hallie kneaded his shoulders, stroked his corded neck and rose on her knees to brush his ponytail aside and explore his back. She absorbed him, learned him, discovered the places his skin was rough and the places it was as soft as a two-year-old's.

The knowledge was no longer satisfying. The tactile information her fingers relayed to her brain stirred a sweet hunger to life, and her self-taught senses responded with spontaneous desire.

Hallie cupped his face in her hands. "Kiss me now," she said on a ragged breath.

Cooper buried his primal craving deep and called on the spirit gods to endow him with the strength this self-denial called for. He knew enough about her to know that she didn't want to be intimidated by a man.

Oh, she was sweet, her curiosity natural, her instincts innocent and sensual. He wanted to know her the same way she knew him. He wanted to undress her and explore her with his hands and mouth. But more than that, more than anything, he wanted her to trust him. Why that trust was so important he didn't know, but rational or not, the desire overshadowed his physical passion.

He raised himself on his knees to meet her, reverently held her jaw, the pulse points beneath his fingertips hammering, and lowered his face to hers.

She met his lips with a soft, yielding sigh and a tightening of her arms around his shoulders. He kissed her sweetly, inhaling her fresh feminine scent, tasting her, fascinated by the unidentifiable sensations that surged within his head and heart. He didn't stop at sweet, but ripened the kiss with an open mouth and seeking tongue.

Instinctively her lips parted and she met him, returning boundless exploration with blissful deliberation. Her soft breasts crushed against his chest, and he knew she must feel him hot and hard between them.

She withdrew in heart-stopping hesitation, parted their bodies and looked up into his eyes.

A little fearful, a little credulous, her dark-eyed expression stole his breath.

He wanted to crush her against him and fill himself with her. At that moment he'd never felt weaker, never felt more selfish or so remorsefully inadequate.

Her black lashes fluttered and her pink tongue darted across her kiss-swollen lips. "Ask," she said.

It took his brain a second to translate the message. "Ask what?"

"Ask starts with an *a*," she said. "Ask for anything."

His overworked heart threatened to stop then and there. She was a boundless mystery, full of surprises and innocent charm. "A kiss," he said. "One more kiss."

A smile of genuine pleasure crossed her parted lips. Placing a hand behind his head, she pulled herself flat against him and kissed him. Breathlessly. Intensely. Confidently.

He would never sleep.

His body trembled.

A groan erupted deep in his throat.

She answered it with the ardent invasion of her tongue.

His heart thundered.

She released him and sat back on her heels.

Cooper stared at her shining eyes, her reddened lips and

the heartbeat at the base of her throat. A log rolled in the grate and the fire hissed.

"Good night," she said.

He forced a response. "Good night."

She steadied herself with a hand on the hearth and stood. With a silken rustle of clothing, she turned and shut herself in her room.

Cooper stared at the door until the fire burned down and the room grew cold. Unfolding his furs, he stared at the ceiling until dawn crept across the beams. And then...he went for a swim in the river.

"We'll leave the horses here and go the rest of the way on foot," Cooper stated. He and Yellow Eagle dismounted carrying bows and slung pouches filled with arrows over their shoulders.

Feeling like an accomplished horsewoman after her second ride, Hallie slid from the saddle, biting back a groan and ignoring both the ache in her posterior and the biting cold wind against her cheeks. Cooper hobbled the horses and the three of them silently climbed a small rise. He and Yellow Eagle crouched low and waited for her to do the same. She stifled a groan at the arthritic pain in her legs and lowered herself.

Yellow Eagle reached the top first and lay flat on his belly. Cooper stretched his considerable length out beside him and both turned to Hallie. She got down on all fours, crawled to where they lay and peered over the wedge of land.

The prairie dogs darted here and there, scampering about playfully and poking their heads in and out of the hundreds of holes littering the expanse of ground.

"Oh, aren't they darling?" she whispered, turning.

Cooper and his nephew exchanged a look and both fitted long arrows against their bowstrings and squinted down the shanks.

"You're not going to kill them, are you?" she asked. They released the arrows with a whooshing sound. Hallie turned in time to see two of the creatures impaled. The sound whizzed past her ear a second time and two more fell. Shaken, she stood and ran toward the holes.

In the blink of an eye all the prairie dogs vanished inside their tunnels.

"Hallie, you scared them away!" Yellow Eagle shouted impatiently.

"I didn't know you were going to kill them!"

Cooper and Yellow Eagle strode toward her. "They're meat for supper," Cooper said.

"But they're so cute...and little...."

"That's why it takes several." White breath puffed from his lips.

"Yeah, well..." She glanced around. "I'll leave the meat for you fellas tonight."

The two slung their bows over their shoulders. "Start looking for your stone, Hallie," Yellow Eagle said.

"It's probably too cold for rattlesnakes, but just to be safe don't stick your hands into any of those holes," Cooper cautioned.

She curled her chilled fingers instinctively. "No."

They had been right. Every so often near one of the mounds of earth, she discovered a rock or two that had been pushed up from the ground by the burrowing animals. An oval one about an inch long with a shiny pink streak running through it caught her attention. Maybe she'd see a better one. She dropped it into her pocket and continued her search.

Most were plain. One had a sparkling vein across the tip, but she was drawn back to the oval one. Something about it appealed to her and she tested its comfortable weight in her palm.

Carrying it to Cooper, she said, "I like this one."

He looked at the stone in her palm and a surprised expression crossed his features. Yellow Eagle joined him and they pored over it approvingly.

"Is it a good choice?" She took it back, still warm from his hand.

He nodded. "Tomorrow we'll ride to the reservation. But you'll need a warmer coat and some gloves."

"Where will I get them?"

"We'll make 'em," he replied matter-of-factly.

That afternoon Cooper did the measuring and cutting. By evening, with Chumani and Cooper supervising, the four of them stitched furs and leather.

Pulling the bone needle through the tough hide took strength, and Hallie's fingers quickly became sore. In her clumsy efforts, she gave herself a good poke and yelped, automatically raising the finger to her mouth.

"Let's see." Cooper stood over her, one palm outstretched.

She held her hand toward him. Crimson blood oozed from the hole. He plucked up a scrap of soft leather from the pile near his chair and pressed it against the tip of her finger, squeezing firmly.

Their eyes met and Hallie thought of touching him the night before, remembered how he'd granted her the privilege of learning the texture of his skin, the tone of his muscled arms and chest. The same thrill ignited in her chest at the memory, and beneath his frank blue gaze her skin grew warm. If Chumani and Yellow Eagle hadn't been sitting close by, she'd have been tempted to try that all over again.

He removed the leather and examined the tiny wound, which was no longer bleeding. "Wash it good," he advised.

She nodded, absorbed by his nearness, his heat, the musky scent of leather and man that was his alone.

"Hallie stand," Chumani said. She carried the back piece.

Hallie tore her gaze from Cooper's and stood with her

arms out so Chumani could measure the garment against her back. By bedtime the coat, gloves and hat were finished.

"We worked through lesson time," Yellow Eagle said.

Hallie wondered if that could have been disappointment she'd heard in his voice. "Your writing lesson time," she said. "But all of you taught me how to make winter clothing."

Yellow Eagle grinned. "So it was a lesson after all!"

Chumani gave her a warm smile, then led Yellow Eagle out the door. Hallie tried out her new coat on her trip to the privy. When she returned she saw that Cooper had cleaned up the bits of fur and thread.

She hung her coat on the antler rack near the door and stared at it for a long minute. Glancing around the room, she remembered her first impression of the house. She'd taken its comfort for granted these past weeks, but it had been built with Cooper's mail-order wife in mind. Her coat hung where he'd planned his bride's to hang. She ate at the table and slept in the bed he'd built for the woman he'd been anticipating.

Considering the disappointment Hallie had been, he'd treated her magnanimously. She warmed her hands near the fire.

He sat on the hearth and lit his pipe.

"Thank you," she said, without looking at him.

"For what?"

"For the coat. For everything."

"It's not much compared to what you're used to."

She turned her head and observed him. He studied his pipe bowl. "What do you think I'm used to?"

His gaze flicked over her skirt and her soft kid boots. "Nice things. Things city women like. You had jewelry before it was stolen. Your clothes are well made. I've never even seen some of the fabrics before." He bit the pipe stem. "Your father has money."

The firelight created prominent shadows in the hollows

of his cheeks. Hallie remembered how that skin had felt beneath her palm. She clasped her hands tight so she wouldn't be tempted to place the tip of her finger on that appealing dimple in his chin. "Money can buy more jewelry," she said on an exhaled breath. "But there are things…important things it can't buy."

He turned to her, his narrowed eyes nearly silver. "Like what?"

"A lot of things. Why do you look so unbelieving?"

He tilted his head. "I didn't expect those words from you."

"We city women are pretty shallow, huh?"

He shrugged and a minute later asked, "What have you wanted that you couldn't buy?"

She considered all the things she'd wanted, the credibility she'd fought tooth and nail for her whole life, the respectability she craved. She replied simply, "A chance."

"A chance for what?"

She shrugged. "Opportunities are for men. I never got a second glance."

"I can't believe that."

"You see?" she said, and ducked her head in exasperation. "You're such a man."

"Shall I apologize?"

She couldn't help a half grin. "No." Then with a rueful tone she added, "Maybe that's what irks me most."

"That I'm a man?"

She smoothed her skirt over her knees unthinkingly. "It's a man's world."

"Men wouldn't be here without women." His tone was matter-of-fact.

"Not a popular thought back East." A vivid memory came to her and she studied the glowing embers. "When I was ten my brothers brought me a puppy, light brown with soft floppy ears. I thought it was the cutest thing I'd ever seen. Charles told me I could name him anything I wanted because he was truly mine. Turner said it was a big responsibility and that the pup depended on me for food and care.''

Hallie glanced at Cooper. He rested comfortably against the stones, and she could tell by the way he studied her and listened that he was interested.

''I felt so important thinking that little dog was mine and only mine, and that he depended on me. I must have thanked my brothers a hundred times the first few days. They rarely paid me any attention, so a gift like that...well, it was special.''

A curl of aromatic smoke drifted between them.

''And then one morning I discovered them carrying bags to the foyer. My father and brothers were taking a trip together. 'I want to go, take me, please can't I go?' I begged.''

Cooper turned to study her in the firelight. Her voice had become childlike and a slight quiver betrayed the story's importance.

''Dusty—that's what I'd named the puppy—needed me, Turner said. He was my responsibility and I had to stay home and care for him. They loaded their bags in the carriage and drove away.'' She composed herself and her voice took on a deliberately calm tone. ''I never came so close to hurting an innocent creature as I did that dog. I hated the sight of it. It was a payoff, a bribe to keep me from underfoot. Instead of kicking it, I gave it to the cook and she took it to her nephew across town.''

She shrugged as if she was over it, as if the incident had been a long, long time ago and didn't affect her anymore, but he knew better. That gift had been a betrayal. What she'd believed her brothers had done out of love, they'd done as a conspiracy to pacify her.

''That wasn't the first time,'' she said. ''I was just too young to realize it before. And it wasn't the last.''

She met his eyes and hers held a sheen of tears.

''That's why I'm here, really,'' she said. ''My father never came right out and ordered me away from the paper.

I think if it wasn't for Charles and Turner, he would have appreciated me. At least, that's what I want to think. They tolerated me,'' she went on, ''for years. I hung around, always underfoot like a pet. I absorbed the business, learned it all by watching and jumping at the least little opportunity.''

She shifted her legs from beneath to her side. ''I told you I was a reporter? Well, that was wishful thinking. I'm just a nuisance.''

Cooper knocked his pipe out against the stones. Her stories had changed since she'd first arrived, and had been quick to relate various women's accomplishments. He understood now why those examples were important to her. They gave her hope.

Gathering her skirts, she stood. ''It's late.''

''They treated you wrong, Hallie,'' he said.

She stopped and listened.

''Don't give up.''

She contemplated him with a quizzical expression.

''You have a strong spirit,'' he said. ''I don't think you'd be you if you changed to suit them.''

''Being me isn't so great,'' she said. ''Sometimes it's downright tiresome.''

He grinned. ''Well, don't change for anybody.''

''Thanks, Cooper.''

''It's getting so cold, we're going to have to start making you a fire at night,'' he said, changing the subject.

''But you'll burn twice as much wood.''

''Can't be helped.'' Their gazes met, then skittered away. The only way to conserve fuel was to sleep in the same room, and that was out of the question. ''I'll start one.''

She followed behind, handing him sticks and finally a log that should last the night. She'd learned how to handle chores competently and efficiently. No doubt she'd be doing it herself by the following night. She caught on fast and never shirked a chance to try something new. Hallie was a wonder. A bundle of spontaneous thoughts and actions. A practical, intelligent beauty. How quickly he'd grown appreciative of her company.

How discouraging that she'd be leaving after winter. "Good night, Hallie."

"Good night."

He left the room and closed the door. With a hollow spot yawning in his chest, Cooper put his pipe away and made his pallet. Might as well take his swim now and get it over with.

He didn't know which disturbed him more: the feelings her kisses and touches had aroused the night before or the gut-deep awareness carved by her honest admissions and the insight into who Hallie really was. He understood a little better, had a deeper comprehension of what had compelled her to throw caution to the wind and take her chances in the Dakotas.

Dawning understanding only made it worse. He respected her now. He admired her.

But worst of all—he desired her.

Chapter Twelve

Bundled in her new coat, hat and gloves, Hallie stayed warm despite the living presence of the biting wind. Chumani traveled with them, chattering to Hallie in Oglala with a few words of English thrown in. Hallie understood her happiness to visit her family and friends.

Crates and barrels filled the wagon bed, but Cooper had left space behind the seat for Chumani and Hallie. Yellow Eagle rode on the seat beside his uncle.

Puffy white clouds in military array filled the northern sky, a sharp contrast to the beds of twisted and scarred rock shapes the mule team carried them past.

"What is this?" she breathed in wonder.

"Lignite," Cooper replied.

"It's been burned?"

"In ancient times. I heard one old trapper call it 'hell with the fires out.'"

"It makes me wish I was an artist."

"It's not that pleasing to the eye," he said.

"No. But it grips the soul, doesn't it?"

Without reply he turned and gave her a thoughtful glance.

"It's incredible to see this much space in all directions." She raised her face to the sunny expanse. "No houses, no lampposts, no buildings or boardwalks or telegraph wires. Nothing that belongs to anyone.''

''Here nothing belongs to anyone and everything belongs to everyone.'' Cooper adjusted his hat against the wind.

''That's quite poetic,'' she called up to him above a howling gust. ''Maybe you'll take to writing now that you have the skills.''

He laughed. The rare sound soared across the landscape and echoed back to lodge in her heart. Chumani gave her a sly, knowing smile before turning her attention to the horizon.

The scenery turned to bare brown hills as they approached the reservation. Hallie pulled herself to her knees and gasped at the encampment of enormous tepees with smoke curling out the tops. A harvested field stretched to the north. Several dogs barked and ran to greet them.

Hallie regarded the patch of land that had been assigned to the Oglala. ''It's not what I expected.''

''What did you expect?'' Cooper asked.

''I don't know. Something more like a fort, I guess.''

Several shouts rang out and children came running. Yellow Eagle leapt from the seat and met them. The youngsters stood in round-eyed anticipation and waited for Cooper to set the brake handle and climb down. He reached for a burlap bag beneath the seat and withdrew handfuls of licorice sticks.

Young voices exclaimed and the children thrust eager hands forward. After he rewarded each of them with a piece of candy, they thanked him and ran back toward the village, Yellow Eagle in their midst.

Hallie and Chumani stood, and Cooper assisted them from the wagon, one at a time. Several men arrived and helped him unload, carrying the supplies to a clearing in the midst of the tepees. Hallie followed. Women appeared and looked on as the men unpacked bags of cornmeal, dried fruit and a crate of bear meat.

At the sight of the meat, their eyes widened. They talked rapidly among themselves, and then to Cooper. He gestured to Hallie.

The Oglala looked at one another. A few whispered and several smiled. Cooper answered more questions, and the men nodded at her sagely.

While the supplies were distributed, Chumani took Hallie into one of the enormous tents and introduced her to an elderly woman. Before long, Cooper came for Hallie and led her to another tent.

"This is Running Elk, my father."

The man he introduced had gray hair, longer and thicker than Cooper's, flowing over a shaggy buffalo robe he wore around his shoulders. Running Elk made the sign for her to sit, and she settled near the fire.

A stoop-shouldered woman brought them wooden bowls filled with dried berries and tough strips of salty meat. "Your mother?" Hallie asked.

Cooper shook his head. "Laughing Woman died several years ago. This is Running Elk's new wife, Miya."

After they ate, Hallie picked up on bits and pieces of the conversation in which Cooper told his father about her. Running Elk spoke to her, and Cooper translated. He shared stories of Cooper as a boy. By the age of twelve Cooper had been as good or better with a bow and arrow than most of the warriors. His skills with his knife were a fond memory for the old man.

"He says my mother died young because she wore herself out making me bigger clothes." Cooper listened a minute. "He says he would sometimes get up at night and watch me grow in my sleep."

Hallie looked from Cooper's face to the old man's. His teak-colored cheeks were lined, but his black eyes shone like a child's. He watched her, gauging her reaction.

She smiled.

He gave a deep chuckle, shaking the fur on the robe, and his leatherlike face crinkled with mirth.

Hallie laughed with him.

The two men were so different physically. She marveled over their apparent fondness for one another and realized they didn't see each other as different. They looked past the skin to see the heart.

"Your father doesn't distrust me because I'm white?" she asked.

"He's trusted many whites," Cooper said gruffly. "That's why The People are here."

"What do you mean?"

"The government makes promises to the Sioux, promises things in exchange for the land. These are a people of broken promises. All those children you saw out there?"

Hallie nodded.

"The treaty promising them a school was signed four years ago."

"And they don't have one yet?"

"No."

"That's terrible." She frowned. "I wouldn't hold it against Running Elk if he didn't like me."

A commotion outside interrupted. Horses whinnied and loud whoops volleyed off the tepees. Reacting instantly, Cooper ran out. Hallie waited for his elderly father to rise, and followed him through the flap. She stayed just outside the tent, Cooper and his father standing ahead of her. Other tribesmen came out of their dwellings.

A dozen Indians atop predominantly white tobinos created havoc, tipping over wash buckets, scattering woodpiles and teasing the dogs. Several slid drunkenly from their horses and beat upon the sides of the tepees with sticks. A smattering of gunfire erupted, startling Hallie.

Last Horse staggered toward them, waving a long-barreled revolver. Hallie cast a look at Running Elk. The chiseled features that had been soft with mirth only minutes ago had hardened into unmistakable suffering and displeasure.

Running Elk spoke harshly in their hard-syllabled language, and Last Horse drew up short before them. His hawklike black eyes, glazed with liquor, raked his father and narrowed on his white brother. They exchanged words and, reaching from beneath his heavy fur robe, Running Elk signed to them. Last Horse's malignant glower slid to Hallie and she cringed back against the tepee.

Last Horse shot his father a parting glare and whistled to the others. It took several minutes before they caught their horses and led them to a corral Hallie hadn't noticed before. She followed Cooper and his father back into the tepee, but the incident had cast a pall over the day.

After supper Cooper indicated they were to go. "It's time for the *Inktomi lowanpi*."

"The what?"

"The spider sing. It's what we came for."

"Oh!" She pulled on her coat and turned to wish Running Elk goodbye, but he was right behind her.

Cooper led them to a huge tepee in the center of the encampment. Many of the village's occupants seemed to have turned out for the occasion, Chumani and Yellow Eagle joining them.

"Hallie, this is Runs Again," Cooper said, introducing her to an aged Indian.

"The Yuwipi man?"

He nodded. An elaborate quill vest covered Runs Again's narrow chest. His brown arms were thin and sinewy. Upon his head he wore a rack of antlers.

Hallie's eyes rose from his seamy, toothless face to the bizarre headdress. "Uh, how do you do, Runs Again?"

He emitted a sharp note. Hallie jumped. The sound turned into a nasal monotone song. She emitted a little laugh and relaxed.

A beat began, and she searched out the man with the drum sitting on the other side of the fire.

She flashed a look at Cooper, and he made the sign for sit. She did so. He lowered himself beside her, Yellow Eagle eagerly squeezing in between her and Runs Again.

Runs Again gathered up a few dried sprigs and rubbed them between his bony hands. The sharp smell of sage met Hallie's nostrils. He took a long, dismantled pipe from a bag, spit on the stem and put it together. Still singing his eerie incantation, he reached into the bag for a pinch of leaves and swirled them in the bowl.

He uttered a rapid prayer, as if he'd done it hundreds of times and the words were a recital. Each phrase started on an abnormally high pitch, his voice cascading down and ending with the same indistinguishable words.

He quieted all at once. The drums stopped.

A baby whined and a soft woman's voice shushed. Seconds later the baby quieted, the cry replaced by loud sucking sounds. Hallie wouldn't look.

Runs Again spoke to her.

"The stone," Cooper whispered.

Delving into her deep skirt pocket, she withdrew the smooth rock and handed it to the Yuwipi man.

His eyes widened at first glance. He examined it closely, his tongue coming out and flicking the surface a few times. He reached for her hand and Hallie suppressed a cry of surprise.

Turning her palm up, the old man placed the stone in her hand and studied it. He turned it over once, curled her fingers around it and opened them back up. Hallie sat perfectly still while he held it to her forehead and looked into her eyes.

He turned, and something unspoken passed between him and Cooper. Hallie looked from one man to the other, mystified by their actions. Apparently satisfied, Runs Again placed the stone on a bed of sage, lit the pipe and passed it to her. Yellow Eagle watched the process with wistful black eyes.

Hesitantly, Hallie accepted the pipe. "What do I do?" she asked Cooper out the side of her mouth.

"Puff once or twice," he replied softly. "Don't inhale."

She turned the long stem and did as he instructed. Hot, acrid smoke bit her tongue and she breathed in, snorting in spite of herself. Cooper took the pipe from her hands and she tried not to cough. Beside her, he puffed solemnly and passed it to the man on his other side.

The drums rumbled and Runs Again repeated the doleful song. A shiver ran up Hallie's spine. The pipe came around again and she managed not to choke. A dizzy sensation filled her head. By the time the pipe returned to Runs Again, he had finished the prayer. He tapped the remaining tobacco from the bowl onto the pile of sage and blew on the embers until they ignited. The fire burned out quickly. Runs Again smothered the fire in the center of the tepee by tossing dirt on it.

Hallie trembled in the total darkness and unfamiliar surroundings. Her head buzzed. She scooted closer to Cooper until their arms and thighs touched.

The baby sucked.

Someone coughed.

"What's going on?" Hallie whispered, leaning sideways and bumping her nose into Cooper's jaw.

"The spirits are placing the stone in the pouch," he replied. "You'll get it back at the end."

They sat for several more minutes, sounds of the other occupants loud in the darkness. Finally a spark ignited and Runs Again instructed the men to build the fire.

"Now an offering," Cooper whispered.

She relaxed and observed the myriad faces in the flickering orange light, each absorbed with the ceremony, and experienced the sensation of going back hundreds of years in time. These faces could have been the faces of men and women who lived long ago. The traditions and beliefs had been passed down from generation to generation. Their lives had not changed until the whites intruded.

Runs Again placed a fist-size roll of what looked like weeds in the fire. A strong tobaccolike odor permeated the interior of the tepee. The drum beat again. Hallie slanted a glance at Cooper. In the eerie light he didn't seem any different from the others seated around the fire. This enlightening glimpse into his spirituality showed her that the inner man went much deeper than she'd understood.

Everyone needed someone or something higher and more powerful than themselves to believe in. These people were faithful to and respectful of the gods they knew. Who had a right to label them heathens?

Runs Again finished singing and sat back.

The men and women rose and left, talking among themselves. Runs Again handed Hallie a small leather pouch on a thong and she understood, at last, the importance of the stone.

"Thank you," she said, rising unsteadily.

Beside her Yellow Eagle beamed.

Cooper exchanged a few words with the Yuwipi man, then turned and escorted Hallie from the tent. In the fresh air her clothes and hair reeked of smoke and tobacco. "Do you suppose I can take a bath and wash my hair when we get home?"

"Tomorrow," he replied.

She stopped.

"We can't travel in the dark. We'll head out at first light."

That made sense. "Where will I sleep?"

"In my father's lodge." He said something to Chumani, then turned back to Hallie. "Chumani will show you where to…attend to…whatever you need to attend to."

He pushed aside the flap and entered his father's tent. When the women returned, he had furs and blankets rolled out. Chumani lay beside her son and pointed for Hallie to sleep nearby.

Surreptitiously, she stole a glance at the tent's other occupants. Running Elk and his wife nestled together in a heap of animal skins. Sitting on another pallet, Cooper removed his boots. They would all be sleeping here together?

Self-consciously, she lowered herself onto the soft furs, removed her boots and stretched out. Yellow Eagle reached across and adjusted the blanket up over her shoulder. ''Now you can pray to the spirits, Hallie,'' he said.

Had the spirit stone been Yellow Eagle's olive branch? Perhaps he really had come to appreciate her instruction. Reading and writing was something anyone with an elementary education could have taught him. Simply some twist of fate had made her the one.

She touched the stone lying heavily against her chest. ''Thank you for the gift, Yellow Eagle.''

He lay back down.

Hallie's gaze drifted. Several feet from her, but close enough to make out his blue eyes through the wavering heat across the fire, Cooper watched her. A slow, steady thrum started in her heart and worked its way down to her belly. A riveting cadence like that of the drums pounded in her veins. Beneath her fingers the stone had a warmth and a life all its own.

Weariness washed over her and her eyes drifted shut. Sometime later she awoke. She imagined that the stone, which had slid to her shoulder, pulsed with a comforting warmth. The fire had dwindled to a glowing pile of embers. Across it, their gazes locked. He turned both his palms upward near his face, one higher than the other.

What was he doing? Almost instantly she recognized the sign for sleep. Hallie closed her eyes and obeyed.

The sky had barely turned light when the smell of cooking woke her. She pulled on her boots, noting that the others were gone. All but Miya. She knelt behind Hallie and patiently worked a comb through her hair.

Hallie sat still beneath the attention and, rather than offend her, didn't object when the woman plaited her tresses into two long braids and secured them with beaded strips of leather. Miya brought a tightly woven basket and placed it in Hallie's hands.

"What would you like me to do?" Hallie asked. "Get something for you?"

Miya brought one palm up in a sign Hallie didn't recognize. She repeated it and added a sign with two fingers up.

"Friend," Hallie said.

Miya signed again and included both hands cupped behind her ears.

Hallie murmured, "Bear."

She waited in uncertainty until the others showed up to eat. Noticing her hair, Cooper raised his brows, but she didn't give him a chance to comment. "Cooper, please tell me what Miya said about this basket."

He listened and obliged. "It's a gift in return for the bear meat."

Hallie gave Miya a warm smile and lowered both flattened hands to say thank-you. After they ate, Cooper and his father bid one another a solemn farewell.

Hallie waved goodbye and left the tent with Chumani and Yellow Eagle. Several Indians intercepted them on their way to the wagon, pressing headbands, beads, wooden bowls and utensils carved from bone into Hallie's arms.

Behind them Cooper, too, was showered with gifts. The items filled several of the empty crates in the back of the wagon. Yellow Eagle and Chumani wished their friends and family goodbye.

Seated in the wagon bed, her coat snugly wrapped around her, Hallie waved. The unforgettable faces of the men and women who returned the gesture ranged from young to old and she remembered their faces around the fire the night before. Leaving them brought a sinking sensation to her stomach. They were a proud and spiritual people. No longer were they allowed to live where they pleased or able to hunt and trap as they had for centuries. Their lives had been vindictively changed forever by men who believed they had the duty to civilize the West regardless of the circumstances.

More clearly than ever, she understood Cooper's dedication to them, and his wariness toward whites. She understood Yellow Eagle's initial distrust…and maybe…maybe she even understood Last Horse's hatred. He knew his way of life was doomed, but unlike Cooper, who had the means to do something about it, Last Horse still fought.

Hallie's blurred gaze turned from the Oglala to Yellow Eagle on the seat above her and then to his mother. Chumani waved to her people, who grew smaller in the distance. Turning back, her black eyes sized up Hallie's hair. She reached into one of the crates and pulled out a headband. Holding it between both hands, she gestured.

Hallie's attention slid from the beaded band to the silver bracelet on Chumani's wrist. The delicate filigree, out of place with leather and quills, caught the morning sunlight. Without thought, Hallie reached for her hand and turned it over for a better look.

A flat signet bore engraved initials. A small slanted *H* and a *C* with a large curly *W* between. Hallie's heart thrust against her breast.

Her initials. *Her* bracelet.

Chapter Thirteen

"Where did you get this?"

Chumani's black eyes widened. She said something and tried to pull away.

"Where did you get this?" Hallie insisted.

Pulling her wrist free, Chumani shook her head.

"Something wrong?" Cooper asked over his shoulder.

Confusion governed Hallie's thinking. "No."

He turned back.

Chumani gave Hallie a wary look and settled onto the furs piled beneath them. Hallie worked at making sense of the situation. Chumani had in her possession the silver bracelet that had been stolen from Hallie during the stage holdup. There could be any number of reasons she'd ended up with it. Whoever had stolen it could have traded it at a post somewhere or even bartered directly with an Indian. Someone at the reservation had ended up with the piece of jewelry and given it to Chumani. Cynically Hallie wondered how much it had been worth for trade.

Where were her other things? Who had spent her money? She mulled over the questions on the way home. Everyone grew tired, but there were chores to tend to once they arrived. By supper there wasn't much conversation.

Hallie ran Yellow Eagle and Cooper through their perfunctory lessons and afterward took herself off to bed still contemplating the bracelet.

In the morning a fine layer of dusty snow covered the earth. The wind picked up and it snowed for days.

A week later the wind still howled at the door. "Will we be snowed in?" she asked one evening.

"It doesn't pile up much," Cooper explained. "Except right against the buildings. The blowing is what's bad. It's not safe to go out when it's snowing because you can't see where you're going or find any landmarks."

Yellow Eagle piped up from his place before the fire. "That's why we gotta have that rope to the privy and the soddy and the other buildings."

The windows had been shuttered, but even so, the fine blend of snow and dust blew between the cracks. Hallie swept it up once or twice a day.

"The evenings seem so long," she said, thinking out loud.

Aware of her restlessness, Cooper studied her profile. She'd behaved strangely for the past week or so—ever since she'd received her *sicun.* Had the naming ceremony bothered her? Did she think him more of a savage than ever?

He would have to find things for her to do—chores more stimulating than sweeping the floor. What could possibly entertain her for the winter? "What does your family do on winter evenings?" he asked.

Her unusual eyes showed her surprise at his question. "My father works," she replied. "Sometimes he and my brothers attend business functions. Occasionally he takes my mother to something that requires her presence, and they entertain often."

"What about you?"

"I write. Once in a while I go out."

"With men?"

"Sometimes."

He avoided her eyes, hating himself for the thread of

jealousy that wove itself into his soul. "But they don't interest you."

"Only as friends," she agreed.

A loud knock startled them. Cooper picked up his rifle and answered the door. "Kincaid!"

Grainy snow gusted in with Wiley's arrival, and Cooper put his rifle away. Hallie hung Wiley's coat on the back of a chair before the fire and laid his gloves on the hearth. "Take off your boots before you catch cold," she insisted. "Our maid used to dry ours out on the oven rack."

Wiley struggled out of his boots, and Hallie carried them away. Chumani brought the man a cup of coffee and gestured for him to sit near the fire. He signed his thanks.

Cooper could tell Hallie was more nervous around Kincaid than she was around her. He spoke comfortably with Cooper and ate cinnamon-and-sugar twists of pastry crust that the women had baked that afternoon.

Chumani refilled his cup and he smiled at her. That smile caught Cooper off guard. He regarded Chumani's reaction, noting her dark skin held a noticeable flush. Hallie, too, glanced between the two of them, and her dark winged brows elevated to the middle of her forehead. She seated herself by Yellow Eagle, but her attention wasn't on the book he read aloud.

Listening to the conversation, she occasionally peeped up at Wiley or Chumani. A scorching smell wafted to Cooper. He sniffed the air and sized up the area surrounding the fireplace, seeing nothing amiss. "Something burning?"

"Oh, my, no!" Hallie shot up as if she'd been jerked with an invisible string and ran to the other end of the room. The others stood and followed. Grabbing a length of folded burlap, she pulled a skillet from the oven.

Black curls of smoke rose from Wiley's shriveled boots. Hallie's mortified expression turned from the smoking footwear to the others' faces.

"I'm so sorry," she said in a tight voice, placing the skillet on the stove and staring at the ruined boots.

Cooper exchanged a look with Kincaid. The side of the man's mouth twitched, dislodging Cooper's restraint. The hilarity of the situation bubbled up inside and a laugh burst forth.

"Are you making fun of me, DeWitt?" she snapped. "If you are, you can go straight to hell!"

At her unladylike language, Cooper guffawed. Kincaid joined him, followed by Yellow Eagle. Chumani covered her mouth with both hands and giggled. Red faced, Hallie gaped at them.

They laughed until tears ran down their cheeks. Hallie's expression softened and seconds later a chuckle tumbled out. Finally she was laughing as hard as they were, a hand pressed to her midriff.

"I have some boots you can wear home," Cooper offered once their laughter died down.

Hallie opened the door and tossed the reeking leather out into the cold. "I'll buy you a new pair," she said, meeting Cooper's eyes. "I have the pay I've earned at the freight company. I don't know how long they'll take to get here, though."

"Don't worry about it," Wiley said. "They were old."

"Well, even so, I feel responsible."

Wiley dismissed her worry with a wave of his hand. Hallie took her place beside Yellow Eagle and he finished his book.

When Wiley prepared to leave, Cooper brought him a pair of fur-lined boots. Wiley bundled up and took his leave. Chumani and Yellow Eagle left shortly after.

"I'll get wood for the night," Cooper said. He returned with a sling full of logs, placed one on the fire and carried the rest into the other room.

Hallie had efficiently started a fire, and sat on her heels before it. Cooper crouched next to her and watched the fire take hold before adding one of the logs. He turned and studied her expression, the light playing over her delicate features. "Are you lonely?"

She appeared to think a minute. "No. Not at all."

"Missing your family?"

She tilted her head. "A little. More than they're missing me, I'm sure."

Though they spent numerous hours with one another, being in this room where she slept somehow made being alone together more intimate. Her hair looked softer, more inviting, her skin radiated the warm glow of the fire. "I know you're bored," he said.

She sat back and hugged her knees beneath her skirt. "Maybe just a little."

The wind buffeted the shutters and created a gust of sparks in the chimney. Cooper glanced at the wide stone hearth he'd built to insure against such a gust causing a fire.

Hallie looked around, too, spotting something behind her and turning quickly forward again. Cooper recognized her bearskin beneath the bed. "You're not using it?" he asked.

"For what?"

"For a rug. Or a blanket?"

She moved her head in a tight little negative shake.

"Why not?"

"Well, I—uh, frankly, it makes me nervous."

"Nervous?"

She nodded.

"How?"

"Those teeth and—oh, I don't know. Why did Wiley leave the head and paws on it? Ugh! I couldn't look at it every time I walk in here." She shuddered.

Cooper couldn't help grinning. "That's the way it's done."

She shrugged and crossed her arms on her knees.

"If you don't like the head and paws," he offered, "I'll cut them off for you."

"You will?"

"Sure."

"I'd love to throw them out," she said.

"You couldn't do that. The Sioux wear claws and teeth and consider them valuable. The whole head and all the paws are worth a lot in trade."

"They are?" Her face brightened.

Cooper nodded.

"You mean I own something valuable?"

"You do." He realized how inadequate a woman in her position must feel without much money. From the beginning he'd been unfair for insisting she was indebted to him.

He pulled the heavy skin from beneath the bed and unfolded it. Drawing his knife from its sheath, he neatly sliced off the offending parts and carried them to the other bedroom, which he used for storage.

Hallie watched him wide-eyed as he returned and lifted the fur, draping it over the bed. "It'll keep you warm. It kept the bear warm a lot of winters."

Hesitantly, she moved toward the bed and ran her hand over the fur. "I really expected it to smell bad, but it doesn't."

"Kincaid knows how to cure the hide," he said. "He did a good job."

Their eyes met, and Cooper wondered if their thoughts had suddenly focused on the same thing. She proved him right when she spoke. "Do you think that since I turned him down, he's taken an interest in Chumani?"

"Chumani is beautiful. She'd be an asset to any man," he replied.

"How would you feel about that?"

"I don't know," he said honestly. "I'd be happy for her to continue living away from the reservation. Her well-being is what's important. He could take care of her and make her happy."

"What about the fact that he's white?"

"I'm white."

She nodded. "But you didn't take her for your wife."

"I couldn't have. I love her as a sister. I couldn't—I just couldn't have." Cooper wouldn't say the thought of sleeping with someone he thought of as a sister had mortified him since the day it became apparent that Last Horse was not going to fulfill his duty. Running Elk had turned to Cooper, and Cooper's insides had lurched. *I will take care of her,* he'd promised his father. *But I won't make her my wife.*

Their arrangement had satisfied Running Elk and pleased everyone else, as well. He and Chumani lived companionably, sharing Yellow Eagle's care, both pleased that there was nothing more expected from their relationship.

Distractedly, Hallie reached up and touched her *sicun.* Cooper's own stone throbbed to life with a heat that spread languorously through his body. He'd known from the minute he'd seen the stone she'd selected that there was something special about it—about the fact that it looked remarkably like his, right down to that pink streak.

"You're different from the men I've known." Hallie perched on the side of the bed.

"I'm certain of that." She was accustomed to gentlemen with fancy clothing and haircuts. Men with white hands who bathed in tubs and depended on pocket watches to tell them what time it was.

"Not just because you wear those clothes and your hair's long," she said. "Because you care that Chumani is satisfied with her life."

"My brother loved her very much. She made him a good wife and she deserves happiness."

"But…" Hallie raised her golden eyes. "You consider her a person. I've heard you ask her advice. You listen when she talks." She gave him a quick smile. "Heck, you listen to me, and heaven knows I certainly don't have any great wisdom to impart."

"Hallie." He touched her shoulder, and heat radiated through his fingers. "You have a lot to say that's worth listening to. You're an important person, too."

A single drop spilled from her bottom lashes, leaving a silver trail on her cheek. The sight did more to his insides than a flood of noisy tears could have done. The evidence of her vulnerability—and his—should have warned him to back off. Instead, he brushed away the tear with his thumb and framed her face. Bending near, he inhaled her glorious feminine scent. "I'm grateful to you for what you've done for Yellow Eagle. And I'm grateful for what you've done for me. You taught me without making me feel stupid."

"You're not stupid. You're one of the smartest people I've ever met."

"Do you always say exactly what you think?" he asked.

Her heart-reaching eyes slid to his. "I don't know."

"What are you thinking now?" His lips were scant inches from her cheek.

"That…" She paused. "That you have the bluest eyes I've ever seen. And that my heart couldn't possibly beat any faster." She licked her lips and the fire inside turned him to molten steel. "And that I want you to kiss me."

He did, leaning over and molding his lips to hers, touching her jaw as though she were a fragile night flower. She emitted a tiny noise that speared his belly with desire. He should leave. He should end this now before any damage had been done and save them both the pain. He drew back.

Her hand rose to his cheek and gently flattened along his jaw, binding him to her in a way no match of strength or strong cords could have. She stared into his eyes, her sultry expression a heady combination of rapt innocence and age-old wisdom. "And I think," she said, her breath against his lips, "that your gentleness gives me power. And I wonder if I would be afraid if you weren't quite so tender."

Her fingers urged his face near for another kiss. With a groan, Cooper complied, taking her in his arms and sinking down on the fur with her beside him. They lay on their sides, face-to-face. She cupped his jaw, her kisses drawing an insatiable yearning from the depths of his soul.

The soft, pliant body he pretended to ignore day in and day out lay pressed along his length. He swept his tongue into her mouth, tracing the silken skin of her inner lips, flattening and curling, possessing her, wanting her. She returned the kiss with an intake of breath and a tightening of her arms around his neck, pressing her sweet breasts against his chest.

Cooper's hand ached to cover those tempting mounds. Instead he circled her ribs, gripped her waist, then kneaded her lower back.

Hallie sighed into his mouth and pressed her thighs to his, teasing, enticing with total naiveté. Cooper teetered on the edge of ecstasy, fire licking through his loins, and captured her breast. Through her clothing her hard nipple pressed against his palm. He worked it beneath his thumb and she trembled in his arms.

He treated the other one with the same attention, skimmed her ribs and caressed her shoulder, coming back to capture the weight of her breast.

Hallie took her lips from his and left him hungering. Her spectacular eyes reflected the firelight. "Cooper?" she said.

His hand stilled on her breast.

"You know how you let me touch you?"

His passion-laden thoughts cleared and he recalled the night she spoke of. "Yes."

"Would it be...? Would you touch me like that?"

His heart mistook her meaning and threatened to burst. "I—I'm not sure..."

"You took your shirt off and let me touch you."

That *was* what she meant! "You don't know what you're asking," he said, his voice rasping more harshly than he'd intended.

"Well, I think I do," she replied. "It felt good to touch

your skin, to learn the warmth and texture. I thought—I thought you might do the same…to me. Perhaps you would enjoy it."

He moved his hand away and reached behind his neck for her wrist. "There's no doubt I'd enjoy it, Hallie. What you don't understand is that…touching you like that would make it impossible for me…for me to…stop."

Her thick black lashes swept downward. "Oh."

He drew her fingers to his lips and kissed them, drawing her feverish topaz gaze.

"Impossible?" she asked.

What was she asking of him? How much tolerance did she think he possessed? He swallowed hard and concentrated on her irresistible body pressed against his. To kiss her was glorious, to touch her would be pure bliss. He could use self-control in order to enjoy this incomparable closeness. Earning her trust was more important than satisfying his flesh. "Not impossible," he said.

Her gaze came back to his.

"You have my word," he vowed. "When you're uncomfortable, we stop."

She sat up.

Her hair spilled over her shoulder and she plucked the pins from it and dropped them over the bed's edge. The dark, fragrant mass fell free.

Cooper propped his head on his hand and watched her fingers go to the front of her blouse. Slowly, as each button was released, the fabric fell apart. She tugged it from her skirt and shrugged her arms free.

Her shoulders were slim, her collarbone a delicate shadow above a white undergarment. His gaze dropped to the pale swells of her breasts pushed upward by a stiff piece of fabric. She unhooked a dozen metal fasteners and cast it aside, revealing the wrinkled cotton beneath.

Cooper frowned in wonder at the amount of restrictive clothing.

Tugging a ribbon free, she worked loose an infinite row of tiny buttons. The material parted, revealing only shadows. His throat tightened and he concentrated. *Breathe in. Breathe out.* If she took it off, he'd be gentle. If she chose not to, he'd be a gentleman.

She took it off.

He forgot to breathe.

He'd never seen skin as pale and delicate looking as hers. Her nipples were tight circles with dusky pink nubs. The crude leather pouch seemed out of place against her exquisite, almost translucent skin. Beneath her breasts remained a mass of imprints from the tight clothing. The first place he touched was that lined flesh. "Isn't that thing uncomfortable?"

"By the end of the day it itches something fierce," she agreed.

"Why do you wear it?"

She blushed. "It's improper to go without a corset. A lady doesn't...doesn't..."

"Jiggle?"

She nodded, her entire chest flushed pink.

He sat up and reached for her. Her eyes fluttered shut. He brushed the skin over her sides and stomach with both palms and Hallie purred. He trailed lingering paths along her tender inner arms, up over her shoulders and back, circling her collarbone, her chest, her wrists and elbows.

Her nipples puckered and her head fell back. Leaning forward, he kissed her neck, sucked at the tender flesh, nipped, tasted. Gently he bit her earlobe and pulled it into his mouth. Against his ear her breath caught shallow and irregular.

Turning his face, he captured her mouth and kissed her hard. Harder than he'd ever kissed her.

Impatiently she caught his hands, pressed them to her breasts and held them there. "Touch me," she demanded.

He complied, kneading her supple flesh, weighing, pulling back to watch his dark hands against the ivory globes.

"I—I can't breathe," she panted.

"I know."

"Did it feel this good when I touched you?"

"Yes."

"I never knew."

He ran his fingers through her silken hair, pulled a fistful to his nose and breathed in her essence. Moving forward, he urged her to her back and straddled her, threading her sable tresses, spilling them in a glorious curtain across the fur.

She beckoned him forward and tugged at his laces. He complied, loosening them and yanking the shirt over his head. She urged him forward again, turning his head and plucking at the thong in his hair. The lace pulled loose and she freed his hair over his shoulders, running her fingers through as he had hers.

A smile trembled on her lips.

Cooper covered her breasts and enjoyed the downward flutter of her lashes. She dropped her hands back onto the bed, palms up, fingers gently curled in. He kissed the blue-veined skin at her elbow, drew a trail with his tongue to her shoulder.

Beneath him, she shivered.

"Cold?" he asked.

"No."

His tongue darted in and out of the indent at the base of her throat. His hair spilled across her face and she swept it behind his ear. The scent and texture of her skin set him on fire.

He closed his lips over one nipple and drew it into his mouth. A gasp escaped her and she brought the back of one hand to her mouth. He toyed with her, worshiped her, winding himself to a needful frenzy. Adoring the other breast in the same manner, he noticed when her hand fell from her mouth, when her breathing changed and her fingers clutched at his shoulders.

Lost in his ravenous desire for her, Cooper cupped her woman's mound through her wool skirt. A cry escaped her lips. She arched upward, and he ground the heel of his hand against her.

She urged his head up and met his lips with a hunger that inflamed him. Their chins tilted. Their tongues meshed. Their bodies strained against one another in an all-consuming burst of realmless passion.

"Cooper," she said against his mouth. "Cooper!" Her cry held an edge of desperation.

"Hallie," he whispered, and eased his hands from the places that caused her torment. "Shh."

She clung to him tremulously. "You said we'd stop when I was uncomfortable, but I didn't know this was what you meant."

"I didn't."

"You didn't?"

"No."

She exhaled and her breath quivered against his chin.

He rubbed her bare silken shoulder with comforting strokes. "I meant if you were afraid or had doubts."

"Should I have doubts?"

She'd never behaved as he expected her to—why should this be any different? He took her hand and placed it over the front of his trousers. "You do know what this leads up to, don't you?"

Her hand molded over his length. "I—I think so."

Cupping her chin, he tilted her head back so he could see her eyes. "I know you don't want a husband. But someday you might. If we were to do this together now, it would take something away from that marriage."

Not to mention that joining his spirit with hers would only lead to wretched pain when she left. He had no business taking her virginity and sending her back to Boston.

Her eyes filled with glistening tears. "But you want me?"

Why did her uncertainty do irreparable things to his insides? Why did he instinctively want to reassure her? He kissed her with all the discipline he could muster, reverently, gently, with none of the hot, wild desperation he really felt, and when her hand moved, he caught it up and entwined her fingers with his.

Hallie swallowed tears of frustration and confusion. Her body wasn't her own. It belonged to him now. Couldn't he see that? Didn't he know? She would joyfully surrender everything she had or had ever wanted, to be loved by this man.

For years she'd lamented being born a woman, she'd damned her femininity and yearned for appreciation and acceptance. For the first time, with Cooper, she'd been grateful for this cursed body. For the first time, because of him, she hadn't wished she was someone or somewhere else.

And ironically, after realizing how wonderful being a woman could be, what good did it do her? He had unerringly pointed out that this awakening she'd experienced wasn't meant for him.

Shame suffused her mind and body. An unbearable ache swelled in her chest. She wasn't here because he'd wanted her. She'd forced herself into his life and house and, most recently, into his arms. She'd asked for this!

Hallie pulled away, covering her naked breasts with her hands. Cooper reached to the end of the bed for her blouse. Ashamed, she clasped it to herself.

"Hallie?"

"Don't apologize for anything."

"I wasn't going to."

"Good."

"I just want to know you're all right."

She didn't meet his eyes. "I'm fine."

"Maybe…" He paused. "Maybe we can talk about this in a day or so. After you've had time to think."

"Maybe" was all she said.

He reached for her shoulder, but she stopped him with an upraised palm. He picked up his shirt from the floor. "Good night."

The door closed softly.

Hallie hurried to her trunk and withdrew a nightgown, pulling it over her head before she removed her skirt and pantaloons. She brushed her hair with severe strokes and picked up her scattered clothing until no evidence of her foolishness remained.

Drawing back the covers, she climbed into bed beneath the heavy fur, its weight and warmth a painful reminder. Outside, the wind whistled through the shutters.

Beneath her cotton nightgown her body still tingled, her breasts sensitive and full. He'd asked her if she knew what their actions led to. She knew. And she knew that's where children came from, too. Thank goodness it hadn't gone that far. Thank goodness he hadn't wanted to go on. The last thing she ever wanted to do was bring a daughter into this stinking world.

Hallie turned over and closed her eyes, forcing herself to relax. She was stuck here for the winter. But first thing in the spring she'd be headed back for Boston. By this time next year, this would all be a bad dream.

Throughout the long night, Hallie drifted into restless sleep…and dreamed of thick fur beneath her back…supple skin against her breasts…unsettling kisses and sultry blue eyes…and in her dreams, she cried.

Chapter Fourteen

Never one to feel sorry for herself, Hallie mustered her determination and prepared breakfast. Since the weather had grown severe, the only meal they ate with Chumani and Yellow Eagle was supper, and they'd taken to doing that in the log house, so Hallie rarely went out.

Cooper came from the other room, dressed in his fringed shirt and trousers, his square jaw freshly shaven. "Smells good," he said.

She let herself look at him, his broad shoulders, his tanned skin.

He met her eyes and gave her a hesitant smile.

Her heart flip-flopped in her chest. "Flapjacks," she said. "I finally made a stack without scorching any."

They sat and ate.

"I have a few things for you to do today," he said. "That is, if you want to."

"Sure. Here?"

"No. Over at the other building."

"I'll be over as soon as the dishes are done."

"I'll help you and we'll go together."

Pleasantly surprised, she agreed.

"What was that look for? What do you think I do when I'm here alone?" he asked.

She shook her head. She hadn't thought about it.

There was an undeniable new awareness between them, something stirring yet tolerable in the way they spoke and talked and carefully avoided touching. She put on her coat and they trudged through the snow to the other building.

"I want to order from these catalogs. Mrs. Kell helped me once." He placed a few books on the desk top. "I'll be able to do it myself soon. But for now, well, I can't make out a lot of words and the prices confound me."

"I'll help," she said.

"And…" He pulled up a chair beside hers and sat. "I want to have items women will want. The brides are here now and there'll be more women next year."

"Good thinking. Will you sell these things to the trading post?"

"Some. Some I'll send with the freighters to other posts and mining towns. But I don't know how to choose things for women."

"Sure you do."

"What do you mean?"

"How about the tea?"

He grinned. "Lucky guess."

"Well, I've enjoyed it. And I know Evelyn liked hers." She opened the first catalog. "How long will it take?"

"To get things? Might be till spring. Mail has to come by dogsled."

"One certainly learns patience out here."

He didn't reply.

"What do you do all winter while the freighters can't get in or out?"

"There are some stretches of fair weather," he explained. "The rest of the time I organize the supplies, oil all the harnesses and collars, make repairs on wagons and fix up the place. I hunt and check my traps. I planned to work inside the house this winter, too. The loft isn't finished."

"What's it for? The loft."

He flipped open another catalog. "Just someplace to store things."

Chumani brought them lunch and ate with them.

Time passed much as Cooper had predicted, with the days growing shorter and the nights growing colder. He kept her busy during the day, making lists and counting items. One afternoon she sat beside a crate, the acrid smell of tobacco overpowering her, and called to him. "Are you sure all these cigars need to be counted individually?"

"I have to know what's here, don't I?" he asked. He eyed the mountain of crates with a frown. "There's more than there should be. I didn't get to move a lot of it because of the robberies. I can only afford so much of a loss before it cuts too deep."

"And you give away so much," Hallie said, thinking aloud.

He turned to her.

"To the reservation," she clarified.

"That's the whole point. That's why I'm here."

"I see that now."

A few nights later Hallie awoke to shouts. She lay for a second, listening to the excited voices, before springing from her bed and peering into the other room at Cooper's empty pallet. She glanced around in confusion. Horses whinnied and she ran to yank open the door. Across the distance to the freight building and the barn beyond, an eerie orange glow lit the night sky.

Fire!

Panicked, she ran into her room and fumbled with her boots, pulled her coat over her nightgown and hurried out. Her breath panted out on white gusts as she closed the distance. Horses and mules, having been turned into the corral, reared in fright. Several others ran loose. Cooper, bare chested and sweating in spite of the cold, wielded a tarp and beat at the consuming flames that licked up the side of the barn.

Hallie stared in horror. Jack shoved a bucket into her hands. "Gather up snow from the drifts," he ordered.

She obeyed, scooping snow and running it back to the blaze as fast as she could. Chumani and Yellow Eagle did the same, and several times they nearly ran into one another. The stench of scorched wood burned her nostrils. Ashes drifted from the sky and turned the snow gray. Cooper worked like a madman, never pausing until the fire was out.

An enormous black hole gaped from his barn. He stared at it, his broad, sweat-glistened chest heaving, his square jaw taut. Finally his attention shot to the animals crowded in the corral and he stalked toward them.

"Chumani!" he shouted, and spoke rapidly in Sioux. The Indian woman turned and ran to the soddy.

"Hallie!"

She jumped, surprised that he even knew she was there.

"Bring clean rags and warm water."

She turned and ran as Chumani had. With an armful of clean rags, she paused, thinking of Cooper in the cold without a shirt. Laying the rags on the table, she lit the lantern and carried it into the bedroom she'd never before entered. There was no bed, no chest of drawers, only several crates, stacks of furs and deerskins, and an enormous trunk covered with animal hide.

Hesitantly she opened it and discovered neatly folded clothing. She chose a deerskin tunic and her fingers brushed a piece of paper. Withdrawing the envelope, she read the postmark. Boston. Hallie unfolded the letter and quickly read Tess Cordell's letter to Cooper. Nothing special, just the facts about herself and her arrival.

Guiltily, Hallie tucked the letter back into its envelope, placed it in the corner of the trunk and hurried out. Cooper's surprise showed when she held the shirt out to him.

"Thank you." He pulled it on over his head.

She assisted him in dressing the burns on several of the horses. Jack hammered tarps over the hole in the barn wall.

Chumani leapt astride a mare and led the loose horses back. Dawn streaked the sky by the time they were finished.

Hallie accompanied Chumani to the soddy and helped her prepare breakfast. Yellow Eagle fell asleep on his pallet. Cooper and Jack came later, washed and dressed in clean clothes. Hallie looked down at her nightgown, and Chumani brought her the green shawl.

Strain shown plainly on Cooper's face. He held the cup of coffee Chumani handed him without tasting it. "We can thank the spirits it's winter," he said. "If it'd been summer, the entire countryside could have been ashes by tonight."

"The whole area is a mass of tracks," Jack said to him. "It hasn't snowed fresh for a week, and what with all those horses loose... Could ya see anything?"

"There were riders down by the river. Shod horses," Cooper clarified. "Boot prints up to the barn and back."

Someone had deliberately set the fire. A sinking fear slid to Hallie's stomach. It could just as easily have been the log house...or the soddy....

Cooper's smoke-reddened eyes met hers and she knew he was thinking the same thing. "Why?" she asked.

He shook his head. "I've asked myself that a hundred times. Could be 'cause I'm considered an Oglala by some." He thought a minute longer. "I supply all the whites from here to Salt Lake City. Why would they do something to cut themselves off?"

"A competitor, then," she suggested. "Someone who wants your customers."

"Maybe. I wouldn't know who."

"The man at the trading post. He gave me the willies." Cooper shook his head. "Reavis isn't that ambitious."

Recalling the state of his filthy, disorganized store, she had to agree. "One of your freighters?"

"I've thought of that, too. But they're all hardworking frontiersmen who have families or need the work because the beaver are trapped out."

"The freight wagons, the stage, and now your barn," Hallie said, ticking them off. "It's almost personal, don't you think?"

Her thoughts slid to Wiley, but she didn't say anything aloud. He'd shown up about the time the robberies were going on. Had he and Cooper known one another before? Hallie wasn't egotistical enough to think that he would take revenge because he thought Hallie was attracted to Cooper instead of him. He'd gotten over her quickly enough and already seemed interested in Chumani.

"You saw the stage robbers," Cooper said, interrupting her thoughts. "Ferlie wasn't much help in describing them."

"They were men," she said with a shrug. "They wore gloves and hats and their faces were covered with kerchiefs. I really didn't see any of them."

"There must be something you can remember."

"I was terrified half out of my wits," she replied. "I didn't take notes."

Silence stretched among the small gathering. The thought of her bracelet surfaced. She would mention it to him when they were alone. She didn't want to put Chumani on the spot; she didn't have anything to do with the robbery.

Fortunately, Cooper had a ready supply of wood and nails, and repair of the barn was under way by that afternoon. Hallie observed his deliberate and steady pace. Thank goodness whoever had done this hadn't gone after the other building at the same time. They obviously didn't know the value or extent of Cooper's holdings. They had, however, known the importance of his livestock.

Before they went to supper, she caught him alone at his workbench. "There's something I need to tell you."

He hung his hammer, weariness evident in his movements. "You didn't really know how to ride a horse."

"No!" She frowned. "Whatever made you think that?"

He shrugged, exhaustion lining his features. "What, then?"

"Remember I told you about the stage robbers taking my jewelry?"

"Yeah."

"I had a silver filigree bracelet with my initials engraved on it."

He waited.

"Chumani wore that bracelet home from the reservation."

His brows lowered into a thunderous frown. "What are you saying?"

"I'm not saying anything. I'm just telling you the facts. It was stolen from me that day and now Chumani has it."

"Why didn't you say anything before?"

"I didn't see any purpose. I know she's not the one who stole it. I'm sure it was a gift or a trade. It could have changed hands any number of times before she ended up with it."

Cooper lifted the lid from a pottery jar, dabbed ointment on his palms and rubbed them together with a rasping sound. "All right," he said. "Do you want it back?"

She shook her head. "The bracelet itself isn't important. It's hers now."

But at supper he asked Chumani about it. She went to her neat stacks of baskets and rolled furs and returned with the silver bracelet.

"This is yours?" Cooper asked Hallie, holding it up.

"It was."

Chumani met her gaze, her eloquent black eyes questioning.

"These letters don't spell anything," Cooper said.

"They're initials," she explained. "*H* for Hallie, *C* for Clair, *W* for Wainwright."

"They're all curly."

"It's script."

Cooper spoke to Chumani again.

"She got it from her sister, Standing Deer. Standing Deer got it in trade from Not Help Him for a tin of beans. Before that, who knows?"

"That's what I figured."

He turned. "No lessons tonight, Yellow Eagle."

"Aww!"

"You had a nap this morning. The rest of us only slept a couple of hours last night. Jack and I are going to take turns getting up and checking all the buildings."

"I can help!" Yellow Eagle offered, eagerness in his young voice.

"You can help by doing exactly as your mother says and not going out alone after dark."

The boy pouted.

"Maybe Hallie will let you come help her with her work tomorrow," he offered, as though taking pity on the youth's boredom.

Hallie cocked her head. What would she be doing tomorrow?

"I have some beaver pelts that need bundling. I'll show you how to do it. You just lay them flat and place them one on top of another in the press. Once they're all stacked, you crank it down and clamp a piece of wire around. It's easy, you'll see."

"Sounds like I'll need help." She patted Yellow Eagle on the shoulder, still uncertain of her tenuous new acceptance. He hadn't said anything rude to her since she'd received her spirit stone.

Seemingly pleased with the arrangement, the boy wished them good-night.

"Tell me about Yellow Eagle's father, Cooper," she said on their way to the house.

"Plenty Wolves was much like Running Elk," he said. "He was a brave warrior, a good husband and proud father.

We trapped together every winter.'' Cooper opened the door and ushered her in.

They hung up their coats, and Hallie checked the fire in the big room while Cooper laid one in the fireplace in her bedroom. ''He was killed during one of our last attempts not to be placed on the reservation. He was taking a message to the army and was shot.''

''That's awful. Do you know who killed him?''

''I know what killed him. An army rifle.''

Hallie thought back over all the things Yellow Eagle had said to her upon her arrival. His bitterness made perfect sense.

''It sure changes the perspective to see both sides of a story,'' Hallie said.

Cooper studied the way the fire caught highlights in her hair. He'd been unwilling to look at both sides of her story when she'd arrived and set his orderly life akilter. Now that he'd had a deeper look at the woman inside, his perspective had changed, too. ''Most people are too narrow-minded to even look at any side but their own,'' he replied.

She surprised him at every turn. She wasn't the helpless, dependent lily he'd supposed her. No, she'd proven herself capable, hardworking and equal to any task. Angus's wife, Evelyn, hadn't even tried to make adjustments. Hallie, on the other hand, had learned the life with an almost obsessive drive.

Part of her being raised with less worth than her brothers, he guessed. He wished he had the right to tell her exactly how beautiful he thought her—and not just on the outside. Her loveliness ran clear through, like the vein in his spirit stone.

She wouldn't want him to appreciate her just because she was a woman. He could say he admired her strength. He could tell her he considered her smart and gutsy and full of wit. But his heart wouldn't allow him the words. She had a goal, and he'd never known anyone more determined. She would take her stories of her Dakota adventure and sell them back East.

"Hallie?" he said, before he knew he was going to say it.

"Yes?"

She wasn't for him. She had a wealthy family waiting. "I hope your stories bring you everything you want."

Her smooth forehead puckered into a frown. "Like what?"

"Your father's approval," he said.

She blushed. "I'm that obvious, am I?"

"I've had time to figure it out."

"I guess you have." She brushed a fold from her skirt. "I hope you get everything you want, too."

"Like what?"

"Enough profit to help the Oglala. A wife."

The word held little appeal, especially coming from her lips. He'd all but changed his mind.

"You still want one, don't you?"

He thought of all the lonely winters stretched out ahead of him—the winters after Hallie. But this life wasn't meant for women like her. Refined women grew discontent, miserable. He didn't know what desperation had come over him to place that notice. He'd known better. He knew firsthand that love wasn't enough to keep a woman here.

Love. That must have come from thinking of his parents' troubled relationship. There was no other reason for the word to enter his head.

He studied the soft, alert smile on her lovely face. She waited for an answer. "I'll be able to read and to figure. If I need a woman I'll probably bring one from the reservation."

Her expression flattened and she avoided his eyes. "At least you know she'd be grateful to you."

"What's that supposed to mean?"

''It means just what I said. One of those women will be glad to get off the reservation and live here.''

Cooper looked around. Not like her, who saw this house as a pitiful excuse for the luxury she was accustomed to.

Hallie stood. ''I'll see you in the morning.''

He nodded.

She closed herself in her room, wondering why his decision disturbed her so. Her chest ached with an emptiness that swelled and filled her throat. Retrieving a nightgown from her trunk, she sat on the bed's edge and stared into the fire. What unspoken glimmer of an idea had she been harboring? That he would ask her to stay? That he would find he couldn't live without her?

Hallie buried her face in the folded gown as if she could hide from herself. Ever since that night here—on this bed— he'd found numerous tasks to keep her busy.

The realization of his purpose pierced her to the quick. She'd thought that counting cigars and tobacco pouches and square-headed nails a trifle unnecessary, but she'd figured he'd had his reasons.

He had, all right. Just the way her father and brothers had found reasons for the tasks they set her to. He wanted to keep her busy—throw her a bone and distract her from what she really wanted.

Did he think she really wanted him? Hallie cursed her boldness. She'd asked to touch him, asked him to touch *her!* She'd thrown herself at him!

And he'd found things for her to do, distracting her from the physical relationship he thought she wanted. *Here, Hallie. Keep busy and stay out of my hair until I can get you back on that stage.*

He'd needed her as long as she could teach him and his nephew to read and write. And she'd done that. She'd served her usefulness and was once again a nuisance.

Well, she'd show him! She didn't need him or his smelly cigars. Angrily she stood and changed clothing, checked the

fire then slipped into bed. She was a writer! She had plenty
of experiences, stacks of paper and a full bottle of ink. She
would write, and to hell with Cooper DeWitt.

"I'll press your furs because I promised Yellow Eagle he
could help," she said the next morning. "But then I would
like some time to work on my stories. I realize I owe you
room and board. But I need some time for myself, too."

He'd worked her morning, noon and night, Cooper
thought with a pang of guilt. She helped Chumani cook and
do laundry. He loaded her down with trivial tasks because
he didn't want her bored, and she coached their studies
every evening. No wonder she needed some time of her
own. "I understand."

He'd said a few pelts, but actually, it took her and Yellow
Eagle a day to press and secure the furs. After that she spent
her afternoons in the house.

For the better part of a week the weather remained mild
and Wiley danced attendance on Chumani. Once Cooper's
sister-in-law realized Wiley's visits were for her, she obviously enjoyed the attention.

Cooper made a visit to the reservation, inquiring about
the origin of the silver bracelet.

During his absence Hallie made herself tea and sat before
the fire with pen and paper. After a bite of lunch, she visited
the privy. Upon her return, she saw that a tall figure waited
in the house. Her heart prepared to lift at Cooper's return,
but instead plummeted to her feet.

Last Horse.

"What do you want?"

He moved swiftly, lunging toward her. Hallie raised her
fist to strike him, but he moved in too close behind her,
stifling her scream with his hand and pressing her back
against his hard body.

Hallie kicked and struggled against his superior strength.
He dragged her effortlessly through the doorway to the west

side of the house, opposite the soddy and freight buildings. Two of his braves waited with rope and kerchiefs.

Hallie's heart pounded erratically at the sight of them. She fought to free herself, but Last Horse held her fast. One of the Indians shoved the kerchief into her mouth and tied another around her head, pulling her hair painfully. Last Horse let loose long enough to bind her hands, then raised her off the ground, while another caught her flying ankles and tied them.

Last Horse picked her up and ran with her as if she was an animal he'd shot. Three horses waited on the frozen riverbank. Last Horse tossed down a fur from the back of his horse, dropped Hallie on it and rolled her up. After that, she couldn't see, could only feel his rough handling, then the sensation of rising and the motion of the horse.

She grew dizzy. She couldn't breathe. The horse jolted her body and she was almost grateful for the cloth in her mouth so her teeth couldn't jar together.

Kidnapped! The words of every tawdry dime novel she'd ever read focused in her mind. Indians did horrible, unspeakable things to white women. She had every right to be terrified.

No. No. This wasn't just any Indian. This was Cooper's brother. Running Elk's son. He wouldn't harm her. Would he? White women had been carried off and never seen again. Some had been raped and killed. Others had been taken into slavery.

That wouldn't happen to her. Cooper would get home and find her missing. He'd been raised with Indians; he could track them.

These Indians no doubt knew how to cover their trail, though, so that even another Indian couldn't find them. But in the snow? Of course there'd be tracks in the snow....

Her one small assurance bit into her thigh. As long as Last Horse didn't discover she had a gun in the folds of her skirt, she had an ace in the hole. When the time was right, she could use it.

The ride lasted forever. They stopped once and Last Horse adjusted her weight, returning to keep her in a new position, for which she was grateful. Her wrists and ankles throbbed. Her ribs ached from the constant jamming against the horse. She should be grateful for the cushioning and warmth of the fur.

At last the horses stopped again and she was lifted down and laid on the ground. The Indians talked among themselves. She made out their movements.

Finally she was picked up again and deposited. Someone peeled back the fur and she blinked, unable to see. It was night already. An orange flame flickered and Hallie focused on a craggy rock wall. They were camped in a small cave. Last Horse sat her up and propped her against the cold stone. She glared at him.

He went to the fire and sat with his companions.

Sometime later, he brought her strips of dried meat and a bag that looked as if it contained water. Untying her hands, he yanked the bandanna from her mouth.

Hallie gagged first, then accepted the water bag, drinking thirstily. He pulled it away and gave her the dried meat.

"What are you going to do with me?" she asked, the words sticking in her dry throat. The others turned and looked when she spoke.

Last Horse glanced from them to her. "Eat."

She watched his back as he returned to the fire. She chewed the tough meat, her tongue painful as she swallowed.

After an hour or so the Oglala men took pipes from their supplies and lit them. The strong tobacco smell reminded Hallie of her father...of Cooper...of security. Fear knotted in her belly. Against the rock wall, far from the fire, cold permeated her body and she shivered.

Pain lodged in her bladder until she could no longer ignore it. She'd seen the others come and go. Her heart pounded with distress. "Last Horse."

His ebony head turned.

"I need to go outside."

Setting his pipe aside, he rose. He untied her feet and led her into the frigid night. "If you run away, I will find you. Or you will freeze and die."

His ominous words sent another chill through her already shaking body. He spoke the truth. This was not the time to use the gun. This was not the time to try to run away. If she wanted to live, she had to plan carefully and stay calm.

She made her way through the snow, stepping over branches and ice-encrusted weeds until she was sure she was out of Last Horse's sight, and hastily relieved herself. Clothing adjusted, she blinked into the darkness. She didn't even know which way she'd come!

Hallie glanced up for the moon, but clouds obliterated any light. She'd be damned if she'd call out to him. She squinted into the darkness. Surely she'd see the fire in the cave's entrance.

A hand shot out of the darkness and grabbed her arm, yanking her forward. Hallie recognized the repugnant smell of tobacco and musk that clung to Last Horse's clothing. The lighted cave appeared, and he pushed her inside.

She hurried to her spot.

Last Horse took the fur she'd been wrapped in and placed it by the fire. "Come."

She'd heard that abrupt word from Cooper many times, but it had never given her the sense of foreboding that it did from this man's lips. Warily, she rose. Her heart hammered against her ribs and her fingertips grew numb.

It would do her no good to run. There were three of them. They were bigger and faster. And even if by some miracle she escaped the cave, she'd be hopelessly lost in the dark

and freeze by morning. Self-preservation brought her forward.

"Lie down."

Keeping her eyes on him, she did as directed. He flipped
the edge of the fur over her and returned to the fire.

The pulse throbbing in her ears slowly faded. Her heart
chugged to a regular cadence. Warmth permeated her chilled
arms and legs and she relaxed. Her hand strayed to the hard
derringer in her pocket, but after a minute she brought her
fingers to the stone against her chest.

You can pray to the spirits now, Hallie.

She didn't know how. But Cooper believed. The wavering memory of that night in the Yuwipi man's tent came
back to her. She heard again the mystical beat of the drums,
smelled the overpowering burning grasses and felt the presence of the strong, solid man beside her, the man she'd
come to trust...and care for. The man who filled her
thoughts and senses and heart. She closed her eyes, and
beneath her fingers the stone grew warm.

Cooper. Cooper, find me.

Chapter Fifteen

Mid afternoon, Cooper returned to the still and silent log house. Even the fire in the fireplace had burned out. Assuming Hallie had spent the day at the soddy, he built up the flame, made himself coffee and thought over the day's events.

He'd talked to Chumani's sister first, and she'd led him to a cousin who named someone else, and so on and so on, until his search led him to Walks Alone, the woman Last Horse visited at the reservation.

Walks Alone had obviously been influenced by Last Horse's hatred for Cooper, because she volunteered no information and held no appreciation for the gifts he supplied The People.

Cooper had ridden home no more enlightened than before. If the bracelet had come from Last Horse, it could have come from anywhere. His Oglala brother had connections with every unsavory whiskey trader and trading post operator in the territory. And he wouldn't be open to Cooper's questioning.

Cooper wasn't even sure where Last Horse and his band wintered anymore.

His stomach rumbled and he grabbed his coat, heading for the soddy. The women would have supper on by now.

Chumani looked up from the kettles over the fireplace and greeted him.

"Hey, Coop!" Yellow Eagle jumped up from his collection of carved animals and leapt onto his uncle's back.

Cooper spun him around a half dozen times before striding to the fireplace with the boy on his back. "Smells good."

"Squirrel stew," Chumani said in their language. "Yellow Eagle shot it with his bow this morning."

"Ah! Yellow Eagle, what a fine hunter you are! You provided our supper." He peered over his shoulder at his nephew's proud grin. "Where's Hallie?" he asked, thinking if she'd gone to the privy she'd have been back by now.

"Hallie must be at the house. She has not been here all day," Chumani replied.

Cooper lowered Yellow Eagle to the floor, a sense of unease rolling over him. "You haven't seen her all day?" He turned to the boy. "What about you?"

"We had our lesson this morning, then I came home. I haven't seen her since then."

"Is Hallie in your house?" Chumani asked, picking up on Cooper's distress.

"No." He grabbed his coat and checked the privy, the freight office and the barn. "Seen Hallie?" he asked Jack.

"Nope." The man stood stirring a pan of beans over the cookstove in his back room. "Didn't see her all day."

Cooper ran to the house. Her new coat hung on the antler rack beside the door. The boots he'd given her to wear over her own for warmth stood beneath. Cooper fingered the sleeve and glanced around the room, fear rising in his gut.

Her papers, pen and ink sat on the table as though she'd just finished with them. Maybe she was sleeping. In her unoccupied room, alarm rose in his chest. Her clothes were neatly folded in the enormous trunk: freshly laundered white cotton, silky rustling garments that had touched her skin. He ran his clumsy fingers over the exquisite fabric and swallowed panic.

A leather valise held books and paper. The carved comb he'd given her sat atop the chest of drawers. Cooper stared at his wavy reflection in the mirror.

Nothing was missing.

Nothing except Hallie.

Hastily he riffled through every drawer.

And the derringer.

With little hope he checked the other room and the loft before heading outdoors. There had been no recent snow, and the accumulation of prints outside made it nearly impossible to distinguish any unusual activity. At the corner of the house he discovered several moccasin prints and the outline of one tiny, pointed boot.

Circling the house and outbuildings in a careful scrutiny, he discovered the hoof marks and droppings on the frozen riverbank.

Cooper ran to the barn for Jack, and together they discarded the possibilities. None of their horses had been near the river for days.

Wiley. Cooper didn't know why the name popped into his head. Though obviously enamored with Hallie, Kincaid had always been forthright. Of late, he seemed to have switched his intentions to Chumani. The hoofprints didn't lead toward Kincaid's place. They followed the river northwest.

"Pack me food," Cooper said to Chumani.

"What has happened?" she asked, following the men out the door.

"I don't know." Cooper saw the alarm in her black eyes and couldn't allow it to affect him. He needed a level head. "There were riders down by the river. Looks like there may have been a scuffle near the corner of the house. All of her things are still in there—her coat, books, clothes, everything."

"She is out in this cold with no coat?" Chumani asked.

A stricken look blanched Yellow Eagle's youthful face. "Can I go with you?"

"No. You take care of your mother."

Yellow Eagle took Chumani's hand and patted the back of it reassuringly. "I will."

"You shouldn't go alone," Jack said as they crossed the yard.

"You need to be here for them," Cooper said, gesturing with his chin to the soddy. "And the livestock has to be looked after." He stopped and stood at the corner of the house. "I'm going to Kincaid's first. If he wants, he can ride with me."

Jack nodded. "You'd better take two horses. I'll get 'em ready."

Cooper packed a saddlebag and rolled Hallie's coat and gloves into his bundle of furs. Dressed warmly, he rode to Wiley's.

Kincaid saw him from a distance and met him in front of his barn. "What brings you out here? Don't have any saddles ready yet."

"Hallie's missing," Cooper stated flatly. "Know anything about it?"

Wiley's mouth gaped. "Well—hell, no! What do you mean, missing?"

Cooper explained the signs. "I'm going to follow the tracks along the river and see where they head."

"Want company?"

"I was hopin' you'd ask." Wiley had obviously been on the frontier a good many years and would be an adequate partner.

"Let me grab my gear."

The amount of time that had passed before they reached the river distressed Cooper. Someone who knew where they were going would be long gone by now. Someone who didn't—well, they'd be hopelessly lost and maybe frozen to death.

The riders had wisely traveled the hard-frozen ice near the bank. There were no tracks, but occasionally droppings told Cooper they'd been this way. As the sun lowered in the sky, gray clouds moved in. If it snowed, they'd lose the trail altogether. He picked up the pace, leading Wiley and the extra horse. The Dakota territory was vast and laced with danger. This faint trail was his only hope of finding Hallie.

Crying wouldn't do any good. Nobody had ever paid any attention to her tears when she was a child; certainly no one would care now. Hallie swallowed the cowardly urge and watched the Indians from beneath nearly closed lids. They'd passed a bottle of amber liquor between them for the past hour, laughing and gesturing. One by one they put their pipes away and went to their pallets.

Last Horse weaved a little when he stood and made his way toward her. She closed her eyes.

Furs dropped behind her and the breeze stirred her hair. He stretched out along her back. His smell combined with the smell of whiskey reached her, and she breathed through her mouth to escape it.

He gathered her hair and her heart jumped, but she forced herself to lie still and silent. He threaded his fingers through her hair, brushed her cheek, leaned over her and pressed his nose into the curve of her neck.

With great restraint Hallie didn't scream or panic or throw up, none of the reactions that came naturally. Instead she pretended she was asleep, pretended she was safe in her bed at home—Cooper's home—pretended none of this was happening and that in the morning she'd wake up from this nightmare and give Yellow Eagle his reading lesson.

Two bullets. When would be the right time to use them? If he tried to force himself on her and she shot him, the others would hear and she could only get one of them—*if* she was extremely lucky.

What would she do? Let him? In order to stay alive?

His rough fingertips skimmed her jaw and a shudder started in her toes and worked its way up until her shoulders convulsed. She thought of Cooper touching her, kissing her, and wished he had fulfilled the act with her so she'd have had one beautiful experience before this man spoiled it for her forever.

She carefully and distinctly separated her mind from her body. He stroked her shoulder, but it was someone else he touched. His liquor-scented breath seared her ear, but someone else felt its damp and heat.

Her fingers crept to the stone around her neck and she prayed to the spirits—to God or Cooper or whoever was listening. *Find me, Cooper. Find me.*

Behind her, Last Horse's breathing deepened and his hand fell slack and heavy on her shoulder. After a time a light snore vibrated the pelts.

Hallie pulled the fur back over her shoulder, dislodging his hand. The animal skins smelled unpleasant, but she was warm and unscathed. Holding the stone and thankful for this reprieve, she drifted into sleep.

The stone on Cooper's breastbone throbbed with warmth. It had only done that a time or two until recently, until Hallie had found her stone. Since then, it had seemed to take on a life of its own. He stared at the dim firelight flickering on the low ceiling of the canvas lean-to they'd constructed at the foot of a butte and touched his *sicun.* An image of Hallie's tense face bathed in orange firelight flickered through his being.

The vision startled him and he released the stone. He hadn't seen anything that clearly since his vision quest, and he'd secretly suspected that vision had been induced by the sacred plants the Yuwipi man had burned and that he himself smoked.

But that had been Hallie's face against an unfamiliar background, and even though wishful thinking could have dreamed her up, the image hadn't seemed like mere imagination.

Once again, with expectation this time, Cooper grasped his stone. The *sicun* was warm in his palm, even through the pouch, and it definitely wasn't his imagination. He closed his eyes against the roof, mere inches from his face, and ignored Wiley's incessant snore.

Her face came to him again, pale, drawn, pleading for something…pleading for him.…

She was afraid, but calm. Warm and safe from the weather. His whole body relaxed.

He pictured craggy stone walls and a fire, and his face turned instinctively to the right. Northwest of where he and Kincaid had camped tonight. Farther up the river.

How had he known that? Were the spirits trying to lead him to Hallie? Cooper thanked them just in case. Nothing more came to him, and deep into the night he fell asleep. Toward dawn he awakened to the mental tug of the stone against his chest.

He held it, but no more images were revealed. In his breechclout, with his hair streaming loose, he greeted the overcast morning and chanted in the four directions, praying for guidance.

"You're going to freeze the best parts of you off," Wiley commented, crawling out of the lean-to.

Quickly Cooper pulled on his clothing, coat and boots. "I know which way they went."

"Is it the way the tracks are going?" Wiley asked snidely.

"Yes. But today we turn away from the river and head west."

Wiley placed a few sticks on their fire and packed snow into the tin coffeepot. "How do you know that?"

"My spirit stone told me."

Wiley looked up at him with one eye squinted shut. "If you think I'm commentin' on that, think again. I knew a métis trapper who could predict the weather each morning by the way his coffee grounds splattered.''

"Good. Then we're headin' out.''

"We don't want to get stranded too far out if it snows,'' Wiley said logically.

Cooper studied the leaden sky with trepidation. "I don't have much choice. I know she's out there and I'm not leaving her.'' He squatted beside the fire. "You can head back now if you want. It's probably the safest bet.''

Wiley pulled a piece of jerky from his pack and bit off a chunk. "Nah. I'm goin' on. Couldn't live with myself if I left her out here somewhere without tryin'. She might not cotton to me romantically, but that don't mean I don't think she's something special.''

Special. Somehow the word seemed too ordinary for Hallie. Extraordinary. Refreshing. Enchanting. Those were words for Hallie. Cooper almost laughed aloud at his own foolishness. What did a frontier man like himself know about describing women?

"There's something there, isn't there?'' Wiley asked. "Between the two of you.''

He'd denied it emphatically before. Denied it to Kincaid. Denied it to himself mostly. He was too cowardly to admit he cared for her and then have to withstand the rejection when she left. "Yeah,'' he admitted to himself. "There's something there.''

Something that ate a hole through his gut when he thought of her hurt or afraid. Something that ripped his insides to ragged pieces when he dared think of the fate that could meet her out here in the desolate badlands. Something that drove him to reach inside himself and peel back all the layers of self-protection in order to use every ounce of strength and ability to find her.

And when he found her he'd hold her until he understood what that something was, until this gnawing fear left.

And he *would* find her.

* * *

Hallie's ribs hurt and her throat was raw from the cold wind. She rode before Last Horse, the buffalo robe pulled around her, his iron-hard arms on either side. He'd given her food. He'd waited for her while she made her necessary trips into the snow-laden brush. He'd never allowed any of the others near her, and for that she supposed she should be grateful.

Often the horses' feet exposed the bones of antelope or deer, but Hallie's mind feared they might be human bones and that hers would soon join them.

The beauty of the bleak countryside mocked her gritty eyes and despair tugged at her heartstrings. In those hours she relived an entire lifetime, hearing the voices of her parents and siblings, seeing her former surroundings and the contrast between her safe Boston home and this desolate windswept vista. Her own helplessness and the gloom of uncertainty settled on her heart like a boulder.

They stopped at noon and ate a cold meal, immediately pushing on afterward. Occasionally the riders before them whipped out their bows and arrows and shot a fox or a rabbit with amazing accuracy. By late afternoon Hallie's feet were numb in her inadequate kid boots and somehow she was dozing when the horses slowed. She opened her eyes and discovered a grouping of white-skinned tepees painted with animals and spirit signs. There were a dozen of them, in no particular order but all facing the same direction. Behind them, an evergreen forest protected the village from the force of the wind.

Dogs met them first, at least twenty of them, their tails wagging low, their ears thrust back and noses sniffing the air. None of the animals barked, however, and Hallie observed their silence with awe.

Men, women and children poured forth next, greeting them with enthusiastic cries. Their manner of dress was bizarre, versatile combinations of color and texture drawn from both white and red man's tastes. One man wore a silk vest upside down, his long black hair divided into two braids with a scalp lock on top of his head. His ears held brass wire rings, and several chains hung around his neck.

Many wore armlets of brass with strings of bears' claws and beads. Several wore what Hallie realized with a jolt were scalps. Her stomach turned and her own scalp prickled.

The Indians stared and moved closer to Hallie. They were straight from the stories she'd read. The harrowing newspaper accounts of whites tortured and slain hadn't seemed real until this moment. Even Cooper had admitted that some of the horrible stories were probably true.

Last Horse pushed her down from the horse amid the throng of villagers. The women crowded around her, pushing and poking. In terror, Hallie tried to draw away, but there were too many of them and they were too strong. One female knocked her backward and wrestled with her boots until she had them off. Another shoved Hallie's skirts up and unrolled her stockings.

Several of them examined her bare feet and cold hands and fingered her hair. Hallie cringed and backed away, confused at their treatment and horrified at their continued explorations.

Trembling, Hallie looked wildly around for Last Horse. She was rudely shoved and rolled about while the women fought over her blouse. She watched the scuffle in shock.

Someone noticed the pouch around her neck and pointed. They spoke rapidly, gesturing and talking about the stone.

They came at her again and tried to remove her skirt. This time Hallie fought like a wildcat, enduring scratches and even several punches to save the derringer.

"Enough! Enough!" she shouted, her panic-stricken voice breaking. "You have everything else! These are mine!"

In the fray, her petticoats were exposed and reluctantly she let them go, a scuffle immediately following. Hallie sat shivering in her chemise and skirt and, by some miracle, the Indian women seemed inclined to let her hang on to them.

They came at her in a blur of dark faces and black eyes, pinching her arms and poking her with sticks, touching the stone on her chest. She endured their abuse, vowing she would live through this so she could go home.

The cold seeped through her thin skirt. Hallie sat on the snow-packed ground, trembling violently. One by one the women lost interest. A few of the men looked her over. Finally Last Horse came for her. He guided her into one of the tepees. Teeth chattering, Hallie rubbed her sore arms and blinked at the dark interior.

"Start a fire," he ordered, startling her.

"Wh-where's the w-wood?"

"I will bring it."

She picked up the buffalo hide he'd left and wrapped it around herself. She watched the tent flap, praying the Indians respected one another's homes and that she'd be left in peace. The hide walls lent a superficial air of safety she was grateful for. Last Horse dropped wood and dried buffalo chips near the fire pit in the center of the tent.

Keeping the hide wrapped around her, Hallie knelt and arranged the wood. "Do you have a tinderbox or some matches?"

He scowled and knelt, lighting some dried moss with merely the friction of a stick twirled between his palms.

Hallie stared in amazement.

"Don't let it go out." He threw back the flap and left.

She got the blaze going well, but smoke backed up inside the tent. Hallie coughed and squinted at the opening above. After a few adjustments, she discovered the poles that opened the flap and arranged them so the smoke carried up through the hole.

The interior grew warm enough to cast off the heavy robe and replace it with a blanket around her shoulders. The shadowy back recesses of the tent were filled with crates and baskets, leather pouches and bags. Cautiously, Hallie inspected a few of them. Beads, crates of whiskey and to-bacco, tinned goods and blankets filled the spaces.

She opened an enormous battered trunk that looked out of place among the more primitive belongings. Inside lay men's clothing, hats, boots and bandannas—items that white men wore. Where had they come from? What did Last Horse want them for?

She let the lid stand open and raised a wrinkled flannel shirt from the pile. Her gaze slid to the black hat and the red bandanna.

A shiver of awareness ran up her spine. She pictured Last Horse dressed in the shirt and trousers with the hat pulled low and the bandanna up over his face. His distinctive hair and features would be hidden. He'd look just like any other man. Like a white man.

Like the men who'd held up the stage.

Her mind rolled back to that day, to the men who'd or-dered the brides from the coach, searched their belongings and frightened the women to tears.

She recalled the man who'd knelt before her and de-manded she raise her dress. His penetrating eyes had been black and unyielding. She'd kneed him and his hat had fallen off. His thick hair…had been black and shiny. Prob-ably tied to conceal its length and covered by the bandanna around his face.

Last Horse had robbed the stage. Stolen her bracelet and money. Robbed all of Cooper's stages and freight wagons. And made it look like the white men he hated.

How very clever.

Hallie slammed the lid and backed away from the trunk.

He'd robbed his own brother…set fire to his barn! What would stop him from killing her? Or letting the others kill her?

She would.

She gathered her wits and hunched down beside the fire.

Last Horse had offered to make a trade for her. That meant in some warped way he was interested in her. He'd asked how it was done among her people.

But he wasn't stupid. She couldn't make the mistake of thinking he was. Whatever she did and said it had to be believable. Her life depended on it.

Outside drums pounded and warbling singing echoed. A celebration was under way. Hallie fought off the terrors and sat wrapped in the buffalo hide.

It was full dark by the time Last Horse returned with a piece of cooked meat for her. She ate it beneath his glittering gaze.

She gathered her courage. "What do you plan to do with me?"

He didn't reply.

"Ransom is profitable. I don't know if Cooper would pay for my return, but my father would. He's a very rich man."

"You said he has no horses."

"He doesn't. No, no horses. When he wants to go somewhere he rents a carriage. Or takes the train. But he owns a newspaper. And a fine big house. He has stock in the railroad, too. My mother even has servants."

"He would trade for you?"

"Sure. I wouldn't be much use to you out here. I'm really not very good at cooking or sewing or anything. Chumani showed me enough to get me by, but I'm afraid I'm a city girl at heart."

He blinked.

"I can read and write." She glanced around. "So if you need anything read I can do that. I can figure, too. Back in Boston I'm a writer for my father's newspaper. That's why I came out here—to get a story. I was planning on going back in the spring, after Yellow Eagle knows how to read and write and do arithmetic.

"So you see, I'm not one of the throng of Easterners

coming out here and crowding you off your land. I'll be going back.''

''What kind of money does your father have?''

''What kind do you like?''

''Not paper.''

''He has gold. Do you like gold? Actually, he has all different kinds of money. Whatever you'd like. It's all the same, really, you just take it to the bank and have it exchanged.''

''Stop! Your words make my head hurt.''

''Sure. I can do that.'' Hallie folded her hands in her lap and watched a column of smoke drift out the hole overhead.

Last Horse took out his pipe and smoked. Hallie sat quietly. Uncorking a bottle of whiskey, he took a long draw. He observed her the way an animal stalks its prey, his eyes hard and glittering.

Hallie couldn't bear the silence. Sitting beneath his penetrating stare drove her crazy. ''I understand why you hate whites,'' she said at last.

''No. You do not.''

''I do. I really do.''

''You could not understand because you are not of The People.''

''No, I'm not, but I can see what it's been like for your people.''

''Can you?''

''Yes.''

''Can you feel how it felt to leave our land and our hunting grounds? Can you feel what it is like to trust again and again and receive lies in return?'' His ebony eyes bored into hers. ''Do you know what my heart felt like when my father accepted a stranger more willingly than he accepted me?''

His stern words hung in the air between them. ''I've never been driven from my home,'' she admitted. ''And I haven't known many broken promises. But, yes, Last Horse,

I do know what it feels like to have my father prefer a stranger over me.''

He said nothing.

"I was hurt. And angry. And more determined than ever to prove myself to him. That's why I'm here—to prove something to him. Or to myself, I don't know.''

"Running Elk took DeWitt as his son,'' Last Horse said. "Taught him the ways of The People. When we were driven from the land, DeWitt turned his back on The People and became just another white man.''

"That's not true. Cooper has advantages that the Oglala don't have. He was able to buy land and start a business and earn money to help them.''

"Money—ha!'' He threw the empty bottle into the flames with such force it shattered and sparks burst upward. "The People don't need money. They need guns and horses and warriors. If we had more guns, Plenty Wolves would not have died.''

Hatred distorted his angular features. "The People are outnumbered, Last Horse,'' she said softly. "That's plain to see. Cooper is helping The People with food for now and education for the future. Even Yellow Eagle sees that he can make a difference if he learns the ways of the whites.''

"You want to teach them your language and make them just like you,'' he said.

"Maybe most do,'' she agreed. "I only wish none of you had to leave your land or learn to live where you don't want to. But I'm just one person, and a woman at that. I'm afraid what I think or wish hasn't made much of a difference in this world until now.''

She stared across the fire and listened to her own words. "But I am one person,'' she said. "And I do have a voice—and an opinion. And if I get out of this mess, I'm going to use my writing to express those opinions and show the rest of the nation what it's really like out here.''

His eyes had taken on a subdued glaze, whether from her

chattering or the liquor she wasn't sure. He shook his head. "Go to sleep!" he ordered.

Hallie moved to her robe and lay down, pulling the fur around her. She didn't know what prompted her to do it, but she signed good-night.

His black brows shot into his hairline and he looked away. Hallie couldn't draw her apprehensive gaze away. His arms and legs were as muscled as Cooper's, but his chest was not quite as broad nor was his appearance as handsome. His skin glowed copper in the firelight, arm bands enhancing his strength and power.

He hadn't harmed her the night before. He hadn't let any of the others harm her. But they were alone now. Alone and in his village. Whatever he'd brought her here for, she was at his mercy.

He put his pipe away and spread pelts behind her.

Grunting, he stretched out. The robe moved and his hand touched her bare arm.

Hallie jumped.

"You are afraid of Last Horse?"

"No." Her heart pounded, confirming his words rather than hers. She reached up and held the stone. "I don't think the spirits are happy about you touching me."

"How do you know this?"

"My *sicun* grows warm when the spirits are active."

He flipped her to her back and touched the pouch at her throat. His eyes widened with an obvious look of fear, and he released her. "This is so! You have powerful spirits!"

Hallie wished she knew more about his beliefs. Apparently, even though he didn't look on anything else the way Cooper and Running Elk did, he had a strong belief in the spirit gods.

"Tomorrow I will make a sacrifice to please them."

"What kind of sacrifice?"

"Tobacco. A dog."

She grimaced in the darkness.

He rolled back on his pallet, and Hallie turned the other way again. Clenching the stone in her fist, she closed her eyes, but slumber eluded her. *Where are you, Cooper?* she intoned silently, and wondered if she would ever see him again.

Cooper lay on his belly in the snow and observed the darkened village. He knew which lodge was Last Horse's. Hallie would be inside. He couldn't wait until morning. It might be too late.

Simply sneaking in and carrying her off as Last Horse had done would be of no use. Last Horse would follow and await his chance to recapture her. Cooper knew it as well as he knew the sun would come up in the morning.

He would have to take her with a show of strength in front of Last Horse's band. The way these people understood and respected.

He slid backward and ran to where Wiley waited with the horses. "She's there," he said.

"Now what?"

"Now I go in for her."

The moon barely shed any illumination. A light snow had begun to fall, and here next to the woods and the buttes the wind wasn't fierce.

"You should wait here," Cooper said. "I can't promise you'd be safe down there."

"Have you asked your spirits for safety?" Wiley asked. Cooper nodded.

"Then I'll take my chances with them," he decided.

Cooper swung up onto his gelding. Wiley followed, and they rode out in the open toward the village. A dog whined and several ran toward them.

A flap was thrown back and an Indian carrying a torch came out. He whistled, and several more braves appeared in the dim moonlight.

Cooper rode directly to Last Horse's lodge and called out. "My brother!" he shouted in Oglala.

Last Horse flung back the flap and straightened, rifle in hand.

"You have the woman that belongs to me!" Cooper challenged. "You will give her back."

Many torches had been lit and carried to the front of Last Horse's lodge, illuminating his angry features. "The woman is mine," Last Horse announced. "If you want her, you will have to take her."

Cooper climbed down from his horse and drew his knife. "That's what I'm here for."

Chapter Sixteen

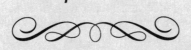

Hallie didn't recognize the words, but something about the familiar voice brought a sob to her throat.

Last Horse had leapt from the pallet of furs and grabbed a rifle before disappearing. She ran toward the opening and was nearly knocked flat when he barged back in. He tossed the gun on the furs, anger flushing his skin and making the veins on his neck and shoulders stand out. He drew an enormous knife, studied the sharp edge in the dwindling firelight and replaced it in its sheath, securing the holsterlike belt at his waist, the only thing he wore besides his breechclout.

"Come." Roughly he grabbed her arm and yanked her toward the flap. "Watch him die."

Hallie stumbled through the opening and blinked against the glare of a dozen torches. In the center of the semicircle stood Cooper.

"Cooper!" she shouted, and attempted to run toward him.

Last Horse jerked her arm and shoved her into a gathering of women. Their hands clasped her and held her securely.

Cooper's relief at seeing her alive entwined with fury at her appearance. Her dark hair hung in a tangled mass, and her face, bare arms and feet were dirty. How had he let this happen to her? Why hadn't he seen her safely home when he'd had the chance? She would never forgive him for the abuse she'd suffered. He would never forgive himself. All that mattered now was getting her out of here and back to her family.

The women clutched at Hallie, but she ignored their grasping hands and tried to pull away.

Cooper glared at the man he'd been raised with, the man he'd shared a lodge and meals with, the man he'd taught his own language and considered a brother. Last Horse had never been able to accept him. He'd resented the love and attention his father had shared with a white boy. If Last Horse had ever seen Cooper as an individual, it had been as one who'd come to damage his position in his father's eyes.

He took a minute to scan the faces of the renegades surrounding them, people he'd grown up with, people he'd fought beside, ate with and played with. People as proud and frightened as those on the reservation, with one difference. These had listened to Last Horse and believed it was better to die fighting than to give up.

Cooper sheathed his knife long enough to strip his shirt over his head. Grasping the bone-handled knife again, he moved forward.

The villagers formed a ragged circle around them. Cooper's attention never left his brother's spiteful eyes. Last Horse lashed out, and Cooper arched his body outward, avoiding the blade. Again his opponent lunged; again Cooper dodged.

He made a sweep of his own, scoring a slash across Last Horse's upper arm.

Last Horse sliced Cooper's trousers and they faced off once again, circling, circling.

Hallie covered her mouth with her trembling fingers, afraid she'd cry out and provide a deadly distraction. Blood streamed from Last Horse's cut, a gruesome shine in the torch glow. She grew dizzy watching the two men bait one another. Light flakes of snow swirled between them.

Last Horse moved in close, his blade leaving a thin streak of blood across Cooper's chest. Cooper's attention never wavered. He never stopped moving or feinting and lunging. Hallie feared her heart wouldn't take the strain. She forced herself to take several deep breaths to keep from fainting or being sick.

Good God, what would she do if Cooper was killed? The gathering would turn on Wiley next, and then her. Cooper should never have come. He shouldn't have risked his life for hers.

Hallie held her breath while the two men wrestled with one another, knife blades gleaming in the eerie flickering light. They landed on their knees, muscles straining, the sheen of sweat on their bodies.

A moment later they sprang apart, Cooper lunging to his feet. Crimson flowed from his side.

"Oh, God!" Hallie sobbed, and clutched the stone at her breast. "Don't let him die. I'd rather stay than have him die."

Cooper panted, his massive chest heaving with exertion, but his stance held life and strength. In the next instant Last Horse rolled into Cooper's legs, knocking him over hard. He met the dirt and came up on his elbow. Last Horse lunged at him and they rolled, vying for the upper position. One of the knives arced through the air, landing out of reach.

Hallie stared in dread.

Cooper came up on top, pressing the tip of his blade against Last Horse's throat. Last Horse, at his mercy, glared upward.

"The woman—is mine," Cooper said between clenched teeth. "Say it."

Hallie scanned the faces of the crowd as they anticipated

what would happen next. Would he say it? Would Cooper kill him?

"Say it!" Cooper demanded.

"The—woman—is—yours," Last Horse growled.

Cooper relaxed his hold.

The crowd seemed to release an audible sigh.

Cooper sheathed his knife and sat on his heels.

Hallie jerked away from the women and ran and held Cooper's head against her midriff, not caring that his wounds bled on her skirt. He enfolded her legs with his arms, holding her against him. She tangled her fingers in his hair.

A little sob escaped her lips and she clung to him for all she was worth, bending to touch her lips to the top of his head, breathing in his strength and masculine scent. She was safe. He was alive.

Last Horse's jerky movement caught her eye as he grabbed the knife. She reacted without thinking, pulling the derringer from her pocket and firing it. Last Horse's body jerked and his eyes widened, but still he lunged closer. Hallie squeezed the other trigger.

Cooper turned at the same time Last Horse fell forward against him. He lowered the limp body to the ground. The knife fell from his brother's hand. Cooper raised his eyes to Hallie's.

"I shot him," she whispered, then dropped the derringer.

Cooper picked it up, looked at her and stood. "You didn't have a choice," he said at last.

Her panicked gaze slid from his face to the crowd of villagers with snowflakes dusting their black hair. Would they kill them now? Would their hair hang from the tribe's belts like so many others before them?

One of the men spoke to Cooper. Cooper replied. A rumble of conversation passed through the gathering.

Cooper spoke again. The men concurred and nodded. Several others gestured and the crowd broke up.

"What did he say?" she asked.

"He said to take you and go."

Relief poured through her.

"I insisted I take Last Horse's body to my father. They agreed."

"They agreed?"

"They saw what happened here. It was a fair fight. I won and let him live. He tried to kill me when my back was turned. Any of these women would protect her man the same."

"Oh."

"Where is your clothing?"

She gestured lamely at the scattered women walking back to their tents.

"Let's find you something."

She followed him into Last Horse's tepee. "There's something you'd better see," she said, and opened the trunk.

Cooper pulled out a shirt. "Wear this. And these." He shoved a pair of boots into her hands.

"Cooper, these are the clothes the stage robbers were wearing," she said, shoving her arms into the oversize shirt. "Last Horse and his men were the ones stealing from you."

His brow furrowed and he studied the items. "Are you sure?"

She nodded. "Once I saw this shirt and hat I remembered what they looked like on him. When I kneed him, his hat fell off and I saw his hair." She met his bewildered look. "I remembered his eyes the most, though."

"I traced your bracelet back to him," he admitted, and she hated to see the way he stood with his proud shoulders slumped. "He hated me that much," he said sadly. "I would have given him anything he needed."

"He blamed you for everything," Hallie said. "Even Plenty Wolves's death."

"I suspected that Last Horse was behind that final rebellion that got Plenty Wolves killed. Someone had tipped off the army to our whereabouts.''

''He was hurting his own people,'' she said, pulling the boots on.

''He didn't see it that way.''

She shook her head.

Cooper carried in her coat and gloves and handed them to her without ceremony.

She glanced from her warm clothing to his shuttered face. ''You brought my things.''

He shrugged. ''Figured you'd be cold.'' He wrapped an additional fur around her and took another to roll Last Horse's body in. He brought a horse from the corral. ''His horse was too tired from riding double, so I traded it for a fresh one.''

Hallie stared at the horse with brass rings pierced through its ears and scalps braided into its tail. ''I don't want to ride behind it.''

''You won't.'' He led her to where Wiley waited with the horses.

''Miss?'' Wiley wore a disconcerted expression.

Hallie hugged him impulsively. ''Thanks for coming with Cooper.''

''Are you all right?'' he asked. ''Did they hurt you?''

''I'm bruised and sore and tired, but other than that, I'm fine.''

''You're right lucky.''

''I don't know about luck.'' She allowed Kincaid to assist her onto the mare while Cooper tied the body to the Indian horse. ''How did you know where to find me? I thought Indians covered their trails.''

''They do. We lost the trail yesterday.''

''Then how—?''

''He said his spirit stone told him where you were.''

Hallie touched her stone and Cooper's head rose. He turned and met her eyes.

"You're cut," she said simply.

"Not bad." He wiped his ribs with a handful of snow and pulled his shirt and coat on. "We have to beat this storm."

She rode behind Cooper, who followed the way they'd come. Behind her, Wiley led the Indian horse. They camped where Cooper and Wiley had camped earlier and slept a few hours.

They awoke and discovered a small group of Oglala waiting for them, women and children and horses among them.

"What are they doing?" Hallie whispered.

"They're following us back to the reservation," Cooper replied. "Last Horse may have been the only thing keeping them out there."

Cooper led them out at first light, setting a persistent pace. The snow let up. They stopped only once to eat, sharing what little food they had with the Oglala. Cooper urged them onward. The moon appeared clear and full and he decided not to stop.

Hallie hurt everywhere. She was so exhausted she couldn't stay atop the horse. The moonlight wavered, and she dreamed of leering faces and burning sticks stabbing her skin. She awoke to the warmth and snapping sound of a fire.

Hallie turned her head and her neck hurt. She tried to speak, but her throat was dry and aching.

Chumani's face swam before her. "Sleep, Hallie, sleep," she said in her distinctive, clipped way. A cool cloth draped Hallie's forehead and she closed her eyes again.

The next time she awoke, the room was light and she recognized it as her room in the log house.

Cooper dozed in a chair by her side.

"Cooper?" she said, trying out her voice. It cracked.

He sat up and blinked, reaching over to place the backs of his fingers against her cheek and forehead. "How are you feeling?"

"Like I was carried over a saddle and beaten with sticks."

"I'm sorry about the way they treated you," he said.

Wincing, she tried to sit up. "It's not your fault."

He helped her.

"How long did I sleep?"

"You had a fever for a couple of days."

"Days!" She glanced down at the covers clasped to her chest and noticed the black-and-blue marks covering her arms. "Where are my clothes?"

"The little you had left were covered with blood."

At that, she remembered his cuts. "Are you all right?"

"I'm fine."

"Show me."

"You're not an easy woman to convince of anything, are you?" He stood and pulled up his deerskin shirt, revealing a light bandage.

"Stitches?" she asked.

"A few."

"Chumani?"

"Kincaid."

"Well." Then another thought. "Where are the Indians who followed us?"

"At the reservation."

"Will the others who stayed make it through the winter?"

"They'll make it," he assured her. "They've been wintering in the cold for as long as the badlands have been here."

"Not this far west, though, have they?"

"There is better land," he agreed. He stepped to the chest of drawers, returned with an envelope and sat on the edge of the chair. "The mail came through," he said softly.

"Dogsled?"

He nodded.

She looked at the letter in his hands. "Who's it from?"

"Your father." He handed it to her.

Hallie took the envelope and stared at the familiar, neat writing. She tore it open and unfolded the paper. A cashier's check fell to the bed. She stared at the amount for a few seconds, then began to read.

Dearest Hallie,
Your mother and I were beside ourselves with worry when we discovered your absence. Your brothers were convinced you'd been to the Piedmont district trying to involve yourself in a story about the boxing tournament. I hired an agent to search for you. When the first telegram arrived, relating your impetuous plan, your mother fainted dead away.

She is highly distressed. The agency will send someone as far as Duluth to meet you and deliver you home. This should be enough to pay someone to get you there. Come home immediately. Your loving father.

"What does it say?"
She handed the letter to him. Frowning, he studied the script. "I can't make out all the words."
"It says he'll have someone waiting in Duluth to take me home."
"Someone you can trust? There's still a long way to go after that."
She lay back. "I'm sure it'll be someone I can trust."
He folded the letter and gave it back to her. "I did a lot of thinking the past couple of days."
She rolled her head to the side to look at him.
"The weather has been fair. If the mail can get through, I'm sure I could get you out of here."
"Is this enough money?"
"I don't want your father's money."
"But I owe you—"
"I said I don't want it."

"Take it for the reservation, then. Buy them clothing and hire a teacher." She held the slip of paper toward him.

He looked at it and back at her face. "I'll take it for them, don't think I won't."

She wiggled the check in the air.

He took it.

"When will we leave?" she asked.

"As soon as you're feeling strong and as long as the weather holds. A day or two. Pack only what you'll need for the trip. I'll send the rest on to you."

Hallie's gaze followed his broad form as he walked to the door. "I'll be ready."

He slipped out of the room and she closed her eyes. It would be that easy, then? In a week or so he'd have her to Duluth and turn her over to another man, who would take her back to Boston. At last she'd be gone, out of his hair, out of his house. He could get on with his life. Perhaps he'd bring home a woman from the reservation.

And what about her? She'd get on with her life, too. She'd have things back to normal in no time.

Normal…begging for scraps beneath her father's desk…trying to be seen and heard above the magnificence of the males in her family…turning down proposals from the young men her father and brothers foisted upon her.

A new thought occurred to her. Maybe she'd marry one of them. Maybe an interesting one would come along, one with blue eyes and skin tanned from the sun. Maybe…

She rolled over and buried her face beneath the covers. No matter how hard she wished, there wasn't a man like Cooper DeWitt in Boston. The longer she thought about it the more convinced she became; nowhere in the world was there a man who would make her feel the way he did. And even if there was, she wouldn't want him. She wanted Cooper. And he wasn't hers to have.

Chumani cared for her after that. The next day she got up and took care of herself. And the following day, Cooper knocked on the door and announced they'd be leaving at daybreak. "Say your goodbyes tonight."

Goodbyes. Hallie hadn't given any thought to telling Chumani and Yellow Eagle goodbye, and she resisted it. But leaving without a farewell would be cowardly and she couldn't bring herself to do that, so she and Chumani prepared supper in the house together one last time.

"I'll send you books," Hallie promised Yellow Eagle at the table. "All the classics."

The boy didn't reply. He picked at his food and excused himself, going to sit by the fireplace.

Hallie laid down her bone fork. No one spoke, and the atmosphere grew uncomfortable. Cooper finished his coffee and Chumani poured him more. Hallie got up and went to sit by Yellow Eagle.

"We all have somewhere we belong," she said softly. "I don't belong here."

He looked up from breaking a stick into tiny pieces, and the hurt in his ebony eyes cut a ragged slice from the brave front she'd constructed. "Where do you belong, then?"

"Back in Boston," she answered. "That's where my family is."

"I guess if they need you, that's where you should be."

She nodded, ignoring the implication of his innocent words. "We'll still be friends, Yellow Eagle," she promised. "You can write to me. And I promise I'll write to you."

"Okay."

Chumani tried to give her the bracelet back, but Hallie insisted it should belong to her. They hugged and said their goodbyes, and Hallie went to bed with a heavy heart.

At daybreak she waved to Jack and, dressed in her warmest clothing, climbed atop the horse Cooper steadied for her. With their supplies tied to two extra horses, their journey began.

The sun reflecting off the snow in all directions hurt her eyes. She pulled her hood low and enjoyed the warmth penetrating her clothing. They traveled fast, but Cooper insisted on stopping for a noon meal with hot tea. They didn't stop to eat again until full dark. Beside a rock formation he constructed a tiny, slant-roofed tent only two feet off the ground, hobbled the horses nearby and built a fire. First he melted snow for the horses and measured each a portion of grain from one of the packs.

Next he opened a tin of meat with his bowie knife and heated it. They shared it and dry biscuits. He showed her how to wipe the plates and silverware with snow, dry them beside the fire and pack them away.

He lit his pipe. "Go lie down."

"What about you?"

"I'll be there in a minute."

She crouched before the shallow tent.

"You'll keep warmer if you take your clothes off and spread them over the top of the furs."

It was no easy task removing her coat and boots and outer clothing in the cramped space. She draped them over the top of the pelts as he'd directed, but kept her underclothes on and slid into the furs.

The sleeping furs smelled better than Last Horse's, their warmth and softness an enveloping cocoon. The scent of Cooper's tobacco drifted on the wind. Within seconds she fell asleep.

For no particular reason she awoke during the night. Cooper lay along her side, his breathing even, his long body relaxed. Their combined body heat kept them deliciously warm. Without moving an eyelash Hallie let herself feel him beside her, inhaled his unique scent, listened to the beat of his heart and his breath.

Slowly and carefully, so as not to wake him, she inched ever so slightly onto her side facing him and placed her cheek against his bare shoulder. She wanted to curl up against him, draw herself as close as she could get and fold herself into his embrace.

As though he sensed her unspoken desire in his sleep, he moved, rustling the pelts and bringing her into the curve of his arm. Hallie snuggled her head beneath his chin and nestled into his arms. She would have time before morning to extricate herself. For now, there was nowhere she'd rather be.

Cooper, waking, delighted in the feel of her soft curving body against his. It was a temptation to thrust his fingers into her sweet-smelling hair and agony not to run his hands over her.

It wasn't enough but it was all he had, and he wouldn't spoil the chance to spend these last few days and nights as close as possible. Duluth wasn't nearly far enough. Nothing had ever had such a sorrowful effect on his heart as the thought of saying goodbye to Hallie.

Before Hallie, he'd been a little lonely, enough to build a house and send for a wife.

After Hallie...a wide open ache gaped in his chest. After Hallie he would know what lonely really was. Enough to tear down the damned house and burn every last thing that reminded him of her.

Enough to make him the bitter, hard-shelled man he knew he had the capability of being. There was something between them; he'd admitted that to himself. He had no doubt he could get her to stay—not because of any appeal he imagined he held or because of his verbal and sensual skills, but because of the mutual attraction that had developed. Because of the explosive energy that radiated between them and the extraordinary link that had been forged.

He could convince her to stay with a simple declaration of love and the obvious physical needs of their bodies. But that wasn't what he wanted. She would stay, yes, but she would grow to hate the land and the life—and him—and that he could never bear.

So he didn't caress her. Didn't kiss her. Didn't fool himself into thinking that love could bridge cultures and heal differences. Lust wasn't what Hallie needed from him right now. She needed his protection, his capability and experience. And he meant to give her what she needed.

Cooper opened his eyes in the pitch-dark enclosure and wished he could see her sable hair and her ebony lashes resting against her fair skin. He needed all the memories he could get.

Chapter Seventeen

During the day they traveled together like mere acquaintances, speaking only of necessary things. At night they slept wrapped in one another's arms, oblivious to the cold, holding the world at bay. But the world grew closer with each passing mile, and each passing day.

The end of the second week they crossed paths with a band of Chippewa hunters, and Cooper traded tobacco for fresh game. Days later he left her on the bank of the Mississippi with the extra horses and crossed the ice, checking for fissures. Hallie waited impatiently, his bulky, dark form growing smaller against the stark white river. What would happen to her if he fell through a weak spot and didn't return?

She reviewed the possibilities, all of them ending in her grisly death, and squinted against the glare. After what seemed like hours, and probably was, he returned for her and led them to the other bank.

"How much farther?" she panted. They'd dismounted at the bank and guided the animals up the slippery incline.

"We'll be there tonight. You can sleep in a bed."

"And a bath? Will there be hot water?"

"I'll find you some," he promised.

This trip was so different than the one that had brought

her here, not only because of the temperature, the scenery and the more direct route, but because of the man she traveled with.

Cooper hadn't been the coarse, smelly old trapper she'd envisioned during the arduous journey west. If only he had been…leaving would have been so much easier.

The smoke from dozens of chimneys and stovepipes curled into the darkening sky. "There it is," Cooper said.

They'd come to a well-traveled road leading into the town.

"Do you think he's there?" Cooper asked. "Your father's man?"

Hallie studied the buildings ahead. "Can we wait until morning to find out?"

She was buying them one more night. One more night before anyone knew where Hallie was and could report back to her father. Cooper agreed, and prodded the tired horses forward.

They found a livery first and left the horses before walking the street lit by yellow lights shining from square-paned windows. Cooper spotted the hotel and led her across the rutted, frozen road.

They entered the building, and Cooper stopped just inside the door. Hallie glanced from his stern face to the rough wooden counter. He didn't make a move, so she crossed and rang the tin cowbell that hung from a wire.

A moment later a robust man with steel gray muttonchops and a shiny bald head parted a faded curtain and peered at them over a bulbous red nose.

"Ma'am," he said, greeting her once she'd pushed back her hood and revealed her hair and face.

"We'd like two rooms, please," she said.

He opened a ledger and turned it toward her, handing her a pen and pushing a bottle of ink forward. "How long will you be staying?"

Hallie signed her name with a flourish. "I'm not sure.

Maybe only tonight, but perhaps longer if the person I'm meeting isn't here yet.''

"Lookin' for somebody in particular?" he asked.

"I don't know his name," she said, hearing how foolish that sounded. "My father is sending someone to see me to Boston."

"You the Wainwright girl?" He squinted at the ledger.

"I am."

"Fella lookin' for you's been here since Tuesday. Said to let him know first thing when you got here."

Hallie gave him her most imploring look. "I would greatly appreciate it if you'd wait until morning. I look a fright and am exhausted from my travels. Could you be a dear and put off notifying him for just a few more hours?"

One side of the fellow's face twitched. "I don't know. Gruber said there'd be a tip in it."

He looked from her to where Cooper hadn't moved from the door. Hallie turned. Cooper's stoic expression was unreadable. She beckoned him forward and finally had to go take his arm. He let his parka fall away from his head. "Sign the book, Cooper," she instructed.

He tugged off his fur mitten and she placed the pen in his fingers.

"This is my cousin, Mr. DeWitt."

The hotel keeper nodded.

"Well, I guess you wouldn't want to lose out on your tip," she said with a sigh, and her gaze slid up to Cooper's.

A flicker of comprehension crossed behind his blue eyes. Parting his heavy coat, he opened a pouch at his waist. He touched a silver coin in question. Hallie nodded and he placed it on the counter.

"Would that compensate?" Hallie asked.

He snatched the coin. "You gotta pay in advance for your rooms, too."

He told Cooper the amount, and Cooper counted the money out.

''She wants a bath,'' Cooper stated gruffly.

''Two bits more.'' The bald man handed them each a key and a candle he lit off the lantern hanging over the counter. ''Nine and ten.''

Cooper dug into his money pouch again, then stared at his key. Hallie took it from his hand and pointed to her satchel and his saddlebags. He picked them up and followed her up the stairs.

She read the room numbers aloud as they passed. ''Nine.''

Unlocking the door, she gestured for him to walk in. ''Leave my bag here.''

She lit the lamp on a washstand with her candle, then blew out the candle.

He set the leather satchel down and looked around. Hallie shrugged out of the heavy coat.

A thin woman tapped on the open door and scurried in with a sling of wood. ''I'll get your stoves going and be back with the tub and water.''

''I'll do that.'' Cooper brushed the servant aside and placed the wood in the metal stove, lighting it with his candle.

''Come on.'' Hallie led him across the hall. The woman appeared again, and once more Cooper did her job.

''I'll be right back,'' she said, and hurried away.

''I'll help.''

Hallie placed her hand on Cooper's chest, stopping him. ''Cooper. It's her job.''

''But she—''

''She works for her pay like anyone else. Let her earn it. Here, take off your coat.''

He draped it over a chair, but remained near the doorway.

His fringed leather garb and knee-high boots won him a long look from the woman when she returned with the metal tub and dragged it into Hallie's room.

"It's a big tub," Hallie observed in a whisper. "Want a bath after me?"

"Do I smell?"

"I probably won't notice until I wash," she said with a grin.

"Maybe I'd better." What would it matter? he thought. They wouldn't be together after tonight, anyway.

"I'll come get you when I'm done." She left him standing in his room, uncomfortable in his surroundings, unwilling to leave her.

Hallie bathed and dressed in clean clothes, luxuriating in the warmth of the stove. She waited in Cooper's room while he used the tub and dressed. Too tired to wait for the woman to dip the water and remove the tub, she wished Cooper a good-night.

"Are you sure you'll be safe alone in there?" he asked.

"I'll be fine. There's a lock on the door. You'll hear if anything happens." What was he thinking? They were in a town now, only feet from her father's hired man. He couldn't expect to share a room.

"Do you have the derringer?"

She pulled it from her pocket and showed him.

"Is it loaded?"

"Yes. Now get some rest."

He glanced up and down the hall. "Lock the door."

"I will. Good night." Closing the door, she turned the key and folded herself into bed.

A rap sounded. Hallie opened her eyes to sunlight streaming through the frayed draperies. Disoriented, she sat and got her bearings.

The rap came again. Men's voices echoed in the hallway. Hallie pulled the coverlet around her shoulders, went to the door and pressed her ear to the wood.

The first voice she heard was Cooper's. She flung open the door.

A tall, dark-haired man in a sheepskin coat turned from an encounter with Cooper. Lines creased his weathered skin. He sported a thick black mustache and a confident manner. "Miss Wainwright?"

"Yes?"

"Tom Gruber." He wrestled a piece of paper away from Cooper and held it out to her. Hallie glanced at the identifying letter in her father's handwriting. "I'm here to see you home."

Hallie stuck her hand into the hall. "Pleased to meet you, Mr. Gruber."

He gave her hand one brisk shake.

"Where are you planning to go from here?" Cooper asked.

Gruber cast him an annoyed glance. "Who is this man?"

"Cooper DeWitt," Hallie said, introducing him. "Of DeWitt Stage and Freight Company. He brought me here from the Dakotas."

"How are you plannin' to go from here?" Cooper asked again.

"I'm gonna head north and follow the coast till we cross the St. Lawrence."

"Hallie, I want to talk to you." Cooper pushed the door open wider and insinuated himself in her room.

"Wait a minute—" Gruber said.

Cooper closed the door in his face. A knock sounded immediately. Hallie gawked at Cooper. "What are you doing?"

"Look, we don't even know him," Cooper said. "How do we know he can get you there safely?"

"My father wouldn't hire someone who wasn't trustworthy," she explained again.

Gruber's incessant rap pounded.

"He's a total stranger, Hallie. Think about it! Think of your reputation. You can't travel alone with him."

She gaped at him. "Since when did you become my mother?"

He scowled.

"And besides that, I've been alone with *you* all this time."

"Oh! You're comparing being with him to being with me? Are you gonna cuddle up in his tent with him at night?"

Hallie stared at him in openmouthed wonder. An angry blush warmed her skin.

The knock sounded louder.

Hallie jerked open the door. "Give us a few minutes here, will you? I'll meet you downstairs for breakfast in half an hour."

Gruber gave her a disparaging look and turned away.

"Thank you," she called after him.

"Cooper," she began.

He faced her silently.

"Thank you for getting me here. Thank you for putting up with me and being understanding. I never apologized appropriately for taking advantage of you, by using the ticket and all, I mean. You had every right to be upset with me, and you were very kind. I don't think..." The words were difficult and she gathered her thoughts and emotions. "I won't ever forget the time I spent at Stone Creek. I won't ever forget Chumani or Yellow Eagle...." Without conscious thought she touched the stone on her chest. "Or you."

He said nothing.

"I think it's better for both of us if we say our goodbyes here and go our separate ways," she finished.

She felt his eyes on her, but couldn't meet them.

"Thanks for everything," she said.

At once the room seemed small and chilly, a bare, empty mockery of the warm, wonderful time they'd spent together over the past weeks. Sounds from the street below drifted up through the closed window. Cooking smells wafted through the floors and walls.

Hallie shifted her weight, and the floorboards creaked beneath her feet.

Without a word, without a touch or a backward glance, Cooper let himself out the door.

Hallie stared at the scarred wood until her vision blurred. Fat, warm drops fell to the hands clutching the coverlet at her chest and she looked down to see tears there. Against her skin, the spirit stone burned hot.

It was over. He was gone.

She'd made the break as painless as possible and had no one to blame but herself for winding up in this situation in the first place. It was too late for "what ifs" and "should haves." The only sensible direction to look was forward… and she did so, without much hope that the aching emptiness in her heart would ever be filled.

Time did wonders for Hallie's outlook. Several weeks later she sat in the tearoom at Miss Abernathy's, enjoying lunch with her mother and her mother's bridge friends.

"You'll be at the musicale tomorrow evening, won't you, Hallie?" Constance Mitchell asked, a dusting of sugar clinging to the fine hairs above her lip.

"Oh, well, I—" Hallie began.

"Of course she will," Clarisse Wainwright replied. "She's looking forward to it, aren't you, darling?"

Constance took a sip of tea, and most of the sugar disappeared. "I'm so glad, because Winfred's young nephew will be there. I just know you will adore him. You've hardly greeted the social scene at all since your trip to Philadelphia."

"Yes, well," Hallie responded. "You know those Philadelphians. They simply wore me out."

Constance tittered and Clarisse gave Hallie a warning look. The truth of her whereabouts over the past months wouldn't have been acceptable in polite society. Hallie's mother vowed that if anyone discovered Hallie had been unchaperoned on the frontier or kidnapped by savages, their entire family would never be able to hold up their heads in public again.

Rather than bring disgrace on her family, Hallie had gone along with her mother's version of a trip to visit relatives.

Among her numerous disappointments was the fact that there hadn't been anyone she could share her tales of the West with. Her mother got the vapors every time Hallie had tried to talk to her. Her brothers thought her the most foolish girl in all the East and her father...

Well, Samuel saw the newsworthy angle, loved the series of articles, but insisted the byline credits go under a fictitious man's name—to spare Hallie's reputation, of course.

And Hallie had sent her first dime novel manuscript off to New York using the pseudonym, as well.

So what had the whole fiasco gained her? Absently, Hallie stared into her cup of tea. A new appreciation for people and life in all its diversities. A newfound tolerance for other cultures...and herself.

Hallie's fingertips touched the bulky, hard lump beneath the prim white yoke of her blouse. Her mother hadn't been able to convince her to get rid of it or even leave it in a drawer. The rock was her link to the governing spirits, a last tenuous thread to the man she'd left in the Dakotas.

She didn't want to relegate that memory to a drawer. As long as she could touch the stone and feel its heat and magic, she could believe he thought of her, too.

She touched the *sicun* through her clothing and his name echoed in her head. *Cooper. Cooper.* What was he doing at this minute? Had he brought a dark-skinned woman home from the reservation to share his bed? Had he read any of the books she'd sent to Yellow Eagle? Did he come home to the log house after checking his traps and feel her absence? Was he sorry he hadn't wanted her to stay?

"—like that lovely blue taffeta," Clarisse was saying. "Too bad it's not spring yet, but you will look stunning in the royal blue crepe with the underskirt."

"It's decided what I'll wear, even," she said to Constance, coming out of her reverie. "I do hope Mr. Mitchell's nephew likes blue."

"He'll adore blue when he sees you in it," Constance cooed.

Hallie held her mother's coat while she slipped into it, donned her own and followed Clarisse to the coach. Her mother chattered and Hallie stared blankly out the crack between the drawn curtain and the side of the window.

A massive form in clothing the color of Cooper's buckskins caught her attention and she jerked the shade up and surveyed the passerby. All ordinary. All occupied with their city business and hurrying along the storefronts.

"Whatever are you doing, Hallie?"

She wilted back against the richly padded seat. "I thought I saw someone I knew," she said.

The carriage pulled up before their house and the driver opened the door, lowered the steps and assisted them to the ground.

Hallie passed the afternoon working on her second novel. Her father and brothers spoke of the war in Mexico during supper and she picked at her meal, listening halfheartedly.

Later, unable to sleep, she padded to the study for a book. Her father still sat in his leather chair, cigar smoke curling around the desk lamp. Hallie stared at the lamp and recalled the one Cooper had ordered and proudly showed her.

"Can't sleep, Precious?" her father asked.

Sitting in the chair before his desk, she pulled her bare toes up under her nightgown. "No."

Samuel leaned back and the chair creaked. "You're different, Hallie," he said.

She shrugged. She knew she was different, but to her it

was all on the inside. To her family she had never changed, never grown up.

"I never would have thought I'd say this," he said. "For so long, I've discouraged you from the paper. I've tried to interest you in other things, introduced you to young men and hoped you'd find an interest."

She looked at him over her updrawn knees.

"Somehow, you going along with all of it now doesn't sit right with me. You're discouraged, aren't you?"

"I guess so. Tired of fighting windmills, anyway."

"Hallie, your articles about the brides were front-page quality. The *New York News* picked them up, for heaven's sake. You can be very proud of them."

"I can be proud of Harold Winthrop," she replied sarcastically.

"You know why we had to use the pen name," her father chided. "Your mother couldn't have gone out in public again if people found out where you'd been."

"Nothing changed while I was gone," she said, getting up abruptly. "So in order to keep my sanity, I'm changing. I've never been what you wanted me to be, Father. Since I had the audacity to be born a female, you would think I could have liked the things girls like, wouldn't you? Instead of picking up grease from the presses, I should have been cutting paper dolls from the previous days' issues. Rather than coming home with ink staining my skirts, I should have batted my lashes and convinced you to buy me Paris fashions."

Moving behind the chair she'd vacated, she gripped the back. "All I ever wanted was to be a part of the paper. I wanted you to be as proud of me as you were of Charles and Turner. I wanted to get in there in the thick of things and feel the camaraderie and the pride. The same love for the smell of the ink and the clack of the presses that burns in your heart burns in here." She pressed a fist to her chest.

"But I'm a square peg," she finished. "Not like Charles

and Turner and Evan. They're nice round pegs, and *The Daily* is nice round business, so they fit quite neatly.''

"Hallie," her father whispered, and she recognized his incognizance. He didn't know what to say, what to think. He'd never known that this side of her existed—hadn't known she was capable of these feelings and desires and wishes.

"You don't have to say anything," she said. "Just don't expect me to leap for joy at the thought of every lame get-together or to fall at the feet of some swain with hands as soft as Mother's." She heard her pain beginning to surface and refused to take it out on her father. "Good night."

She turned and fled to her room.

Hallie perked herself up the following day, determined to enjoy the evening, in spite of the Mitchells' nephew. She loved music, and the presentations at the opera house were always enjoyable.

She begged off when her mother tried to get her to go along for some late-afternoon shopping. Her father was still at the paper and Hallie preferred the time to work on her story.

The shadows grew long. Hallie lit the lamp and stretched, heading to the kitchen to make herself a cup of tea.

A rap sounded at the door as she reached the foyer. Hallie glanced around, noting the servants were otherwise occupied, and opened the door.

Her breath stopped in her throat and her heart skipped several much-needed beats.

A wild, primitive man stood on the stoop, his stance like that of one about to encounter an enraged animal. An enormous fur coat enhanced his size, and the rifle slung over his shoulder lent fierceness to his already rigid expression.

Elation washed away Hallie's surprise. "Cooper!"

Chapter Eighteen

His sky blue eyes swept her hair and clothing, returning to her face.

"What are you doing here?" she asked in amazement. Never in a lifetime had she expected to see Cooper DeWitt on her doorstep.

"I came to see you. To talk."

"Miss Wainwright?" The maid spoke from the doorway.

"It's okay." Hallie turned and waved her away. "Well…" She glanced over his shoulder at the brick-paved street and then behind her. "Come in."

He took a step forward. "Can we talk alone?"

"It's highly improper," she said automatically. What other choice had been available to him? He had no idea of how to send a message or arrange a meeting in an appropriate location. The supercilious intricacies of society were foreign to him.

On the street a carriage pulled up before the house. "Mother!" she gasped. "My mother's home!" He started to back away, but Hallie grabbed his sleeve and pulled him in, closing the door. "Come with me. Hurry!"

She dragged him up the staircase and down the hall, ushering him into her room and closing the door. "I'm sorry, Cooper, but my mother would never understand."

He stood in the center of her room and regarded his surroundings. Hallie saw the cabbage-rose wallpaper and fringe-tasseled draperies through his eyes. Next to her silver dresser set lay handmade baskets and beaded jewelry. The quill-decorated dress Chumani had helped her make had been draped over a silk-painted dressing screen in the corner.

The four-poster bed with the white ruffled canopy had always seemed huge to Hallie, but the furniture diminished in size next to Cooper's immense form.

"Take off your coat."

Leaning his rifle against the wall, he shrugged out of the coat and Hallie held it, relishing its weight and the warmth from his body. She had to resist burying her nose in the rich fur. Cooper's familiar fringed tunic and pants outlined his muscular frame. She hadn't thought she'd see him again. Hadn't dared dream he'd be close enough to talk to…to touch.

Her knees grew shaky and she perched on the edge of her bed, his coat on her lap. She didn't care if he ever spoke. Just looking at him filled her heart with pleasure.

"I got home safe," she said finally.

"I know."

He knew? "How are Chumani and Yellow Eagle?"

"I'm not sure."

She frowned. "What do you mean?"

"I haven't been back yet."

"You haven't—! Where have you been?"

He tried to hide a sheepish expression. "I went to Quebec for a time. Made arrangements with some of the French traders."

"Quebec! What were you doing in Quebec?"

"I told you…I had some business dealings…"

"You followed us!"

He met her gaze levelly.

The surprise wore off and the meaning sank in. "Why did you follow us?"

"I felt responsible for you."

Idly, she smoothed the fur beneath her hands. "Why did you come here?"

He glanced around. "I had this crazy idea…"

"What?"

"That maybe we could find somewhere halfway… somewhere in between where we could…"

"What?"

"It was a crazy idea. Duluth wasn't so terrible, but Massachusetts is…"

"What!" she said, too loud this time.

"I could never stand it here."

She tried to reason out his words, his thinking. Her heart lifted. "You were thinking that maybe there was somewhere between your world and my world where we could find a compromise?"

He nodded. "But I'm not foolish enough to think love is the answer to everything. I could love you as much and as hard as there was strength in me, but I'd still hate it here. I wouldn't fit and you would be ashamed of me."

"I could never be ashamed of you, Cooper, but I wouldn't want you to fit. There are any number of gentlemen in Boston who 'fit,' and I don't want any of them."

He studied her, and his stoic mask seemed to have slipped a little.

"Hell of it is, I don't fit, either," she said with a wry twist of her mouth, and refocused her attention. "What was that you said about how you could love me?"

"I said that, didn't I?"

She nodded. "Do you? Love me?"

"I do."

Elation rose in her chest. "Why didn't you tell me?"

He moved to sit on the bed beside her. "I didn't want to tie you there…where you'd be miserable."

"I wouldn't be miserable."

"Hallie, my father brought my mother to the Dakotas and she pined her time away being miserable and missing her city life. She couldn't stand it, and my father moved her farther and farther east until finally she left him. Then he followed her. I never even heard from them again. I don't know if he found her, if either of them lived. She hated it so much she ran off and left us."

"I'm sorry about that," Hallie said sincerely. "But I'm not her. I'm not like her. I didn't miss the city for one minute while I was at Stone Creek." She laid her hand on his arm. "My problem was that I still had an unrealistic pipe dream that I had a future as a big-time reporter waiting for me."

"You don't still want that?"

"It's not going to happen." Tears filled her throat and threatened to spill from her eyes. Rapidly she blinked them back. "Instead, I'm going to be just like my mother."

Her worst fear. "Maybe there's a way," he said, hoping to give her what she needed.

"Oh, there's a way," she said. "I could renounce my family and be scorned by society and make a fool of myself. Not an option I'm willing to take."

Cooper's chest ached with inadequacy and hesitation. "You're not happy here?" he dared to ask.

She shook her head. "I'm not happy here."

"What about your friends? The things you like to do? The shops?"

She raised her lovely eyes. "What are you asking?"

"Could you be happy in Stone Creek?" he asked.

"I was happy in Stone Creek. I just didn't know it."

"Could you love me?" he asked. Something glorious and sparkling rose in her eyes, and Cooper wanted to wrap himself in that moment. He wanted to keep this wondrous new discovery fresh and alive and never let it tarnish.

"I do love you, Cooper," she said on a shaky sigh, and a tear escaped her lashes, followed by another…and another.

He framed her velvet-soft face with his hands and knew an all-consuming, breathtaking emotion of wonder and joy he'd never dared hope for. A sob escaped her throat and she closed her eyes against the rush of tears.

Hallie. Hallie, who'd taken on stage robbers, faced Indians and shot a grizzly without a tear. Hallie, who'd survived a kidnapping, brutal treatment and fever without breaking down, now cried. Great rolling tears and sobs that shook her slender frame and punctured his soul; tears because a rough, unpolished frontier man loved her.

"Hallie, I need you," he admitted in an unsteady voice. "Marry me and come home with me."

Shoving the coat to the bed behind her, she flung herself into his arms and met his kiss. "What about an Indian wife?" she asked against his lips.

"I don't want anyone but you."

"She would be easy to get along with and know how to cook and cure hides and ride horses."

"But she wouldn't do this," he said, pressing her hand against his heart. "Or this." He led her hand lower and Hallie caught her breath. "Or make me laugh."

Elated, she pressed herself against him and they fell back on the bed. Hallie kissed him long and hard and pulled back to study his sun-darkened face against her pristine white coverlet. She kissed his high, angled cheekbone, the fair crest of his brow, the dip in his strong chin, and covered his lips in an all-encompassing, tempestuous kiss of love and desire, knowing she wanted him, needed him, had to make him hers.

Breathing hard, she drew back and untied his hair, running her fingers through the silken length. He did the same, and hers spilled over her shoulder and draped across the side of his face. He threaded his fingers in the tresses and pulled her down for another protracted clash of lips and tongues.

"Take your shirt off," she said impatiently, sliding to his side.

He glanced from her face to the rest of the room. "Here?"

She nodded and unlaced the ties.

He yanked the leather garment over his head. "What if...?"

Hallie forced her attention from his sleek, muscled chest long enough to jump up and fumble in her jewelry box for a key. She found it and reached the door at the same time Cooper did. She inserted the key and twisted it. He stepped to her nearly ceiling-high armoire and shoved it in front of the door with a look of unbridled determination on his flushed face.

Hallie laughed.

He smiled and met her beside the bed.

She unbuttoned her blouse and pulled it from the waistband of her skirt while he removed his boots. He slid the blouse from her arms and tossed it on the floor. Together they unfastened her skirt and pushed it down. Cooper knelt and pulled her boots and stockings off, taking time to unroll them and run his palms over each inch of skin he uncovered. Hallie's body tingled with delight and anticipation.

She unfastened her corset, tossing it aside, and Cooper kneaded her breasts through the wrinkled fabric of her chemise. He kissed her tenderly, touched the tip of his tongue to her earlobes and the base of her throat, tasting her, testing her, teasing her.

Hallie slid from his loose embrace and pulled back the covers. Behind her, Cooper removed his trousers. She turned. He wore only the soft flap of leather that barely contained him. He knelt on her bed, burnished skin against crisp white linen, and she smiled.

"What's that for?" he asked.

"Last night I told my father I wouldn't marry a man with soft white hands."

His head tilted ever so slightly.

"Nothing soft or white about you," she said. Without any fear or hesitation, she untied her chemise and pulled it off, then sat back and removed her pantaloons.

His feverish eyes surveyed her body and returned to her face. "Does this mean you'll marry me?"

"Cooper!" she said in a stricken voice. "Of course. I thought we had that settled."

"You never said yes."

A long, expectant moment passed between them. "Yes," she said.

He reached for her and they fell back against the soft feather mattress. Cooper covered her breasts with his hands, kissed them, teased her nipples with his tongue. Passion washed through Hallie like a flash flood, pounding in her veins, setting every nerve ending alive and on end.

She stroked his supple skin, kneaded his flesh and wrapped her arms around his shoulders in an attempt to pull herself inside him. The skin of his back and hips was a delight to her sensitive fingertips. In her exploration, she fumbled over the leather thong and he showed her where it untied.

"Wait," she said unexpectedly.

"What?"

She disentangled herself and reached to the foot of the bed, spreading his coat between them. "Now," she said, and moved to lie on the fur. She pulled the thong that released his last scrap of clothing.

One side of his mouth lifted. "What's this? A fondness for fur?"

"I want the feel of it beneath my back and you against the front." She pulled him down and felt his matching excitement humming through his muscles. "It reminds me of home."

He settled in the apex of her thighs and she gripped his biceps. He reached between their bodies and guided himself to her. Hallie almost panicked at the first sensation of his hot, hard sex against her tender, untried flesh, but he soothed her with a kiss and the erotic stroking of his knuckle.

A shiver of delight spread through her body, and a tremulous exultation made her feel as though she were swelling around him, absorbing him. He removed his hand and thrust into her hard, his own body trembling, and brushed the tears that slid from the corners of her eyes with his thumbs.

Miraculously, her body stretched to accommodate him and he moved against her, drawing a groan of pleasure from each of them. His body was hard and powerful, tension and excitement transmitted to her with each stroke. He needed her. He needed her, and she gave herself to him completely, fulfilling her purpose, at last understanding her femininity. For the first time, she rejoiced in her womanhood, filled with its power and headiness.

He rocked their bodies with tormenting ecstasy, and she clung to him, arched against him, made frantic sounds of pleasure and frustration against his lips and his neck. A sublime madness overcame her and she begged him to stop it, to prolong it, to take her with him on his shimmering ride to bliss.

And he did.

Hallie held him tight and quaked with the force and beauty of their shared love. With a last convulsive shudder, he collapsed and rolled them to their sides, their bodies heated and slick. She brushed his hair from his face and kissed his eyes, his nose, his chin. "I love you, Cooper."

"I love—"

"Hallie!" Behind the armoire, the doorknob rattled and her mother's voice called. "Hallie, what are you doing?"

Hallie sprang from Cooper's embrace and gaped about the room in horror.

"Hallie?" Clarisse called.

Leaping from the bed, she tore through the heap of sheets and discarded clothing. "Here," she said, shoving Cooper's pants at him and jumping on one foot to get into her pantaloons. "Get dressed, hurry!"

A frantic pounding sounded on the door this time. "Hallie, answer me!"

"I'm fine, Mother!"

Her sense of urgency infected Cooper and he pulled on his trousers and shirt. Hallie stuffed her corset under the mattress and stepped into her skirt. Cooper tried to sit on the bed to pull on his boots, but she shooed him away to haphazardly arrange the sheets and coverlet. He hopped on one foot at a time.

Hallie buttoned her blouse, tucked it in and gathered her hair into a loose knot.

"She was behaving oddly last night, Clarisse," her father's voice said. "I don't like this."

"Hallie, open this door at once or your father will break it down!"

Hallie faced Cooper. He raised a brow and she nodded. Wedging a shoulder against the armoire, he moved it aside. Hallie turned the key and the door burst open, hitting the wall.

"Hallie! What is this all about? Why, whatever has happened to you?" she asked, taking in her daughter's disheveled appearance and flushed skin. Turning her head slightly, she encountered Cooper's massive form. Seeing his wild unfettered hair, his primitive clothing and the intimidating way he stood with his feet spraddled, she blanched. Her hand flattened on her bosom. "What—who—?"

"What the hell are you doing in my daughter's room?" Samuel asked.

"I can explain," Hallie said.

But before she could, Cooper moved and picked up his rifle leaning against the wall. A startled look crossed Samuel's face and he took a step in front of Clarisse.

Cooper handed him the rifle, butt first, and pointed the barrel at himself. "I'm afraid you'll have to insist I marry your daughter, sir. I've compromised her."

Hallie stared.

Clarisse swooned, and Hallie helped her to the edge of the bed.

Samuel stood with the gun leveled at Cooper's heart. "Is this loaded?"

"It is," Cooper confirmed.

"Is this true, Hallie?" her father asked.

"It's true," Cooper insisted. "I slept with her in my arms every night between the Dakotas and Duluth."

Hallie's skin burned and she sputtered. "It wasn't—"

"Who the hell are you?" her father thundered.

"Cooper DeWitt."

"Shall I kill him?" Samuel asked.

"No!" Hallie left her mother and ran to stand between Cooper and the gun. "You don't need the gun, Father. I want to marry him. I love him."

"What about him?"

Hallie stepped aside and looked at Cooper. "Ask him."

His eyes left Samuel and rested on Hallie. "You don't need the gun. I want Hallie for my wife."

She turned into his arms and held him tight, his heart beating wildly against her cheek.

"I guess that's settled," Samuel said, and rested the rifle over the arms of a chair.

"Whatever is this?"

Hallie turned to her mother and recognized the leather thong between her thumb and forefinger. She met Cooper's eyes. He raised his brows and shrugged and their shoulders shook with laughter.

Epilogue

Hallie stood on Stone Creek's new boardwalk and studied the gold lettering on the window of their new building: *Stone Creek Daily News*. Hallie Claire DeWitt. Editor-in-Chief. Her father had shipped them the old press he'd stored in a back room for years. Hallie knew how to run it, and Yellow Eagle was learning to set the type. Lowell Heckman, the blacksmith, turned out to be pretty fair at repairs when something needed work.

"Mornin', Mizz DeWitt!"

She turned and waved at the Howards, Wiley's relatives who'd moved to Stone Creek last spring. They entered the trading post. Old Reavis had had to clean the place up, what with the advent of women and families in the territory. And the fact that another family had put up a building and were running him some competition, calling themselves the "mercantile," had been adequate incentive.

Wiley had asked Chumani to marry him, and a wedding was planned for the fall.

"You working or admiring your window?" Cooper sat atop his gelding, a few feet from the boardwalk.

Her heart tripped a little, as it did each time she saw him. "A little of both, I guess."

"Did you forget lessons this morning?"

Three days a week they rode to the reservation and Hallie taught the youngsters. "I didn't forget. Just a little slow these past mornings."

He dismounted and tied the reins to the hitching rail he'd built outside their newspaper office. "Any particular reason for that, do you suppose?"

"Might be." She walked inside the building, and he followed her to the Franklin press. She picked up a paper and held it so he could read the bold headline.

"DeWitts Expecting First Child," he read aloud. "We're havin' a baby, Hallie?"

"We're having a baby."

An odd expression crossed his features.

"Are you happy?" she asked.

He pulled her into his arms. "Couldn't be happier. And you?"

She nodded against his chest. "If it's a boy, I'll make him buckskins just like yours."

"If it's a girl, she'll be a hellcat," he said. "We'll teach her to ride and hunt. And you can show her how to run the presses."

"Our children can be whatever they want to be, can't they?" she said wistfully.

"That they can."

"That's what the loft is for, isn't it? Our children?"

"Until we have to build a bigger house. Stone Creek Family Builds Mansion," he said.

"Keep trying," she teased. "You'll have to stay up nights to top my best headline."

Reluctantly agreeing, Cooper glanced at the paper she'd framed and proudly hung on the wall. The headline read, Badlands Bride: She Got Her Story—And Her Man.

* * * * *

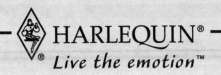

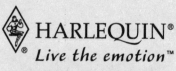

HARLEQUIN®
INTRIGUE®

BREATHTAKING ROMANTIC SUSPENSE

Shared dangers and passions lead to electrifying
romance and heart-stopping suspense!

Every month, you'll meet six new heroes
who are guaranteed to make your spine tingle
and your pulse pound. With them you'll enter
into the exciting world of Harlequin Intrigue—
where your life is on the line
and so is your heart!

THAT'S INTRIGUE—
ROMANTIC SUSPENSE
AT ITS BEST!

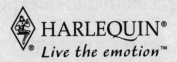

HARLEQUIN®
Live the emotion™

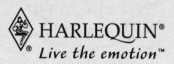

Harlequin® Historical
Historical Romantic Adventure!

*Imagine a time of chivalrous
knights and unconventional ladies,
roguish rakes and impetuous
heiresses, rugged cowboys
and spirited frontierswomen—
these rich and vivid tales will
capture your imagination!*

*Harlequin Historical...
they're too good to miss!*

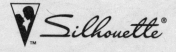